TURF OR STONE

PARTHIAN
LIBRARY OF WALES

Margiad Evans (Peggy Whistler) was born in Uxbridge in 1909, and lived in the Border area in Ross-on-Wye. The border was central to her consciousness, and she adopted the Welsh nom de plume, Margiad Evans, out of a sense of identity with Wales. She attended Hereford School of Art, but although she continued to paint and draw until late in her life, writing displaced art as her primary work. In addition to *Country Dance* (1932), her novels include *The Wooden Doctor* (1933), *Turf or Stone* (1934) and *Creed* (1936). She also wrote numerous articles and short stories, some of which were collected in *The Old and the Young* (1948), and two collections of poetry, *Poems from Obscurity* (1947) and *A Candle Ahead* (1956). Her *Autobiography* was published in 1943 and *A Ray of Darkness*, an account of her experience with epilepsy, appeared in 1952. She died in 1958.

TURF OR STONE

MARGIAD EVANS

PARTHIAN
LIBRARY OF WALES

Parthian
The Old Surgery
Napier Street
Cardigan
SA43 1ED
www.parthianbooks.co.uk

The Library of Wales is a Welsh Assembly Government
initiative which highlights and celebrates Wales' literary
heritage in the English language.

Published with the financial support of
the Welsh Books Council.

www.libraryofwales.org

Series Editor: Dai Smith

Turf or Stone first published in 1934
© The Estate of Margiad Evans 1934

Library of Wales edition 2010
Foreword © Deborah Kay Davies 2010
Publishing Editor: Penny Thomas
All Rights Reserved

ISBN 978-1-906998-28-8

Cover design: www.theundercard.co.uk
Cover image: *He Takes Me by the Shoulders* Peggy Whistler

Printed and bound by Gwasg Gomer, Llandysul, Wales
Typeset by Lucy Llewellyn

British Library Cataloguing in Publication Data

A cataloguing record for this book is available from the British Library.

LIBRARY OF WALES

FOREWORD

It is my pleasure to introduce this book to you. Beware; it is a rough read, a demanding journey, an amazing, fantastical, invigorating experience. And what more can you want as a reader? Margiad Evans' warm, eloquent voice, her unequivocal exploration of the extremes of human behaviour, of cruelty, lust and ultimate redemption, her stunning evocations of the natural world, may well leave you unsatisfied with anything less in other writers.

I sat down to read one rainy weekend. Immediately I was tipped into a strange world. It's a freezing morning. A cart lumbers along a country lane driven by a one-armed man (a very Margiad detail) who is oblivious to the elements. I was unsure which century we were in; the snow-salted fields gave no clue. It occurred to me this could be medieval England, or even a Grimm brothers' fairytale. There are a few huddled people about, three yews under a net in the back of the cart. And a lone woman limping wearily along the track. A woman who is elegantly dressed and obviously deeply troubled. Not entirely beaten down however. We read she responds contemptuously to a friendly drover's enquiries, whilst favouring the carter with a gentle gaze; she needs him, or at least his cart, to get to her destination. So we meet Mary Bicknor, the book's not entirely likeable heroine.

Mary has been a cosseted quasi-servant to an old lady. During her stay in the big house this old lady had 'spoiled

ix

and petted her, dressed her expensively... and easily persuaded her to give up all thought of marriage with her own natural equals.' Mary '...used to carry herself very proudly' and 'snort at callers...' It is a shock, then, to read the throwaway line: 'Then one day Mary confessed to her mistress she was pregnant.' And to take in the fact that Mary has fallen from grace. A hasty marriage is arranged to Easter, a groom, the father of the child she carries. This is obviously a union that Mary believes is beneath her. And the story proper begins.

This story, told many times over the centuries, is a narrative that could only start to change with the advent of the contraceptive pill. Here we have the haughty beauty, unmarried, cast out when pregnant, humiliated and impoverished, forced into a marriage she detests for the sake of convention. It would not be many years before other narratives take over. Margiad Evans is on the cusp of change. Even so, the book encompasses divorce, or at least separation, and the possibility of a new life for Mary – an outcome almost unheard of for someone of Mary's class before the twentieth century. This duality between the ancient and the modern, between the unchanging countryside and the teashop and magistrates' court, kept me alert. I had to continually reappraise what I knew and understood about the story. Patterns that seemed familiar – the woman brought low, a ruffian for a husband, the upper-class lover – are subverted by Margiad Evans; twisted and squeezed to extract a fresh, startling newness.

Throughout the book we see Mary through the eyes of the men she encounters. The carter examines her bowed head and takes in her 'fresh lips' with their 'hint of a voluptuous pout suggesting a caress... and red hair which showed... beneath her hat.' A little later, asleep in her new husband's bed, he surreptitiously observes '...her naked shoulder' whose 'blooming flesh shone with pearly lustre against the harsh white sheet'. Thirty pages on, Matt, the disaffected squire, sees Mary for the first time. In his room later he recalls '...Mary's eyes, her long neck, her hollow cheeks, her mouth, tempting yet severe'. So far so predictable, you might say.

But Mary is more than the stereotypical tempting woman. She is her own person: awkward, ungrateful sometimes, a character who grabs new experiences unwisely and wholeheartedly. The disquieting relationship she has with her cruel, enigmatic husband Easter is mysterious and engaging. She is no pallid victim, even though at times she breaks down under the onslaught of his sadism. His behaviour, whilst she never welcomes it, is understandable to her. His passion awakes similar reactions in her. Despite herself she responds to his physicality because it matches her own.

There are issues arising from this almost entirely external appraisal of the main female character, I think. Because she is largely unknowable – and what we do know about her character is not always appealing – we may not connect with her experiences in a way that Margiad Evans would like us to. We have no idea about her upbringing. No clue about her early dreams and struggles. Yet Easter has several poignant passages in which we see him as a ragamuffin, tagging along with the gypsies. His mother dies when he is sixteen and he is almost feral. He grows up famished, full of energy, and constantly abandoned by the people he should be able to rely on.

On the night of their comically disastrous wedding Easter watches Mary while she sleeps. We are told how he examines her underclothes, amazed at their delicacy; '...feeling the silk with his hard, dirty fingers'. He is thrown back in time and remembers his mother hanging things like these out to dry. 'He used to carry the empty basket back to the kitchen along a path between blackcurrant bushes.' He recalls '...the little daisies under (his mother's) feet'. And along with this early domestic memory comes a desire for '...tenderness, he wanted to be soothed, he longed for (Mary) to caress him, to be his entirely'. Of course, Mary wakes and vehemently squashes his advances – and who can blame her? He'd grudgingly taken a ring off his own finger for the vicar to use in the ceremony, snatched it back, pinched her arm and pushed her over into the frozen mud, then promptly hopped on a bus and left her to find her own way home.

Yes, Easter Probert is a vile, ungovernable man whose behaviour is reprehensible, but because we are given so much information about the workings of his damaged mind, and supplied with such lyrical details about his neglected childhood, we understand him. We consider his inarticulate yearning for warmth, and subsequently we may care about him in a way we can't about the cold, snobbish Mary. We know he will never be able to obtain what he craves – he is too warped – but we can't help but sympathise with his utter aloneness. And this ambivalence also touches the way we feel about his appearance. He is like a 'goblin', 'a panther', but he has '...beautifully sound teeth', 'hair growing back from broad temples', 'deep-set eyes' and is 'graceful and rakish'. There is more than a touch of Heathcliff or Rochester about him. The subconscious ambivalence that permeates the book, this blurry, uncertain mix of messages, adds depth and richness. It challenges the reader.

The marital struggles of Easter and Mary, horrifying, pathetic and childish as they can be, are mirrored more subtly and alluringly in the relationship Easter has with the squire's intense older daughter Phoebe. She is the pure, serious, unworldly maiden in this quasi-fairytale. And it is her developing, barely-there connection with Easter that Margiad Evans does so well. The first time I read the book (I read it three times in all, each time it became more rich and strange and believable to me) I did not understand why Phoebe was given so much attention early on. I interpreted the imbalance in the text as a lack of discipline on the writer's part, an inability to control her obviously teeming ideas. But on reflection, it is clear that Phoebe is crucial to the story; we need to know her obsessive, striving character to understand her selfless act at the dénouement.

There is a psychological truth also in her confused feelings for Easter. When she is a girl of fifteen she is exposed to a grotesque vision of Easter as he peers through a tiny window in an attempt to gain access to a serving girl. This encounter; '...the odd tinge to his skin ...the upper teeth were showing and a large spider's web... seemed ...to be hanging from his mouth' doesn't frighten Phoebe as one might expect. She wonders about him, and from that time on cannot be near him without shrinking. When he looks at her it is with '...the long, knowing stare that made her feel so uncomfortable'. He has awakened feelings in her that she is ashamed of and fascinated by. In her journal she writes 'Yes, I'm haunted. Else why should strangers look at me with Easter's eyes?'

It is the strength of this reciprocated, unconsummated attraction and the way that it mimics the book's other male-female relationships – Matt and his lazy, luxurious wife, Dorothy; Mary and the greedy, consuming passion she shares with Matt – which breathes clear, fresh air through the pages. Quite early on in the narrative Phoebe modifies Easter's behaviour by merely leaping up and casting him a look both '...courageous and imploring. In response 'He averted his eyes and his expression changed...' She has the power to calm his temper. In every other encounter he is driven to fits of cruelty and viciousness that border on madness. Later on in the book he touchingly ties her dropped handkerchief around his wrist like a knight who takes the favour of his lady into battle. Most importantly, it is because of his connection with Phoebe that Easter performs his one truly altruistic act, and finds a grubby, hard-won kind of redemption.

Turf or Stone is wonderful. I have not touched on the shining passages of nature writing in the book, such as the description of an expedition to the river that Phoebe and her sister, Rosamund, take one hot summer day. It is perfect. They play in '...a slowly turning pool curved into the red clay, overhung by fresh young alders thick with leaves whose dipping branches swept the water'. The girls swim in the gleaming river, careful Phoebe 'swam froggily... her head far too high'. No-nonsense Rosamund has '...nerve, and a passionate love of flinging herself into water'. At other times the countryside turns threatening, or gloomy and thunderous, often lashed with rain. Always the descriptions seem true. Margiad Evans has rightly been called a consummate nature writer.

It is also true to say that sometimes she may over-embellish, as if she is unable to resist the impulse to decorate each surface with grotesque detail. No mean roof is without its quota of fungi and weeds; no bit-character is without a smattering of hideous warts, or '...skin that resembled wet clay', and even, on one occasion, an extracted glass eye whose '...blue stare (is smothered) in a handkerchief...' But this embellishment is essential to the success of the book. Yes, it is extreme, elemental, nightmarish even in its uncompromising intensity, and that is as it should be. The reader is constantly pushed and pulled, drawn in and repelled, but never, ever bored.

Deborah Kay Davies

TURF OR STONE

I

Early one February morning a tip cart, which was plastered with dried mud and driven by a man with one arm, turned out of a lane some eight miles from Salus, and journeyed slowly along the main road towards the town.

Heavy clouds retarded the progress of day, but at length the man pulled up, sprang to the ground, and opening the lamps, extinguished them with two vigorous puffs. He then mounted once more, settling himself on the front, his feet on the shaft.

The cart contained under a net three ewes, whose breath rose steamily in the cold air. The man, bareheaded, broad-shouldered, sat easily swaying to the movement of the shaft, expanding his chest though the east wind was blowing. He seemed indifferent, durable, hard as the cart itself. It was freezing again; there was dust on the grey road. The few people who were about walked with their heads bent, huddling their shoulders. From his seat the man could see the rounded frostbitten fields over the hedges and the vague encompassing hills patchy with lingering snow.

An hour later, when it was still three miles from Salus, the cart overtook a flock of sheep, and was obliged to come to a stand close to the path while the drover cleared a way for it. The carter noticed a young woman walking past, and struck by her weary air – she limped – called out to know whether she would be too proud to take a lift on the front with him.

The woman who was jaded in spirit rather than in fact, and whose painful meditations were the true brake on her steps, was about to answer him haughtily. She raised her eyes, hesitated, and suited her reply to the gentle gaze which met her own.

'Thank you,' she said, looking up at him. 'I should be glad enough, but I haven't far to go now.'

'How far, miss?'

'Fown Mill.'

'Get up... it'll be a bit of a rest.'

Leaning forward he extended his one hand. Darting a contemptuous look at the smiling drover, she put her hand in the carter's. He swung her up: she sat beside him silently. He examined her sideways without turning his head. She was an elegant woman with a sombre expression, whose long neck shone warmly white against a dark fur. Her face was thin, without colour, her nose inclined to a downward curve, the wide nostrils nervously dilated. Her fresh lips protruded slightly, and this hint of a voluptuous pout suggesting a caress, lent her hollow countenance fascination. She had red hair which showed on one side beneath her hat. In her hands she held a prayer book and a clean white handkerchief. She wore a loose grey coat almost like a cloak which flowed over the rail. Her crossed feet in high-heeled shoes hung some inches above the shaft.

The carter saw that she had been crying, and he felt sorry for her. But he did not speak to her because she was a stranger and he admired her.

They proceeded thus the best part of a mile, until they reached a broad tarred lane branching off to the left. A granite war memorial, in the shape of a bleak grey cross, stood on the corner, garnished with a tattered laurel wreath. There she asked to be set down, thanked him, and drew away, wrapping her coat tightly across her as the wind whisked round the corner.

The carter slapped the reins on the horse's back and it broke into a clumsy trot, jerking the cart backwards; balancing himself he gave a long sigh of relief which yet had in it some regret. It was not until he reached Salus, that he discovered the prayer book inside the cart where it had fallen and been trodden on by the frightened ewes. She must have let it fall when she turned round to get down.

He opened it: there was a name written on the flyleaf.

'Mary Bicknor,' he read, and then he remembered he had heard about her.

She was half servant, half companion, to an old eccentric lady who within the last year had taken a house at Buck Castle, a small hamlet on the outskirts of Fown Mill parish where she was a complete stranger. The old lady, whose name was Tressan, spoiled and petted her, dressed her expensively, even submitted to her dominance, and easily persuaded her to give up all thoughts of marriage with her own natural equals. Without actually saying as much, she really expected Mary to remain single. Mary used to carry herself very proudly, snort at callers, regulate Miss Tressan's friendships from her own front door. Indeed, they were both very foolish and everybody laughed at them.... Then one day Mary confessed to her mistress that she was pregnant. The old lady did not desert her, but she instantly withdrew her affection, nor did she at all approve of the hastily arranged marriage. She thought it a calamity with a preposterous ending, and as well as she could she ignored it. The vicar of Fown Mill brought the couple together. He took great credit to himself for this.

The carter recollected some of these circumstances. They were wasted on him. Being no gossip he was generally regarded as a shy, taciturn fellow without a great deal to say for himself. He went to the market carrying the white prayer book in his pocket.

*   *   *

Mary did not discover the loss of her prayer book until she reached the church. She was thinking of her mistress, whom she had left lying in bed.

When she took up the tea as usual, at eight o'clock, she saw Miss Tressan regarding her mournfully and steadily over the bed clothes. She pulled up the blinds, keeping her back to the bed.

They did not know what to say to each other. At last,

as Mary was closing the window, the old lady stammered: 'Is it a fine day?'

She had asked this question first thing every morning for fifteen years, and no other words seemed possible. Mary told her it was freezing. She drew the sheet tight under her chin and shut her eyes: 'I'll have the fire and stay in bed today,' she said resolutely.

'Shall I light it?'

'No... no... keep your hands clean this morning. There, go along, and shut the door.'

But as Mary passed the bed with averted face, she suddenly sat up, tendering her an envelope. Her lips trembled.

'Take this. You must. I insist.'

'No, no, I can't.'

'You must... I insist.' She repeated like a feeble cry.

Mary felt the envelope pushed into her hand and Miss Tressan's fingers close over her wrist for a moment in a loose clasp. Then she drew away her arm suddenly and lay back again, shutting her eyes.

'Goodbye,' she said bitterly.

Mary dropped the envelope on the floor.

'That's no use, no help at all.'

She looked around the room at the silk curtains, the cushions, the pictures, the soft carpet, the emaciated figure flat on the bed, and having looked, with a kind of sick disgust, went out and dressed for her marriage to a groom. She wept.

Descending the steep hill to the church, she met two women carrying baskets to market. She pulled herself together, she had cried for hours before she left the house, and her eyes were swollen. The women stared at her. The heavy baskets packed with butter and eggs had made them tired – they had missed the bus. One ejaculated loudly: 'Some people have no shame,' and the other cast down her eyes.

Mary cried: 'What have I done to you?'

Before misfortune had overtaken her she would not have spoken to them.

They threw up their chins and trudged on up the hill, exchanging glances.

Mary could not understand herself: it seemed as if she wished to descend as far as possible, to roll in the mud.

Rounding the bend, the church came into view, a small, renovated edifice with a Saxon tower. A straight walk, shaded by cut yews, led up to the porch, where the man she was about to marry stood talking to the vicar. She approached them nervously and the bridegroom, Easter Probert, came towards her swinging his arms.

He was peculiar in appearance. He did not look like a man who had ever had anything to do with horses except in a thieving, gypsyish, wayside kind of way. He might very easily have been a travelling kettle-mender. He was small; his skin shone faintly, through a yellow-brown tan, and his large black eyes protruded from the sockets, although they were set deep in the skull. His square-seamed forehead was marked by strong brows a shade lighter than the hair, which grew stiffly and tuftily back from the broad temples. The features were harsh, the cheekbones prominent, the mouth sunken. A mauve scar, triangular in shape, showed clearly a little below the right eye. When he talked or laughed his upper lip lifted at the corner, exposing beautifully sound teeth. A strange wary face, alert, hungry, malicious, subtly mournful. His movements, as he went to meet Mary, were very graceful, but suggested insolence; for a short man he took long strides, which lent him a rakish, high cockalorum air.

The same odd individuality marked his clothes: he wore a greenish coat, brown trousers, old and dirty, and a thick, twisted, silver ring on a little finger. It was said that his mother had been a gypsy, but of this no one could be certain, as he was a love child and she was dead.

He strode towards Mary and took her hand as he turned to walk beside her. They walked so to the door, where the vicar stood pulling his lips and staring at them dimly.

The vicar, an old man of seventy-odd, recalled some corrupt, degenerate idol which had decayed in a jungle. Fat, bloated, yet withered, he stood, his legs shaking visibly beneath the cassock, his head sunk between shoulders which had lost their outline and become mere pads of flesh. He wore a smile. Having attained his object he felt ready to be affable; he wished to speak kindly, but Easter's expression was so ferocious, Mary's so defiant, that a doubt crept into his negligible mind: 'Surely this is wrong and cruel! These people do not love each other,' he said to himself.

Then he thought of the child.

'No, it is too late. But God help them,' he concluded his momentary reflection.

He held out his hand. Mary took it, let it go, and drew a pair of clean gloves from her pocket. As she began to put them on she noticed the loss of her prayer book which Miss Tressan had given her years ago on her confirmation.

Tears again rose to her eyes. The vicar saw them. In spite of himself he pitied her profoundly, following them into the dark church.

She lifted a prayer book from the shelf. 'You will not need that,' the vicar informed her. She dropped it again in a confused and hasty manner.

The verger, sniffing, stepped from a pew under the pulpit, where he had been sitting half asleep, and the clerk who was to be the other witness, came out of the vestry with an impatient air. He cast a hurried glance through the open door as he passed it, for he had tied his dog to a tombstone, and feared that it might howl. But it was lying quietly asleep on the grass.

Fown Mill church stands on the road, and there is a short cut to Salus through the churchyard. Being market day the parish was astir, so that throughout the service people were continually passing. Their conversation could be clearly overheard, and one or two looked in at the door. A small boy stood for some time by the font with his cap on, while the clerk made energetic signs to him to remove it. He grimaced, swung on his heel, and walked out, screwing up his nose. The clerk boiled with futile anger.

When the time came for Easter to fit the ring on Mary's finger it was discovered that he was without one. She turned paler, bit her lips, stared stonily at the altar. The service paused. Easter suddenly drew off the silver ring and slipped it on her finger. She was obliged to shut her hand to prevent it from falling to the ground. The ceremony concluded without the vicar taking the couple to the altar. This he had determined he would not do. When Mary took a step forward he shook his head, folding his lips tightly and moved resolutely towards the vestry; the clerk and the verger, who were prepared, followed the couple ungraciously. The church had not been heated. Mary trembled visibly with the cold, her very heart beat languidly and her hands shook so that she could hardly sign the register.

The verger had built up a fire in the vestry, a weak, smoky slack fire which smelt acrid. The smoke blew out and tasted bitter in their mouths. She dropped on her knees before it, holding out her hands. Seeing the ring she began to cry again, bending her head to hide her face from the men.

'Don't cry,' said the vicar in a low consoling murmur. He leant forward and touched her shoulder.

'Why are you crying? Come on, let's go,' Easter suggested, stepping restlessly to the vestry door. He looked at the east window, pretentious painted glass, purple, blue, and red, with no depths to the colours, at the varnished pews roped off with red cords for the important families, the arrogant brass eagle beating the open Bible, the pale pulpit, the snowdrops on the altar. Mary wept and wept, heedless of whispers and sympathetic glances. He wished he were outside in the wind.

'Let's go,' he repeated impatiently. The vicar glanced at him reproachfully, rolling his dull eyes under which showed livid smears. 'Can't you wait a little until your *wife* is better?'

Easter spoke harshly: 'Give over, Mary.'

She took no notice. His voice was affliction. Lifting his eyes he caught sight of the thick bell ropes which hung temptingly near his hand. He seized one in both hands and

11

gave it a strong pull. Above their heads an unseen bell vibrated like a huge gong. It made Easter think of his master's, hanging in the hall, a bland brass circle between two foxes' masks with pointed teeth.... 'Dinner!' he shouted.

The verger clutched his shoulder, the vicar was scandalised, but Easter laughed aloud as he shook himself free. Again he tugged – he'd give them something to remember! This time the bell rang out full and true.

'What are you doing?' the clerk stammered, shocked. A fantastic humour possessed Easter and gleamed in his puckered eyes. He felt it glowing, he felt he wanted to outrage and distract these stuffy people who had tied him up to that crouching woman: they stank, like the church itself they reeked of damp cold stone and the clammy tombs of dead institutions. Again he pulled the gay red and white bell-rope, interspersing himself between the verger who reached out to grab his wrists. The verger retreated.

'I'll ring my own wedding peal!'

Booming, the bell answered him. Mary lifted her head, her face shining with tears.

'Easter!'

'He's drunk,' said the vicar angrily. His practical ignorance was colossal.

At that moment the bell's powerful motion wrenched the rope from Easter's unpractised grip; with a terrific swing it leapt the vestry partition. The verger and the clerk both held the vicar, who had quite lost his head. They forced him down.

'Be careful, sir, it's coming back,' the clerk cried, and they all cowered to avoid the blow. The rope slapped

12

against the wall, jerked once or twice and became still. The bell vibrated. Easter pulled up his trousers and jeered at the vicar. The vicar puffed out his cheeks and his eyes were vicious.

'This is outrageous.... I must speak to you outside,' he expostulated, smoothing the top of his head.

They went out.

The verger pushed a poker under the fire and it burst into roaring flame. Mary drew back from the heat. Her head ached, and, forgetting that she was in a church, she took off her hat, which had pressed her beautiful red hair close to the sides of her head: it clung to her temples and the delicate, prominent bones below her ears. The clerk watching her thought of Mary Magdalen, for to his mind this woman with her pale, miserable face still wet from tears, her full trembling mouth, her wan and working features, resembled his favourite saint. He poked the fire again and touched the cold hand lying in her lap. Like the carter earlier in the day, and the vicar, his pity stirred.

In the porch the vicar repeated that he considered Easter's behaviour outrageous: he really could find no other word to describe it. It seemed poor enough to a man of Easter's violent vocabulary. He smiled.

The wind blew the vicar's cassock against his legs and he wished he had not left the vestry without putting on his coat. He turned blue – the veins showed on his cheeks, he rubbed his freezing hands.

Easter disliked men, who were, most of them, larger than himself. As a rule he avoided them. When that was impossible he quarrelled with them, or ignored them. He felt neither shame nor repentance: he regarded the vicar boldly, not troubling to dispel his disapprobation, and making no attempt at a connected conversation, he broke into speech abruptly.

'I want my ring back. And then I must go. You've married us, there's no more to be done in there? Well, then, we'll be off. I gave the money to the clerk.'

The vicar flushed: 'In this case I shall of course, accept no fee. Good heavens, don't you feel the disgrace,' he burst out in a flood of indignation.

Easter smiled at him, cruelly, enigmatically silent. The vicar examined the face before him, the half-bared upper teeth, the dangerous eyes, and his mind grasped at reassurance.

'I hope you will be good to your wife?'

Easter raised his shoulders. He walked away between the trimmed yews to the gate, leaned over it, spat into the road, and taking out a cigarette, stood waiting for Mary.

The vicar returned to the vestry: 'A pariah,' he muttered full of resentment. Mary was standing up. The vicar went up to her as close as he could, so that he might probe the texture of her skin with his dim eyes... women fascinated him.

'Your husband is waiting for you. But don't hurry,' he added vindictively. Once more he held out his hand, which almost trembled with emotional sympathy, and taking it, Mary said dully: 'Thank you, I'll go,' fixing her swollen eyes on his face as if she were dazed from her weeping. He continued to hold the outstretched hand, slightly squeezing the palm and working his fingers towards her wrist, bare and warm above her glove.

'My child...' he murmured. His voice was tender, but

14

he could not go on because Mary's vague gaze was so indifferent. He felt too embarrassed.

The clerk and the verger thinking he wished to be alone with her, took up their hats and went away, rather downcast by the doleful ceremony. The clerk untied his dog, which jumped up at him playfully, then leapt the churchyard wall and ran up the road, ahead of his master.

*   *   *

Easter turned back to the church, scowling and blowing smoke.

Would Mary never give over? What in hell could he do? He was beginning to be very angry when at last she appeared.

'Come on,' he said.

As they walked away together the vicar watched them, distressed and helpless. He was obliged to tell himself that he had done the right thing. He said it once, and that was enough for him. Later he repeated it three times to his wife, and still she was not convinced.

Easter said: 'I want my ring back.'

'Take your ring then.'

He put the ring on his finger and looked at his wife as she walked sadly in the wind, wrapping her loose coat about her, hard and desolate. And she looked at him with disgust; at that moment they both remembered the night of their mating, she shameful of her traitorous flesh, he quickening to desire. Her tears were no longer falling, but she could hardly speak. Her voice sounded rough and thick, her breath shuddered: her features were slightly swollen,

15

her under lip was moist and parted from the upper; the tear marks, though dry, still glistened on her pale skin. Her eyes, heavy and cast down, were sullenly averted.

He had taken her when for a while she had put aside her airs and abandoned herself to caresses. She seemed without airs now... she wanted to yield, she would yield....

Easter loved women who were sad and gentle, and suffered him. He came close to her, put his open hand on her side: 'Let's go home, Mary.'

She hastily retreated. He pursued until she pressed against the frosty hedge and cold flakes fell on her upturned bitter face. He threw one arm around her, his large eyes burning eagerly, approached her own. She pushed him away, evading the kiss.

In an instant he was enraged, and no longer wanted her. He pinched her arm, wrenching at her clothes in spite, and gave her a rough shove which caused her to stumble. She fell sideways to the ground, on the frozen grass and mud. Easter's teeth gleamed.

Then she cried out; she complained aloud in tense misery between groaning and screaming. On market days buses run along the country roads to and from Salus. A few minutes later one approached. Easter stopped it, and leapt in, leaving Mary standing shaking the frosty leaves off her coat.

'You can go home by yourself – or not at all. No loss,' he shouted.

Mary was aghast at his brutality. He had been a peculiar unsatisfied lover. He bid fair to make a terrifying husband. She stared through the windows of the bus, and women leaning over their heaped-up baskets stared back openly.

The bus moved on. Mary stood absolutely still until it had gone. Then she followed. She walked to Salus by the river. Before the frost had set in there had been floods, and they had left the low water meadows gritty and littered with rotten sticks. Bundles of brushwood like untidy nests were tangled in the withy branches, draggling in the red swift river, whose turbid water poured with solid volume through the arches of the bridge. The path through the meadows was solitary; beneath the rusty wishing-gates which squeaked and creaked on their bent hinges, were puddles of ice; the grass, the empty iron seats, all were the same dismal brownish hue. A few ponies with their long, youthful manes flowing, hung their faces mournfully over a gate into the high road.

*   *   *

The carter, having concluded his business, stood with his arm on the rough counter of the canteen in the cattle market, his hand on an empty pint measure which he was pushing across to the man on the other side. The man, huge, a tower of fat and irritability, was a bit of a bruiser. You had to be careful what you said to him! He grabbed the measure and attended to other men.

The carter's eyes swept over the market square. A little boy was running the length of the pig pens, switching every pig in reach with a thin, supple stick; a cow was bellowing; across on the greensward two cheapjacks were trying to shout each other down. Their hoarse blaring voices cut across the general din. A crowd had assembled about them, throwing in words now and then, jeering or facetious, but seldom buying. Pink and grey pigeons waddled between the marketers' feet, pecking at wisps of straw from the cheapjacks' crates, and sidling in a deliberate heavy fashion away from the traffic. Close to him three or four men in leggings and heavy boots inclined their heads towards a drover who was binding his hand with a green handkerchief. The carter saw big blood stains forming. The man must have a bad cut....

He did not want another drink yet. He strolled out of the market up the steep hill, into the Town. Salus was busy – thronged with women in groups on the pavements, an outer circle of parcels and baskets projecting so far from their backs that it was impossible to get by without stepping into the road. The market hall swarmed. It was too early in the year for the colourful flower stalls... the bartering was for carcasses and butter and eggs.

The women held all the centre of the town. In the high street before The George, men spread right across the road. The glass doors opened and shut; it was barely twelve o'clock and custom was waxing.

Neither nature nor necessity hurried the carter: leisurely in movement, as in disposition, he made his way to The George and drank another pint. Emerging, he saw Mary on the opposite side of the street, by the saddler's. She was walking away from him fast; before he could get clear of the crowd she was a long way ahead, work as he would with his powerful, thrusting shoulders, in spite of the unexpected sinuousness he displayed in gliding through narrow apertures, where rough and ready shoving would have been the only means employed by smaller and more avid persons. He attained the opposite pavement in time to see her turn into a teashop which had been newly established in the Ticestor Road. He followed her, feeling conspicuous and ashamed. He stayed several minutes outside the shop before he could make up his mind to go in, gazing through the glass window at the people inside... he saw an expectant-looking waitress in a green linen dress standing with her eyes fixed on the door, and another very young girl who, with her slender arm stretched out, hung intent over the tray of cakes in the window. Behind her there were hints of easy forms reclining in coloured cane chairs, cigarette smoke floating lightly up to the ceiling. These sights interested him, but now his errand seemed ridiculous. He hesitated: 'What, frightened of the women? Shall I stand here and wait till she comes out and then hand her the prayer book? No, I'll go in. I'll buy a bag of doughnuts for the children!' His face lightened at the thought; he pushed the door open. A woman in furs was coming out, with a little veil dropping from her hat over half her face. Beneath, her painted mouth was parted. He stood aside to let her pass, and she was so close to him that he smelt a sweet dusty perfume, and saw the line of rouge along her lips. She turned her head over her shoulder, smiled at him, simply and gaily. This farther encouraged him, and he entered without awkwardness.

While the fragile ladylike waitress piled doughnuts into the bag with surprisingly thick fingers, he looked around the room for Mary.

She was sitting at a small table in the corner, drinking coffee, and holding a cigarette in her drooping hand. She looked cold and pale, with dry lips and heavy eyes. The carter regarded her, sighed, and took his doughnuts absently:

19

he drew the prayer book from his pocket and, going across to her, laid it on the table beside her plate as the best means of indicating his presence and the reason for it.

She glanced up, astonished at the sight of her book and the rough hand on the tablecloth, and recognised the carter who had taken a pace backwards. She smiled. This man was now her equal. Such folk would be the only ones to cross her threshold. Formerly she would hardly have acknowledged a good day from this labourer, least of all in front of gentlefolk – of whom she had always considered herself – now she was almost effusive. She wanted familiarity that she might press the insult close like a corrosive iron upon her tenderness, and burn away all feeling – once and for all.

She spoke loudly and easily. Everyone could hear.

'Have some coffee with me?'

He shook his head, and peered at the bag in his hands on which warm grease stains were appearing.

'No, thank you. No, thank you, miss.'

'Oh, you must!'

'I must be off. I picked that up in the cart this morning after you'd gone. It's a pity the ewes 'ud trod on it. I'm sorry.'

'That's nothing,' she touched the soiled leather cover, and for a second or two seemed to forget his presence. Her fingers smoothed the dog-eared leaves. He would have gone away silently. He was out of place here – it would be better to return to The George.

'Tell me your name.'

'Dallett, miss... William Dallett. I works over at Gillow. Good afternoon, miss.'

20

'Don't go. Please sit down, and have some coffee with me.'

She saw that he was puzzled and for the first time it occurred to her that she might be making him look a fool, might be hurting him. Several people were regarding them. Immobile from bewilderment and fright he repeated that he must be going.

'Sit down, please. Or won't you have anything to do with me?'

He hastily sat down, but refused everything she offered him, nor would he open his mouth. Mary continued to smoke. She pushed the packet of cigarettes towards him.

'Would you like to please me... would you? Then take those cigarettes.'

Dallett was more abashed than ever: 'I don't want to rob you, miss.'

'There... I don't want them. Put them in your pocket.'

He did so.

'Thank you, miss.'

'Don't call me "miss". I was married this morning.'

He gaped.

'I hope you'll be very happy.'

She felt a thrill of anguish. She spread her smooth hands on the table.

'Look!'

'Why, where's the ring?'

'My husband married me with an old worthless one of his which he took away as soon as we left the church. What do you think of that?'

'Tchach!' the carter ejaculated contemptuously. The waitress thought them a most peculiar couple, the man

21

without a collar who sat looking between his knees and the elegant woman who sometimes spoke so loudly that her voice could be heard in the kitchens, and at others almost below her breath, sinking her head as if she were ashamed.

Dallett sat a while longer, gradually regaining his composure. Mary found his company soothing. Her eyes dwelt on his face, on his large features, his hanging brow as rich in colour as his brown and scarlet cheeks. His own eyes were cast down but when he raised them they did not waver. She wondered why she should feel so grateful for his compassion. His empty sleeve terminated in a pathetic hook. At last he stood up to go: she was sorry.

'See here,' said he, extending his one hand, 'this might be useful to you.'

He was offering her a thin metal ring of strange dull colour.

'What is that?'

'It's made of gun-metal. I brought it home from the War. Take it; you needn't be ashamed to wear it. I took your fags.'

'I'm not ashamed! I'll wear it. Thank you... gun-metal!'

Thoughtfully she put it on her marriage finger. When she looked up, the carter was about to leave the shop. As he went out the waitress called after him pertly: 'You haven't paid for the doughnuts.'

He felt very small.

II

Easter's master, Matt Kilminster, led an increasingly blank existence. He was sometimes tortured by the vacancy of everything. Lately he had taken to drinking....

'As an example to others,' he declared. He drew a fairly large income from Welsh breweries.

People noticed the depression which was beginning to grow upon him. His body seemed inert, and his gloomy eyes seldom followed anything beyond the direct frontal line of vision. He had pleasant manners verging on indifference.

He was the only son of a well-to-do north Herefordshire gentleman, who had married his housekeeper late in life. The blood was running thin from its antique source, and in this case was but erratically strengthened. Matt was queer – shiftless, easy going, vehement. He ran away from school twice, he refused point-blank to go to the

University. When he was twenty-four his father died, a doting old man who was, with difficulty, prevailed upon to leave his property to his wife and son, instead of bequeathing it on maudlin conditions to a widow in the village who used to send him flowers from her garden.

Mrs Kilminster, relieved, threw the last futile withering bunch on the bonfire. Eighteen months later she died. Matt was married to a Cardiff doctor's daughter. He sold the house and the two farms, and came down to live in south Herefordshire.

His house was five miles out of Salus in Brelshope parish, a red brick Georgian building which looked out of place amid the surrounding fields until on approaching its dilapidations became more apparent. With it he possessed three hundred acres of land which he let to a tenant farmer, who was his nearest neighbour.

It was known by a peculiar name standing near a crossroads, where there had been a gibbet; it was called The Gallustree, and it was said that a portion of the cross beam had been worked into the porch. Built on high ground which rose sharply from the river valley and the water meadows, it could be seen for a considerable distance, a graceful construction with a rank walled garden. Seen thus it looked well, but a nearer view exposed its painful demission. Money was freely spent on clumsy unskilful repairs: the paint on windows and door was new, thick, white; the most beautiful thing about it, a wall in the form of a cupid's bow, four feet high, which separated the narrow front garden from a strip of greensward beside the road, had collapsed in one place, and been mended with rough stone blocks projecting far

24

beyond the original curve; an old urn, missing from among its fellows on the high garden wall, had been replaced by a modern monstrosity almost orange in hue; an atrocious, a terrible excrescence of pale green glass and white painted wood adhering to one side completely destroyed its delicately calculated proportions. Inside, moulded ceilings had been tampered with and valuable fireplaces mauled. The house, decorated throughout in vile standard taste, testified to the plebeian strain in the inhabitants. People, gentle and simple, who had lived in Brelshope for generations, mourned over the time when it had been an unadorned farmhouse, falling to ruin perhaps, but accomplishing that with mellow grace: they looked askance at its owners.

The house was overshadowed by a group of fine elms which grew on a grassy mound on the opposite side of the road. It was supposed that Danes were buried there. A path, no more than a few yards in length, traversed the front garden from gate to doorsteps. Cars were obliged to draw up outside. Dorothy Kilminster considered the possibility of constructing a glass passage to save her visitors' hats on a wet day. The visitors, however, did not appear in great numbers, and the idea collapsed. Yellow crocuses, old lavender bushes, and a monkey tree grew in the front. The stables and outbuildings were at the back, divided from the house by a sloping lawn and a thick, low, laurel hedge. A young sycamore tree sprang from the centre of the lawn girdled around with a circular iron seat; in fine summer weather, Dorothy Kilminster spent much time beneath its boughs reading and doing her embroidery. Even in winter she was sometimes to be seen sitting well wrapped up in her fur coat, a scarf over her blonde head, her hands folded in her lap, gazing over the hedge. Easter hated this practice; he fancied she spied upon him. Her eyes followed him as he worked.

Matt refused to run a car – he disliked them. He kept only one hunter, a hack, and two ponies for the children, so that Easter filled in time doing odd jobs. At present the title 'groom' as applied to him was in sober reality more ambitious than true. Easter looked after the horses; he also drove the children to the station and back – they went to school by train – milked the two jersey cows, and even worked in the garden.

At one time Matt had a pack of otter hounds kennelled in his empty stables, but Mrs Kilminster objected to the noise, and the smell made her sick. He very reluctantly gave them up. Since then the yard seemed very empty. Easter and his master shared a secret grievance; they had both loved the hounds and missed the wild floating cries which had awakened them in the early mornings.

* * *

Easter brooded on the coming night.

He sat in the harness room before a little red fire cleaning some mouldy harness which Matt would not sell. His stained hands flew; visions violent or poignantly gentle filled his imagination. The door was open; he constantly turned his head to see if Mary were coming into the yard. It was dark. Matt Kilminster was walking about on the lawn. He had nothing else to do and he found his wife tedious. There was raw fog in the air.

He watched Easter through the open harness room door, rubbing the leather across his knees. The firelight exposed his high arrogant features, his broad working shoulders. Matt had given him a holiday.

'Strange... he was married today. What made him come back to work?' the watcher thought. He smoked cigarette after cigarette, consumed by ennui. His mouth was dried up. The dinner gong roused him; yawning, he turned towards the house and as he did so Easter emerged, locking the saddle-room door behind him.

'Goodnight,' Matt called. He liked Easter, and paused for a moment to question him, but he walked away rapidly, striding rakish and assured across the yard.

'Goodnight, sir,' he answered carelessly.

Matt saw him mount the wooden steps to the two rooms above the old brewing house, which he had inhabited since he came to work at The Gallustree, three years before. No lights showed. Matt wondered.

The gong again rang. He threw away the end of his cigarette, and returned to his house, which harboured its own peculiarities.

Easter shut and bolted his door. He wished Mary to entreat that he should open it and let her into the bed where she had lain in his arms the whole of one autumn night. His neck swelled. He laughed, took off his boots in the dark, and sat for several minutes thinking about it, while his teeth tore at a ragged fingernail; but he was ravenously hungry, he craved for food.

He felt about on the table for the lamp which he always left ready to be lighted. He could not find it so he struck a match, and his eyes flitted over the room suspiciously.

On the table, bare and unscrubbed, with dark rings on the wood, like a dirty pub's, were the remains of a baked fish, a vinegar bottle, and several broken crusts of brown bread; there were also an enamel teapot, half full of cold tea, and a cup without saucer or handle. Nothing had been touched since the meal he had had in the morning.

The match expired... Easter crammed the crusts into his mouth and went into the next room. The full moon, newly arisen, was shining through the window on the bed, a muffled light, dimmed by the raw vapour outside. He was able to make out a woman's shape beneath the bed clothes. His wife had come home, sneaked in secretly. All blanched, she lay there huddled, her knees drawn up, her hands clasped under her chin, as though she were cold, or afraid, or perhaps, in pain. The light imparted a rigidity, a sculptured rhythm to her outline, but the sheet over her breast moved mysteriously. He bent down to look closely at the face on the indented pillow.

She was dead asleep, too weary to feel his breath on her neck and her naked shoulder – the bare, blooming flesh shone with pearly lustre against the harsh white sheet. He saw a narrow satin ribbon.

She was wearing a chemise, and the rest of her clothes were folded up on a chair beside her; her coat was spread over her feet.

He whispered close to her face: 'Mary, do you hear me?'

She did not; at first he thought he would wake her, then he stood up straight and considered. No hurry.

Slowly, very quietly, he examined the clothes, holding them in the light, feeling the silk with his hard, dirty fingers, which reeked of harness cream and stale leather. He remembered his mother washing clothes like this and hanging them out to dry... in that instant he recollected her lean figure strained up to the line, the clothes prop with dried bark peeling off the wood, and even the scrubby grass, the little daisies under her feet. He used to carry the empty basket back to the kitchen along a path between blackcurrant bushes. He heard the twigs brushing against that withy basket – twenty-five years ago.

He rolled the clothes up and threw them behind the chest of drawers. All the pockets in the coat were empty. The belt of moonlight across the room lengthened, began to creep up the door.

He went and sat down in a dark corner where he could watch Mary without being seen, if she should awaken, planning how he would wake her, and leap out and clasp her, so that she could not breathe. Spite and desire, which could not bear delay, contended within him. He held his chin in his hands. Practically invisible, he sat smiling away in his corner.

She awoke before he was ready, and turned over on her back. For a moment she felt peaceful, comfortable and warm; a lamb's thin shuddering cry, a horse moving, were all the sounds that she heard. Then Easter sprang from the darkness, his hand and arm barred the window, his silver ring glittered. He closed the shutters.

The shock almost deprived Mary of her senses; half erect in the bed, she let her head fall on her supporting arm, and put out her hand defensively as he came towards her in the utter darkness. Her fingers encountered his hot mouth, he shut his lips over them so that she could feel the point of his teeth pressing lightly on her skin. He murmured indistinctly, the wordless mutters of extremity, and his hands touched her bosom. Instantly her passionless limbs kindled to his as though she were a joyful woman welcoming a beloved man. In disgust at herself she leapt away from him, out of the bed, and once more opening the shutters wide, stood revealed, trembling and half naked. Easter looked at her bare thighs, her straight, slender legs, and he changed his mind as he had that morning when she resisted him. He wanted her tenderness, he wanted to be soothed, he longed for her to caress him, to weep, and to be his entirely, as if his own spirit animated her.

'Mary,' he said, 'Mary, Mary, Mary...' He moved his hands jerkily. She slowly turned her head towards him and looked at him. He jumped to his feet.

'No,' she said inflexibly. She flung her head back, holding him off with rigid arms. Fuming and thwarted he thrust his fingers into her long hair, and tugged at it until the tears ran out of her eyes; she seized his wrist and her whole frame stiffened in the effort to tear away his hand. Suddenly he let her go. He did not want her. He gave a deep sigh, walked out of the room, and locked her in.

For two hours he wandered about the fields, keeping close under the hedges – the wind was still bitter. At ten o'clock he returned angry, and ready to be vicious. She was sitting wrapped in blankets at the foot of the bed. He threw off his clothes, lifted her bodily to him, and lying down beside her put his arms around her. The contact betrayed her into a renewal of love, but all night she moaned and her face was wet with tears. He tasted them

30

on her mouth, salt and biting, he felt them on his own face, his neck, his breast.... They slept. The moon set, the day broke. As soon as it grew light enough to see, Easter got up and began to dress. His expression was lifeless, the yellow tinge in his face had deepened. Mary could not bear to look at him. A terrible longing after happiness took possession of her.

He raged unsatisfied.

*　　*　　*

In the house one other person was awake. The eyes of anyone passing might have lifted to an upper window where a young girl was sitting, her arms crossed on the sill, her solemn gaze on the grey east.

She wore a white nightgown with long, loose sleeves; her shoulders were covered with an eiderdown. Her lips moved, for she was saying her prayers.

After a few minutes she drew back, closed the window, and disappeared. There was a poor light in the room, such as might be given by a single candle.

This serious girl was Matt Kilminster's elder daughter. He had at this time three children, two girls and a boy. His elder daughter, Phoebe, was just fifteen, the younger Rosamund, ten. Philip was nearly six.

Phoebe suffered agonies from a nervous temperament which she rigidly controlled. She was a girl of serious, even pious, disposition, and very grave demeanour, altogether an astonishing contrast to her family, who beneath their inconsequent disorderliness and turbulent self-assertion, were remarkably well balanced and self-centred. From

31

blows that would have prostrated less elastic souls they sprang erect, with the exception of Matt himself, whom Phoebe resembled in many ways. She was gifted, not alone among them, but particularly. She saw far and truly; she was growing very fast and her quick perceptions often made her very gloomy. There was much which tended to develop this side of her character; Matt, like a great many of his neighbours, frequently drank himself sick and stupid. His wife wept and reviled him at the top of her voice as they lay in bed, rising and running about the room, sometimes throwing her brushes and scent bottles at his head, or stamping her feet while she called the children to look at their father. She would tell all her friends that it was impossible to go on – they must separate. No woman should be called upon to live with a drunkard. She confided everywhere. Then a day or two later, perhaps sooner, they would become reconciled, for they were really quite attached to each other, and everything went on in just the same old slapdash, slovenly manner. Phoebe's natural reverence for her parents suffered severely.

Rosamund detested her spoilt little brother (once at six years old she had attempted to kill him by rushing him round and round the orchard in his perambulator, until she dropped to the ground exhausted), quarrelled with him, continually exasperated her parents, and distracted her teachers. She was a fierce, sullen child; the servants feared her, people never teased or played with her, the girls at her school were in awe of her. Only animals loved her, particularly dogs, because she defended them from all cruelty with zealous pertinacity, and saved up scraps for them from her own meals, which she hoarded up for them in the wood shed.

She had once gone otter hunting... the hounds had worried a rabbit... she could not forget the red strips down there among the trampled reeds by the stream. She had gone to Matt's room, taken out his blue coat, cut off the gold buttons, and slashed the cuffs. The cap she stuffed into the kitchen range. The cook – a new one – who attempted to stop her, received a basin of embryo apple fritters, full in the face – oh, what an uproar! Matt intended to whip her.

Undoubtedly a great share of the violent scenes that shook the household were due to her, and to Philip's querulous exactions. All the outbreaks of temper, the unrestrained self-indulgent exhibitions, served as so many vent holes, but Phoebe had no outlet save her work, her own nature denied it. She studied incessantly, and fought all her battles in her soul.

While she was still very young she began to make curious conduct rules for herself, and she kept to them strictly. This peculiar characteristic, at first merely puerile and absurd, developed and became gallingly restrictive. The child made up her mind not to climb a certain tree, not to say 'what', not to sit on the kitchen table: the girl set herself to work four hours in the evening after a full school day, to practise scales for an hour before her seven o'clock breakfast, to turn herself into a housemaid on Saturdays.

She was gentle, obstinate, sensitive and more passionate than anybody suspected. She was brilliantly clever. At school she was far ahead of her contemporaries; she seemed to fly where they walked.

Most of the qualities she displayed, and many that she concealed, were unique in the family. The fact was, she resembled Dorothy's mother, a remarkable Welsh woman.

The resemblance did not extend to appearance; the grandmother had been a beauty, Phoebe was plain, overgrown; there her sister had the advantage of her. Rosamund was a handsome child, compact and well made, with large narrow eyes, and full, soft lips; Phoebe was tall and bony, with a sallow complexion, a harassed expression, and long, perfectly straight hair, which she wore in two plaits. A gold wire confined her teeth, her thin hands and feet were large and red. But she also possessed a sonorous, roomy voice, both speaking and singing, beautiful, deliberate, even haunting, like the voice of a mature woman.

This, at present, was her only attraction.

* * *

Phoebe stretched up her cold arms to pull down the window. It was loose in the frame and made a noise loud enough to wake Rosamund, who slept in the same room. She closed and parted her lips, with a faint smacking sound, as a sleeping child does when it turns over.

'What are you doing?'

'Getting up.'

'It's not morning yet.'

'Yes, it is. Go to sleep.'

Phoebe pulled her long nightgown over her head. She stood naked in the candlelight, shivering in the icy dawn.

'You're all goose-fleshy,' Rosamund murmured. She turned on her back, her half-shut eyes on a cobweb in the angle of the wall. A little cat sleeping between her neck and shoulder, half under the twisted bedclothes, stood up on her chest and arched its back, sweeping its tail across her mouth. She shut her eyes and dozed.

Phoebe brushed and plaited her hair.

The corners of the room were in darkness; the furniture, the heavily draped curtains, the sleeping child in the disordered bed, were almost indistinguishable. A silver Christ on his ebony cross hung catching the light; the knees, high cheekbones, ribs, and clenched fingers sparkled. Phoebe's hair shone with a soft yellow splendour, hanging like long tassels from her weaving fingers. The dawn was advancing in sound as in sight.

Rosamund made an abrupt movement.

'I've had a horrid dream, Phib. I dreamed worms were coming out of my nose... long ones.'

'How beastly!'

Phoebe put on her white blouse and her short tunic, which did not set off her long neck, sloping shoulders, and narrow bony fingers. She thrust her thumbs behind her heels into her cold, heavy shoes, and pulled them over her chilblains, gritting her teeth with pain. All her movements were spasmodically rapid, but two or three times in the course of dressing she stood arrested, absolutely still, as though thinking deeply, and her face took on in those moments a remote peaceful expression, very lovely in its profound calm. When strangers saw this look they wondered what she was thinking about; sometimes they asked, and she would come to herself and laugh, or turn very red, and the nervous worried frown, the restless glances, would return directly.

When she was dressed she left the room quietly, walking on her toes in case her tread in the passage should awake the others. But a moment later Rosamund awoke to find her leaning over the bed trying to twitch the cat from her warm nest. Mrs Pussy, privileged matriarch, gave forth a lugubrious yowl. Rosamund raised her damp face and sat up; with one hand she firmly retained the animal, while she planted the other on Phoebe's chest, to push her away. Phoebe drew herself up, her hands dangling.

'She's made a mess...'

Rosamund scowled.

'Don't be silly, Ros. Let me take her – you know she's got to be punished.'

'She's *my* cat, and I'll punish her.'

'No, you won't; you never do. And in the end she'll have to be drowned.'

'Yes, and you'll give Easter a pot of jam to do it, like you did with my darling Tibbins.'

'Oh, I never did!' Phoebe expostulated, her mouth aghast.

Rosamund's narrow eyes flashed.

'You did... you did! And he shoved him in a sack and threw him over the bridge, lovely Tibbins, who never did any harm, only had worms in his poor little tummy. Just you try it again, that's all!'

She threw herself back on the pillow, snorting and clutching the cat. Her angry voice dropped: 'Go away... leave me alone... and shut door... so can't hear... piano,' she muttered disconnectedly. Her lips fell apart, she sighed deeply, turning her head over her shoulder, and went fast asleep still clasping the cat.

Phoebe went downstairs to get a shovel from the kitchen. It was empty and cold as a cavern; the curtains were drawn across the long window, bulging over the geraniums on the window sill, the strip of drugget in front of the range had been rolled back. From a saucer on the fender, half full of congealed white fat – a concoction of melted soap and cold cream, used by the young cook for her complexion – arose a sweet, sickly smell. An old round wooden clock suspended over the mantelpiece pointed to five minutes to six.

As Phoebe stooped to pick up the shovel the handle of the back door moved as though somebody were trying it. There was a pause while she watched the brass knob turn, but the door was locked and bolted, and the person outside found it impossible to enter.

'Lily, open the door.'

It was Easter's voice. He was speaking below his breath, but distinctly as though his mouth were close to the keyhole.

'Open the door,' he repeated after a moment of silence.

Phoebe did not move. She heard him drag something across the cobbles. Above the door, a little more than a man's height from the ground, there was a square of glass. She lifted her eyes to it in a strained, expectant stare, and saw Easter's face. The greyish-green colour of the dirty glass lent an odd tinge to his skin; he looked livid, the upper teeth were showing, and a large spider's web, really on the inside, seemed at that distance to be hanging from his mouth. A light wavered over his jaws thrown upwards from the lantern he had set on the ground.

He fixed his eyes on Phoebe. She had recognised his

voice. She was not very frightened but it was a fact which only lately she had discovered, that she could not see or hear or be near him without shrinking. Her lips formed words which she did not utter aloud: 'Curious, fantastic man – you're like a goblin.'

And truly he did look very much like a goblin.

After a moment he disappeared. Phoebe snatched the shovel and the candle.

After she had rectified Mrs Pussy's mistake she went to practise. The piano was a little out of tune. Mrs Kilminster spent a great deal of money on clothes, cinemas, cats, or any other luxury which appealed to her at the moment, but she paid little heed to household matters. The piano's shrill tone hurt Phoebe, who possessed an excellent ear.

It was an old walnut grand, with yellowing keys which jammed in cold or damp weather. The day before, Phoebe had placed a small glass cup, filled with purple violets, on the lid. She smelt them directly she opened the door, and before she began to practise she lifted them to her face, plunging her nose among the blossoms while she inhaled the fragrance. She looked at them... looked at them smiling, thinking of the spring that was coming and the sheltered border where they grew. She lit the candles on the piano, and beat her hands to warm them.

She played minor scales because she loved them – she was apt to neglect the others. The whole vast realm of music held no greater magic for her than the exquisite minor fall; in a sense one could progress no farther, it was heaven attained – by ten cold fingers exercising on a senile keyboard. Her mouth opened a little – she forgot everything. The room in which she was sitting looked over the lawn. It had been given to her as a study for her own special use, although like nearly all her possessions, it was shared by Rosamund. Here Mrs Kilminster crammed all the furniture she particularly disliked; anything she considered ugly found its way to Phoebe's study. Against the walls there were two carved bookcases, a fragile china cupboard, with glass doors, rejected as being too plain to stand comparison with the inlaid drawing-room furniture (which indeed it was), a wrinkled leather sofa boasting a chenille fringe as a decoration, several cane chairs which did not match, and a little mahogany table lacking a leaf. A square polished table occupied the centre of the room. On it was a glass lamp with an empty bowl – Phoebe had worked late – a neat pile of exercise books, a few textbooks in brown-paper covers, a fountain pen, and a ruler. Two satchels dangled behind the door.

A blue carpet covered the entire floor. Long, stiff curtains of green and gold brocade were looped back from the narrow window. The piano took up the whole of one corner, and its tail jutted almost into the middle of the room, so that the housemaid, who was plump, had to squeeze herself uncomfortably between it and the table.

Phoebe played scales without looking at her hands, her eyes were fixed on the window, but it never occurred to her to extinguish the unnecessary candles.

Presently the servant came in to light the fire. When it had caught she rose from her knees on the hearth, pushed her cap off her forehead with her ashy fingers, and began to dust the mantelpiece. Her figure and movements were clumsy. She had a peculiar habit of grinding her teeth while she worked, which made it difficult for her to keep a place.

She began to talk, turning her head towards Phoebe, who had ceased playing and sat resting her aching wrists. From time to time she coughed, and afterwards she always hit herself hard on the breast, cleared her throat and shook her shoulders impatiently. She seemed out of temper with the universe. Phoebe asked her if she had a cold.

'Yes, miss, indeed. And I've been blowing the kitchen fire till the smoke got in my throat... the bellows is gone into holes. It seems there was a wedding yesterday?' she suddenly concluded, rubbing the table with both hands.

'Yes, Easter was married.'

Phoebe gave the servant a penetrating glance: 'Did the smoke get into your eyes too?' she asked gently.

'Yes, the tears streamed. Are they red?'

'A little.'

The girl rubbed her eyes with her knuckles.

'That'll make them worse,' said Phoebe, 'spit on your fingers. Look, like this.' She had done it before.

The servant allowed the saliva to dry on her swollen eyelids.

'Have you seen the "bride", miss?'

'No,' said Phoebe. She sighed and struck an octave. She did like her old piano.

'They say she's quite a lady... rather a come-down for her to live in a loft! There's been a lot of talk... I hope I never have to get married.'

She coughed again and slapped her chest.

'Lily,' Phoebe demanded abruptly, 'has Easter... did he...?' She broke off.

The servant stood close to the table, leaning her hip against its edge. She had twisted the duster into a long tight tube, and without looking at what she was doing, she tied it into knots. Phoebe could not see her face. 'There's no good in that Easter,' said Lily hoarsely, 'he'd get any girl into trouble quicker than she'd understand – an' then he'd be off. But thank God there's nothing the matter with *me*, nor never will be so far as he has anything to do with it. "Easter," I says, "don't you go thinking you've a common farm labourer's daughter to deal with, nor a charity girl that's been taken in and sheltered by a silly old woman that can't see she's playing the fool... don't you think that." I saw him go white,' she proclaimed with a vindictive glance, grinding her teeth most viciously.

'I may be a servant, but so far I've kept myself... I've kept myself away from that. And it wasn't for want of chances. I've had some tussles!'

Mrs Kilminster did not believe in enlightening her children. Phoebe did not altogether understand. She recognised the allusion to Easter's wife.

'What do you mean?'

'Why that I might be where that woman is.'

'Easter's wife?'

'Easter's...' she did not say the word; after a moment she continued furiously: 'six weeks ago nothing kept him away from that back door. He lived there. "Lily, let's get into the barn... I'll look after you..."'

She coughed so wildly that she was forced to stop.

Phoebe regarded her with a most mournful and moved expression; it was remarkable that her face wore a piteous pleading smile. But she was quite silent while the servant cleared her throat and blew her nose. Again she laid her hands on the keys.

'Miss Phoebe, he come this morning to the kitchen and he says, "Lily, this wedding business makes no difference, it was forced on me. Open the door just a little way for me to tell you something." So I did, and he stuck his ugly yellow face in, laughing and showing all his teeth.

'"I'm married," he says. "What do you think of that?"

'"I know it," I says, "and I pity your wife."

'"Do you?" he says, and he comes right in and shuts the door after him, "you've no need. Last night while you was lying in your bed alone we were together with nothing between us… flesh against flesh, and with our arms round each other." He says, "Have you ever had someone lying so close to you that their breath was like dew on your skin?" Then he begins to tell me about… her, and… all the time he was talking, he grinned and laughed, and held me fast against the wall. If he was to die I'd say it was a judgement and rejoice!'

She stopped, glaring and choking, and thrust one hand down the bosom of her dress, tearing it open as though she were longing for air. There was a ripping sound, the worn material hung in a jagged triangle over the bib of her apron. Her face and the skin which the opening exposed were suffused with red. The next moment she ran from the room. Phoebe followed, half expecting to see her fling herself headlong down the stairs; however, she was standing at the foot of them, biting her lips.

'Lily,' said Phoebe softly, behind her. She bent forward.

'Are you sorry for me?' Lily asked, in a hoarse, muffled voice.

'Yes, I'm sorry for you.'

'You needn't be. There are better fish…'

She turned to look up at Phoebe whose poignant slight smile was at once so miserable and so compassionate.

'Don't think about it, miss, and for the Lord's sake don't tell anybody.'

'Of course I shan't tell.'

'I'm going to leave...'

Phoebe did think about it. She could not help it. She feared Easter, and he occupied a place by himself in her mind, a troubled corner where his dark image stirred restlessly, threateningly. She perceived his cruelty, and she could not understand it. She had seen him drowning kittens in a bucket, laughing at their feeble clawing, poking them under the water with his fingers, pulling them out and re-immersing them.

When he came to work at The Gallustree, Phoebe had been twelve years old. One day she was standing in the yard, watching him unharness the pony. He was whistling and taking no notice of her. She asked for a ride. Easter nodded, smiling kindly. He put her up with the harness still on, holding the reins. The buckles hurt her, and after a quiet turn round the yard she wanted to get down; but to her alarm he led the pony into the paddock... a sudden slash with the reins and the pony broke into a gallop, tossing her up and down on the buckles. She never forgot Easter's laughing face as he ran, holding the long reins. When they stopped she slid to the ground stupefied by his unkindness.

'I wanted to see if you were afraid,' he said, looking at the tears in her eyes. His expression changed and she fled, terrified. He could persecute her with a glance; she knew he was aware of it. When she thought about him she felt self-conscious, and a pang went through her as though he had touched her. She saw him walking insolently, staring out of the corners of his eyes, smiling. 'He's spiteful, scornful, mocking. I am afraid of him.'

She went off into a long wandering meditation, which made her very unhappy: her shadowed face looked almost haggard.

* * *

At a quarter past eight Easter drove the trap round to the front gate. As no one was there waiting he climbed out and stood near the pony's head. He wore shabby grey breeches and leggings, and his head was bare. He waited, the eyes scanning the windows, grinding his heel into the weedy road. The east wind blew violently, harder than the day before, roaring in the branches of the elms on the Danes' Mount. Dead twigs fell to the ground. The desolate monkey tree, the long unpruned rambler shoots, the young firs, even the snowdrops so close to the earth, trembled and waved. Some lavender bushes growing by the wall looked like brittle grey skeletons.

Easter beat his hands on his shoulders. Mrs Pussy lay under the wall, rolling and scrabbling in the dead leaves. She rushed up a tree and lay along a branch; the high wind had infected her with temporary madness. Easter stooped and picked up a pebble which he intended to throw at her, but seeing Rosamund run down the steps he put the pebble in his pocket. Phoebe followed her, buckling the strap of her satchel, and they all got in.

It was a governess car. Phoebe sat beside Easter, so that in driving his back was three-quarters presented to her.

She chose her position because she could not see his face. Rosamund sat opposite, her round knees in darned brown stockings, thrust indifferently between his.

She peered at him.

'Aren't you well?' she demanded.

'There's nothing amiss with me,' he replied. He was a horrible colour. He turned his head over his shoulder and gave Phoebe the long, knowing stare that made her feel so uncomfortable.

Rosamund sat crunching an apple and blowing on her fingers. On reaching the station a few minutes later she gave the core to the pony, and at her leisure followed Phoebe along the platform.

III

On her birthday, which was the seventeenth of March, Mary left The Gallustree for the first time since her marriage. She went to Salus, and having walked from the station, returned about six o'clock. As she entered the yard she heard a woman's furious voice, and Easter growling in reply. The sounds proceeded from an empty loose box, which was used for storing wood. A wheelbarrow containing several logs was standing on the cobbles outside the open door. Following a particularly loud outburst when both voices, grumbling and screeching reached a climax, when they were indistinguishable, Lily emerged stumbling, her arms thrown out as if there were force behind her. Her face was distorted. She approached Mary and stared at her with the eyes of an angry cat.

'I should think you'd be ashamed to come out!'

'Say something pretty for a change,' Easter jeered.

Mary caught sight of him as he stood leaning against the wall, a log balanced on each hand. He hurled them into the barrow. Lily left the yard at a run: she was leaving on the morrow and had been having a final scene with Easter.

'You've got to take Lily to the station,' the cook told him next morning when he walked into the kitchen with the milk. Her cheeks were smothered with a white grease, her soft fine hair was pinned in a slatternly knot on the top of her head. With one foot on the fender she shamelessly adjusted her garters. Mrs Pussy was sitting on the table; the cloth, stained and torn, lay in wrinkles. Easter came close to the young cook, and taking the poker jabbed it between the bars till the sparks fell in showers.

'Warm your legs,' he said, smiling sidelong. The cook jerked her skirt from his fingers.

'Now then, behave yourself! You heard what I said, didn't you?'

'What time?' he asked morosely.

'Catch the ten-forty. You'd better clear; I hear Miss Phoebe. She's in and out of the kitchen all day Saturdays.'

'I'll drop in tonight and make the acquaintance of the new girl.'

'No, you won't. You stay in the yard or get off to The Dog, but keep clear of the kitchen for a bit. Mrs Kilminster can't bear the sight of you – you'll have to be on the look out for a new job soon. She give me a real rowing about you being in here so much, and I'm not so anxious to see your face...'

She turned her back, planted her feet firmly on the floor, and reaching for a handkerchief began to wipe her face. As he went out she muttered it was all his fault and then,

47

hearing the postman, rushed away to see if there were a letter from her regular young man who was respectable.

Much later in the morning Matt and his wife were sitting at breakfast. A glass door led into the ugly conservatory, where she kept her birds. They kept up a continual piping, interrupted now and then by a shrill cry whirring like clockwork running down.

Dorothy did not, as a rule, interfere with her husband's concerns; indeed, she took no interest in them. He was astonished when she suddenly asked him to dismiss Easter. He pushed his chair away from the table and let the newspaper fall on the floor.

'I shan't do anything so ridiculous. Why ever should I?'

'Very well,' said Dorothy disagreeably. Then she began to upbraid him with Easter's morals. 'And you,' she shouted in her thin, high voice, 'what sort of an example are you?'

'I'm a chaste man, aren't I?'

'God knows, I don't. You're a drunkard.'

'Easter's not.'

Matt leaned back in his chair, clasping his hands behind his head. Dorothy rejoined:

'Oh, isn't he? That's where you're wrong. I've watched him... I've seen him in the harness room drinking out of a flask. He keeps it hidden behind the stove.'

'Good luck to him,' Matt exclaimed, but his face was serious. He immediately got up, left the house and went to search in the harness room. He found nothing. Returning he said: 'You see you're wrong. Why do you want to make a scene?'

She had lighted a cigarette, and sprawled across the

48

table on her elbows, blowing out angry jets of smoke. Even at breakfast her cheeks were rouged, high up under the eyes. Anger flushed her deeper.

'I tell you I've seen him when he could hardly stagger across the yard...'

'Will you be quiet?'

'Get rid of Easter and that woman. With my own eyes...'

'Oh, damn your eyes, and hold your tongue!' But she would not. She railed at Matt until he too began to show signs of temper. A rumour of foot-and-mouth had put a stop to hunting; after all, it was something to do. The altercation waxed into a bitter dispute, and waned into a final sulky silence, which might take days to break.

The inner door opened and through the narrowest possible aperture a little boy, with a white subtle face and black eyes, set very close together, slipped into the room. He was absolutely naked except for a pair of plaid bedroom shoes, and he carried some clothes in each hand.

Dorothy gave him a long tender smile, holding out her arms. She took him up on her knee and he buried his face in her neck. After he had slightly relaxed a throttling embrace, she leant forward to the fire, still clasping the child with one arm, and held his garments to warm. Meanwhile he was helping himself to sugar and lighting another cigarette for his mother.

'What have you been doing, my darling?'

'In bed,' he drawled.

'Lazy little boy!'

'Phib told me something funny about Cal-pur-nia.'

'Well, who was Calpurnia?' demanded Matt, inwardly contemptuous of Phoebe's choice. Philip answered: 'A

49

frog. She has a house in the hedge with Mr Caesar. *This* is how they talk: "Good morning Miss Cleo-pat-ra, is it going to be a fine day?"'

He drew in his breath, talking in a grating backwards voice. His eyes goggled: 'Cleo-pat-ra is a snail.'

'Oh,' said Matt. He looked at the mother and child – a pretty, self-indulgent couple. Dorothy was thin, slender, and very small. Her face interested him no longer. The smoothness and lack of shadows or lines, the little nose and mouth, the dull pink flush beneath the light changeless eyes, might have held great appeal for a younger man. She wore her fair hair in profuse curls on her neck, and when she bent her head it fell over her cheeks and forehead, so that sometimes she singed the ends while she was smoking. Wherever she went she carried with her an odd, rather pleasant, smell of cigarette smoke, expensive perfume, and slightly burnt hair. She loved bright, unconventional colours, and rich fabrics. Her clothes were usually heavy, clinging, and gaudy, even in the mornings. She was wearing a sea-green silk robe, with huge fanlike sleeves, a pearl necklace, and high-heeled brocade shoes. She was a costly person.

She dressed the child slowly. He jumped off her knee and squatted in front of the fire, sipping cold coffee. She rose, smoothed his straight, black hair with a caress, and holding her own curls back from her high forehead, stared at herself with bent head, in the low-hanging mirror. She had two inseparable companions: her son, and her own mirrored face. She could not rest long away from either.

Presently she turned away, taking a few lumps of sugar for her canaries. Matt went after her. She broke into a

50

whistle. There were several cages hanging from bars, and to reach them she had to stand on her toes. She poked the sugar between the bars; the cages swayed lightly, her sleeves fell back from her bare arms. Philip was plunging his hands in the goldfishes' tank, which was overgrown with ferns and moss. The sun shone through the green glass roof, obscured by a plumbago.

Matt had felt a feeble impulse to speak to her. It passed before any definite words came to his mind, for he was drugged with inertia. He went through the outer door, shutting it behind him, and leant against the frame. He closed his eyes, but the brilliant spring sunshine penetrated the lids like a red film.

A large man, somewhat delicately made, he seemed to lack energy of any sort. His face was stiff and expressionless, his features long and fine. The eyes, set obliquely, reflected no more light than a pair of grey pebbles; yet two sharp grooves, running from the wide nostrils to the upper lip lifting it in a keen, fierce curve, indicated a temperament which was by no means phlegmatic. Matt had been passionate, and he could still be violent.

He opened his eyes and looked up into the clear sky. During the past two weeks he had been madly drunk three times. He would be madly drunk again tonight, but he would approach the climax slowly.

He made his way to the stables. Sparrows were hopping about the clean-swept yard. Easter's red-headed wife was descending the loft steps. She wore a long apron and carried a pail. With slow steps she walked to the pump.

The water gushed into the bucket. He went up to her.

51

He was nervous with women whom he did not know. She paused.

'Where's Easter?'

'I don't know, sir.'

Matt regarded her; she was exceedingly pale. He turned away his eyes, took the bucket, and without finding a word, carried it across the yard and up the steps. He caught a glimpse of a spotless room. She thanked him, surprised. Then she closed her door softly.

Matt saddled his own horse and rode away thinking about her. It was the first time he had spoken to her.

A week ago he came upon her at dusk in the disused brewing house, beneath the loft, and her wan face framed in the gloom startled him.

He rode slackly at a walking pace, occasionally greeting people on the road. One round-shouldered youth with a rough skin, huge red ears, and a squint, sidled towards his horse and snatched at the rein. The animal shied, threw up its head, and sprang forward. The idiot crouched under the hedge, frightened at the flurry.

A mile from The Gallustree the river was spanned by an iron toll bridge. Matt rode across it and paid the due to the leery old woman who opened the gate.

He was lost, not exactly in thought, but in the effort of inward contemplation. There are moments when it is necessary to use all pictorial imagination to assemble the features of one face; the entire mind is given up to materialisation. It is an effort. Matt dwelt on Mary's eyes, her long neck, her hollow cheeks, her mouth, tempting, yet severe. Gradually he called up the last glance she had given him as she shut her door, a look obstinately calm

52

and haughty, as though it would take many such insignificant kindnesses to win her good will.

For some reason the vision embarrassed him. He felt a premonition of difficulty and temptation. He pulled himself up, broke into a rapid trot, which quickly brought him to his destination and resolutely put her away from him.

A marked trait in his otherwise elusive character was a strong leaning towards democracy. He associated with anyone whom he liked. A year ago he had rubbed shoulders in some pub with an unsuccessful dissipated farmer, and this man had since become his chief companion. It was towards his farm he was now riding.

Arriving at a huddle of wretched outhouses, which looked more like shacks than farm buildings, he dismounted and tied his horse to a gate. The assembly was crowned by a new Dutch barn on a slight rise, whose corrugated iron roof was painted a dull red. The house lay beyond the yard, behind a round wooden shed, where the shafts of a wagon protruded from the dark interior into the sunlight. A little girl with a solid round face was sitting on the shaft nursing a rabbit. When she saw Matt she jumped up and ran towards him, dangling the rabbit by its ears.

'Father's in the yard,' she squealed before she was asked. Matt nodded quickly. He walked into the yard, which was festering with muck, calling out, 'Davis!'

The farmer appeared, his hands black and greasy, dressed in an old army service coat, and a very dirty pair of flannel trousers. Beside him Matt appeared to advantage in breeches and a tweed coat. Davis too had a rather ridiculous figure, short and rotund, while Matt's legs were so long that people, seeing them and his sharp features, were surprised that he should possess such wide shoulders.

Davis was smiling cheerfully.

'More trouble,' he announced, indicating a chaff cutter, which he had pulled to pieces just inside the barn. His wife was sitting on a ladder, a thin sharp-faced woman, whose black hair grew horribly low on her neck. She waved her hand casually.

'Did yer leave yer 'orse outside, Matt?'

'Yes.'

'Margie'll stable it for yer. Bill's just off to Chepsford. Yer'll go along?'

'Why, yes, I will.'

'That's right,' she said heartily, as she got up and shook the bits of straw from her dress. She was a queer woman who liked her husband to carouse and bring others home to share the fun. Davis was proud of her. He had told Matt as much. Matt studied her. He came to the conclusion that she was kind-hearted, but rather repulsive. Dorothy was better, though more stupid. He had never regretted his marriage, but to think of it was like blowing on dead embers: only dust arose.

'I was wondering when you'd be round agen,' Mrs Davis said, leaving the barn without any farther farewell.

Davis looked at his watch. He wiped his hands and face on some rags, took a coat off the chaff-cutter wheel and put it on, instead of the khaki garment he was wearing. He was then ready to go to Chepsford.

They walked the mile to Brelshope station, fully aware of their common intention to get drunk. Neither mentioned it. Davis walked, turning his head from side to side, his inquisitive gaze taking in everything. Matt's eyes were downcast, and he seemed disposed to silence. As they drew near the station Davis began on a subject curiously near Matt's thoughts.

''Ave you found a new man, yet?' he inquired, as he scrambled along with quick steps which took him over the ground wonderfully fast.

'Eh... what do you mean?'

'You're getting rid of Easter Probert, aren't you?'

'B—!' ejaculated Matt in sudden hot exasperation at his groom's intrusive name. Davis opened his eyes.

'I tell you I've had enough of that fellow,' Matt continued sulkily.

'Shouldn't 'ave thought you'd mind him.'

'Mind? I don't think about him; why should I?'

'Well, if you've given him the sack...'

'I haven't. I'm not going to.'

Without being aware of it he had fallen deep into thought again, and slackened his pace to a saunter.

'Come on! We'll miss that train,' shouted Davis, sprinting on ahead. Matt roused himself. Now it was Easter who occupied his brain.

'Why should you think I was going to sack him?' he demanded, catching Davis up.

'Heard it somewhere. Thought you must've turned moralist. Mind, he's a queer chap.'

'Yes... perhaps.'

'No doubt of it. Saw him last night.'

'Where?'

'Walking with a woman.'

'His wife?'

'Shouldn't be surprised. Red haired, and not bad-looking.'

'Yes, she has red hair.'

'Well, they didn't know I was there. I watched them, and once I was on the point of jumping out at him and letting him have it. Depend upon it that bloke's a brute. I don't care for him,' said Davis emphatically.

They concentrated all their energy on speed. They did not speak again until they were in the train. Then Matt asked why Davis thought Easter a brute. He had never seen any signs of it before. Davis grimaced, scratched his nose, and swung his feet, in their dirty, neglected boots, up on the seat. They had a carriage to themselves. He began to trim his dirty nails with a small instrument, which was fastened to his watch chain. Matt repeated the question.

'When a man throws stones at his wife I call him a brute.'

'I don't understand... you saw Easter throwing stones at his wife?'

'I saw him.'

'Why, good God, she's...'

'That's plain. Your groom's a b— scoundrel, Kilminster.'

'Was she hurt?'

'Don't know. She didn't make a sound. I'd no sooner made up my mind to have a go at him than he ran up to her, and they seemed to be all right. I was some distance off, so I couldn't see much.'

Matt seemed aghast, and said no more. He was struck by the number of questions he had asked. So was Davis.

*   *   *

At ten o'clock that night Dorothy sent for Easter. Being perfectly aware of what she wanted him to do he deliberately took his time before answering the summons. On these occasions it pleased him to feel the Kilminsters in his hands. Dorothy was lying on the hearthrug in the drawing room, collecting the pieces of a jigsaw puzzle which Philip had thrown at Rosamund. Over-tired and peevish they had gone to bed. Phoebe sat on a stool near the fire, a book upside down on her lap, murmuring poetry. At each disconnected audible mutter Dorothy twitched her brows with annoyance. The white light of the unshaded lamp made them look drawn and unhealthy. The room was chilly, the carpet littered with chocolate-box shavings, and children's crumpled comic papers.

Phoebe stopped, and Dorothy jerked herself upright. Through the door they heard scolding and broken jeering laughter.

'There he is, mother!'

Dorothy walked across the room and glanced along the passage, which was almost dark. With the light of the hall lamp behind him, Easter was coming towards her, and there was something dangerous in his aspect, something wild and out of control. His features still gleamed with fitful mirth, and his unholy eyes were shining excitedly. He stopped very near to her, bending so close to her bare shoulders that she took a quick pace backwards. She wore a long amber-coloured satin dress, which attracted him, but he disdained her. She had no character, no strength, nothing to give or to teach.

'You have been a long time,' she said.

'I came as soon as I could, madam.'

Dorothy surveyed his slovenly clothes and ill-shaven face impatiently.

'How many times have you been told not to loaf about the kitchen?'

'I was killing a rat.'

He answered impudently; pulling the dead animal out of his pocket he swung it round jauntily by the tail.

'Its neck's broken,' he added, with a secret glance under his arched eyelids, 'I caught it a clip with the tongs as it run over the fender.'

He held it out for her to see. She was disgusted, and he returned it to his pocket with a contemptuous grin. A horrible odour indicated that the rat was in reality much staler than he made out; in fact, it was a dead one which he had picked up for a purpose of his own.

'Bring me a cigarette,' Dorothy suddenly demanded.

Easter could not see any.

'On the table behind you, in that box.'

While he turned round she dwelt on him, the fierce, impertinent man whom she could not endure.

He found the box and passed it to her without opening it, and she shook it so that they could hear the cigarettes rolling about inside.

'Don't you think you should have opened it for me? Now, a match!'

'I haven't a match,' Easter exclaimed loudly. All at once he felt furiously angry as though he must strike her or spit into her face. The mood blazed in every feature, and made itself clear in his voice. Phoebe heard. She sprang to her

58

feet, and coming to her mother's side leant forward and lit the cigarette. She cast a wavering nebulous glance on Easter; it seemed as if she were aware of his impulse and would take the insult herself. She looked both courageous and imploring. He averted his eyes, and his expression changed from a scowl to a sullen moroseness.

Dorothy smoked and stared him up and down. She gave her orders: he was to drive over to Davis' farm and find out if Mr Kilminster were there. If he were, Easter was to bring him back. On no account to let him ride...

'Oh, you are impossible!' she broke out, 'you haven't shaved, and your clothes are awful – disgraceful. You look like a sweep.'

'They're good enough for my work.'

'That's enough. You can go.'

'Of course.'

'How *dare* you!'

Phoebe's heart was beating terribly fast.

Easter roared with laughter. Standing in an absurd attitude on the tips of his toes he took the ends of his coat and held them out between finger and thumb, opening his arms, which were remarkably long, as far as they would go. The dead rat fell to the floor. He picked it up, made a ridiculous bow to Dorothy, and went away leaving her petrified with astonishment, until her rage burst. Almost beside herself, she took Phoebe by the shoulders and shouted, 'Who can I appeal to, answer me that? Eh... fancy that creature having the face... oh, your father...'

* * *

The night was frosty. Above his bare head the sharp stars flashed. He held the reins in his cold taut hands. Who'd think things were growing? Who'd think there were animals as warm as lambs in the hard fields?

The old woman at the toll house had gone to bed ill, her daughter told him as she opened the gate, a lantern hanging from her wrist, a shawl over her head. Was he coming back? Yes. Well may as well leave the gate open now, must be close on eleven. He heard the old woman coughing up there in her bedroom. There were nice warm lights in Brelshope. Easter passed. Down one hill holding up the pony, up another, down another. He got out, went up to the rickety gate and shook it roughly till the pony turned its head. The gate was fastened with string. Easter took out a knife, cut through the many strands and led the pony into the yard. He knew exactly what to do. Having taken it out of the shafts and led it into an empty stable he pulled one lamp from the bracket, and carrying it, made his way towards the house. As he approached he heard a confused muffled tumult and the random straying notes of a tinny piano. He nodded, and screwed his mouth to one side.

Descending a couple of shallow steps behind the wagon-house he followed the path under a high stone wall, then turning sharp to the left came upon the house, a solid old sandstone building, as heavy and irregular as a red crag. It was divided by a paved passage with doors at either end, which were never locked or bolted. He marched up this passage, his lamp swinging, his long stride echoing, until he reached a window, then pushing his face forward, he peered through the uncurtained glass into the room.

It was full of men, most of whom he knew well by sight, intimately by tale. They were dishevelled, squalling, vehement, their hands and faces red, and their throats bursting with wet laughter. Only one woman was present – Mrs Davis, sitting at the table pinching the wick of a candle, while her eyes, bright with joyful life, flitted from one hot face to another. Matt himself sat on the table so close to her that his knees pushed into her shoulder: a green velveteen curtain draped his head and arms, and he continually twitched at it, fingering the tasselled fringe which fell ludicrously over his forehead and nose. His eyes were swimming, his skin damp and very pale. He was silent.

Davis himself in his shirt sleeves, a cap on the back of his head, sat at the piano, his open arms extended the whole length of the keyboard, lolling in a very easy attitude. The others leant against the walls or straddled across chairs. What would have astonished almost any observer was the sight of Marge in her cotton nightgown fast asleep on the knees of one of them, her little arm and relaxed fist thrown backwards against his cuff. Easter saw a great many bottles, not only on the tables and the floor, but sticking out of the empty parrot cage. Everyone was drinking, bawling, and gesticulating, excepting Matt and Mrs Davis, who, having smothered her fingers in candle grease, now folded her hands beneath her chin and observed the party with a pleasant expression.

Suddenly, however, a thunderous frown blackened her brow; she sprang across the room and grasped the arm of a man who was about to pour the dregs of his drink into the open piano, too late as it happened. Easter heard her

61

yell, saw her lifted off her feet, twisting and kicking out her legs, and then pandemonium broke loose. Easter observed that Matt made no attempt to throw himself into the row; his head had fallen forward, and his hand relinquished the glass, which lay on the floor in pieces. The groom reflected: he was in no hurry and the thought of Dorothy waiting up in her drawing room for her drunken husband was pleasant. He retreated from the window, walked back to the stable and, mounting a wooden ladder flat against the wall, which led up to the loft through a hole in the boards, threw himself down on a pile of hay from whence nothing was visible but the star-speared square of sky through the unglassed window. He extinguished the lamp and quickly fell asleep. He had a strange dream.

He seemed to have gone very far back into childhood, as far back as he could remember, when he lived with his mother in a sort of encampment with other half-bred gypsies. He thought he was lying in their own shelter made of bent withies and tarpaulins; he thought it was raining outside and he was alone in the hot dark, and if he put up his hand he could thrust the roof away from his face. He felt he could not draw his breath, and a burning, dusty smell crowded his throat. He was choking.

'Mammy,' he cried in his sleep. He fancied he heard her coming, but when the sack across the opening was pushed aside, it was not his mother's brown hand that he saw. The sweat broke out.

'Who's there?' he cried aloud.

'Phoebe,' her voice replied as distinctly as if she had really spoken in his ear.

He awoke terrified, and found that he was lying face downwards and might easily have been smothered in the hay. For a moment his senses gibbered, then he swore, spat out the bits and ends that were in his mouth and sat up. During his sleep, which had been much longer than he knew, his body had sunk deep into the hay. Now he was hot, his throat was parched with grassy particles, he was soaked with sweat. He coughed and coughed until his forehead swelled, felt for the light, and climbed down the ladder feeling ill and sensitive to the dark. The dead rat smelled like a dirty drain. It was one in the morning: a light now showed from an upper window of the house, a window which must have been ajar, for Easter distinctly heard two voices. His own was dry and harsh as though it had been scorched as he shouted down below, 'Who's there?' like an echo of his dream.

Mrs Davis put her head out. The groom yelled in reply: 'Easter Probert. Where's Mr Kilminster?'

'We're putting 'un to bed.'

'Then you're doing my job, and I hope you like it.'

'Fine, thanks,' Mrs Davis replied, peacefully and without irony.

'What'm I to tell the missus?'

Hereupon she sloped her head towards someone behind her, and murmured a question. After a moment her full face was turned once more towards Easter, but a yawn so far distended her jaws as to render her incoherent. The groom waited, his heart singing curses. Mrs Davis repeated: 'Say, we couldn't send 'im back tonight. 'E went stupid. Tell 'er that. Goodnight.'

The window shut and the light withdrew from her head,

travelled across the ceiling, and went out. Easter went across the yard to the pump, splashing in the muck. He drank deeply, drenched his head, and yawned to the stars. The sweat dried on him, his terror began to abate. He had felt, for one spasm, when Mrs Davis had shut the window, that he should scream. His hair had risen on the back of his neck.

He harnessed the pony and drove him rather slowly. He was very late, for on reaching The Gallustree, he found no lights showing. Mrs Kilminster had evidently given him up. That didn't trouble him.

Mary was not asleep. She lay in bed, waiting for Easter. Curtains were drawn across the window; the bedroom was a box of black darkness. Mary lay on her back, turning over her bitter, resentful thoughts and counting her grudges. She would not speak, and when he sat down by the bed and put his head on the pillow, she did not move.

'Haven't you been to sleep yet?'

'Leave me alone.'

'But I've a surprise for you,' he whispered, and stretched an arm across her throat. She was still, absolutely still. He hated her hardy self-command.

He struck a match: in the light her face appeared white and dragged. It was the fifth month of her pregnancy. By the brief flickering of the little yellow flame burning like a searchlight on her face, he looked at her and wanted her to be kind. But she had lost all her kindness, which at the best had been dictatorial. She closed her eyes, the match burnt out, and Easter cast away the glowing end. Throwing up both arms, he brought them down crashing with clenched fists on either side her body. The bed sprang.

'You're what I hate most... you're what I hate most!'

64

He cursed her passionately while she lay inert, breathing hard and straining her eyes, his weight on her legs. He returned to his sing-song whisper: 'A surprise for you. You wait!'

With a swirling movement he rolled the bedclothes towards her feet, and then she felt something furry burrowing into her neck beneath her ear. It was stone cold. There was a dreadful smell.

'What is it?'

She began to writhe and scream. A little dead head snuggled hard under her chin.

'Easter, Easter, take it away!' She pulled at his wrists, her round, tossing hip hit him over the heart.

'Take it away. I'm going mad! Please...'

'It's a dead rat. That's what it is. Its eyes are running, there are flies' eggs in the fur, the tail's half off. It's only a dead rat.'

And he pushed it deeper and deeper into her flesh, till, hanging round his neck, she dragged herself up, and with the poisonous little carcass crushed between them, seized him by the ear and tugged. They struggled furiously in the darkness. He did not strike her; he half carried, half dragged her across the room and poured a jug of water over her head. She relaxed, one mighty quake shook her, and she burst into shuddering groans. She fell prone on the floor, her wet hair over his feet. When he bent to lift her she crawled away from him and hit her head against the wall. She cried like a thrashed animal in snarling despair.

Easter struck another match: 'That's what you'll get when you try to fight me. Stand up!' he shouted. 'Stand up and I'll kill you this time.'

His lip writhed exposing the white teeth, and he lightly swayed his shoulders as if he were actually waiting for her to spring up and aim a blow at him. He touched his sore ear. Again the match expired; he struck another and another and another in a frenzy, not waiting until they went out, but throwing them down and stamping on them with all his strength. The boards cracked, the jug and basin rattled. Easter's stiff hair stood on end; he yearned over Mary in the attitude of a murderer, which the intermittent illumination rendered still more horrifying. She remained on her knees. She pressed her face against the wall, her arms hung down, and there was a great wet patch over her back and shoulders, grey on the white nightgown. She shivered, cowering, her sobs becoming more pitiful. Her soaking hair looked black.

After nearly ten minutes had passed, he lit the candle.

'Get up, Mary.'

He went to lift her. She moved her arms in a sudden shocked gesture towards herself.

'The child's leaping!' she cried in rational terror, turning her face up to him.

His heart jumped.

'They always do...' he stammered, crouching beside her. She muttered: 'Help me to the bed.'

Leaning on him, she crept into the bed. They were both very frightened. She lay down and Easter covered her up.

'Is it quiet?' he asked.

'No.'

He was afraid to touch her whom a moment ago he had dragged across the room.

She was ignorant.

'Is it going to be born now?'

'No... no. They all jump about months before they are born,' he exclaimed, listening to her chattering teeth. She heaved great sighs, her whole body was tense, and her tears ran down the side of her face among her hair.

'My hair's wet!' she moaned after a while, 'I'm wet all over. Go to the drawer and fetch me a clean nightgown.'

He did what she asked him. She raised herself, let the wet garment slip over her shoulders and lie round her waist, pulled on the dry one, and began nervelessly to rub her hair with the towel he brought her.

As they were feebly moving with disjointed activity, something scratched at the outer door.

'What's that?'

'Only one of the dogs.'

'I want it,' she said. It whined.

'It's been off rabbiting.'

'If it comes and lies down on the bed I'll go to sleep.'

Easter let the dog in. 'Now lift it up.'

A mongrel, filthy, weary, its short, whitish curls clotted with earth, its eyes blinking, it lapped at the pool on the floor. Easter flung it on the bed. Hot and panting, it stretched out its ugly body and fell asleep. Mary lay back gently screwing the almost hairless chilly ears between her fingers.

Easter was swamped by voluptuous tenderness. He clasped her in his arms, softly moving his head between her breasts, his eyes closed. A gentle, timid woman he might have loved with real intensity, and perhaps even constancy, since his promiscuous rovings were something in the nature of a search.

67

Mary listened for repentance: among the kisses and the quivers there was no keen word of self-reproach. Exhausted, more bitter than ever, she went to sleep in Easter's arms.

When he took the milk up to the house in the morning, the cook twitted him on his looks. Sloppy, tumbled, his brilliant eyes all but extinguished beneath the heavy lids, he listened to her for a moment without a smile, then offended her by walking away abruptly. She said he needn't be in such an unusual hurry. He took no notice; she had to run after him. Mrs Kilminster wanted to see him.

'Is the lady up?'

He usually spoke of Dorothy as 'the lady', dragging the words like a gypsy. Of course she wasn't up, and wouldn't be for the next two hours, the cook said, crushing a snail under her shoe. The master was out all night. She gave a loud cry at the sight of the wretched dog who had followed Easter from the yard.

'Full of fleas, the dirty brute!' She drove it into the kitchen; 'If it comes in like this, I'll leave.'

She had to bath it.

Towards midday, Easter saw Dorothy. She was in the glasshouse, stroking a young pigeon's splendid green and pink neck. She jumped up, scaring the bird which was lame and could not fly, until it hid itself behind the hot pipe.

While she was talking she roamed about restlessly, uneasy and irritable. She felt a cold growing on her, and her eyes were rather red.

'Why didn't you bring Mr Kilminster back last night?' she demanded in an angry voice.

'He'd gone to bed.'

'Who told you?'

'Mrs Davis.'

'Oh... so you saw her?'

'Yes, madam, I did.'

'Then I suppose you went in?'

She wants to know everything but she's ashamed of her questions, he thought.

'No; Mrs Davis leant out of the window for a minute. She was putting him to bed.'

Dorothy went crimson. She opened her mouth, raised her hands, and twisted the pearls round her neck.

All day, waiting for Matt's return, she grew more and more furious. She kept all three children near her, alternately scolding them and running down their father, her sharp, high voice blurred and hoarsened by the cold. She made the new housemaid (who was afraid of her) light fires all over the house so that she might wander from room to room. She shut all the windows, smoked endlessly, and refused to let the children go out in the drizzle. Stupid with aching foreheads and pale cheeks, very bewildered, they followed her about, carrying their books and games and her bright-coloured embroidery. It was a procession headed by the little talking woman in a fantastic geranium-red dress. The glow in her face did not diminish; she burned, and her fingers were so transparently white that they seemed to sparkle. She had a very bad cold.

Towards six o'clock her throat became so sore that she could only speak in a lifeless undertone and infrequently, which was a relief to everybody. Phoebe tried to make her go to bed; however, Dorothy was always obstinate with her. Rosamund, who was always very kind to sick people, ready to do anything for them, managed to get her upstairs. She sat on the edge of her bed, shivering and hanging her head.

Rosamund ran down to fill a hot-water bottle; encountering Philip, she took her first opportunity that day to beat him for chalking in one of her picture books. Philip rushed to his mother. The two of them sat on the bed together in a bundle, crying and gripping each other round the neck. Dorothy, presented with the hot-water bottle, threw it at Rosamund. It burst. In walked Matt. He was not quite drunk.

'Well...' said he, sleepily. He leaned against the wardrobe, unshaven and hollow-jawed.

Dorothy pushed her head forwards with a curious snakish movement.

'Philip, my darling son, ring the bell for mother.'

The boy jangled the bell and fell back on her breast, covering his eyes with his fists. After a moment the submissive new housemaid appeared, out of breath from running upstairs.

'Ask Miss Phoebe to come here.'

Phoebe came.

'Now you're all here,' said Dorothy excitedly. She strained her voice so that for the moment it was thick and strong.

'Philip, sweetheart, sit up and look at daddy. Rosamund... Phoebe, look at your father. He's drunk. He can't stand up. Isn't it horrible. Isn't it disgusting?'

'Yes, it's disgusting...' Matt admitted in a faint, far-away tone. He seemed as if he would have added a long speech to these few feeble words, but Dorothy interrupted.

'You beast! you make a beast of yourself, d'you hear? Ah, how shall I live... how can I bear it? Think of it, the

70

terrible humiliation of a drunken husband!'

She pointed at Matt, speaking through red, rough lips: '*That* always near me, *that* owning me...'

'He doesn't own you. Nobody owns anybody,' shouted Rosamund, waving the hot-water bottle.

'That's daddy,' said Philip positively.

'Yes, that's daddy,' said Dorothy, with bitter imitation.

'Father, why don't you go away?' Phoebe urged, touching his arm.

'Mind your own business, Phoebe!' cried Rosamund.

Phoebe's eyes opened wide in bright, angry surprise. Then, commanding her temper, she left the room and Dorothy called after her: 'Come back,' she shouted, springing from the bed: 'you *shall* share my miseries. I *won't* be left to bear everything alone. You shameful, disgusting man,' she continued, addressing her husband while she shook his inert shoulders, 'where have you been all day?'

He did not answer, but gazed at the carpet sodden and melancholy.

Phoebe did not return; they heard the piano – a succession of loud ringing chords.

'Ah, you can all get away but me! Tied up for all my life, and what do I get out of it?' Dorothy lamented. She gathered Philip into her arms and kissed him wildly under the ear. He stared at Matt, subtly, laughing.

'Daddy, I hate you,' said Rosamund.

'What, you too!' he burst out, 'and I thought we got on well together. Damn you, you little beast; get out!'

He took her in a really cruel grip, overwhelmed by the abrupt rage that sometimes put fear into Dorothy. Rosamund screamed with temper and pain until all their ears rang. He gave her a couple of savage slaps and put her outside the door.

'Now I'm master of the situation,' he thought.

He was very muddled.

'Philip, come here.'

'Philip will stay with me,' said Dorothy.

'Philip, come here,' repeated his father emphatically, '*let him go*!'

Dorothy clutched the boy, but she wished the row had not gone so far. She remembered Matt violent....

'Are you going to hurt him, Matt?'

'Let him go.'

She released him. He sat down on the floor.

'Come here,' said Matt.

Philip went to him inscrutably.

Matt folded him in his arms, and stood holding him against his shoulder. He bent his head, swaying as though he were rocking the child to sleep.

'I want to get down.'

'No; stay here.'

They rocked together; there was deep silence in the room.

* * *

The cook interrupted the story of Gladys' abortive courting.

'We all have our troubles,' she declared, her fists on the table. She wished with all her heart the new girl wouldn't remove her glass eye at meals, smothering its blue stare in a handkerchief which remained beside her until they carried the pudding plates into the scullery. Mary, in the loft, kept her misery to herself. She had received a letter from Miss Tressan; it was cool but anxious, and it contained five pounds. She returned the money that same day without acknowledgment or message. To be offered the sort of sympathy that any unlucky servant might excite, from a woman who had for some years almost yielded obedience, put an exquisite edge on her resentment.

*　*　*

Dorothy did not speak to Matt for nearly a week, most of which she spent in bed. It was not so much sulkiness as a deliberate attempt to find out how well silence would serve her purpose. Lying soothed in her room which reeked of 'Dernier soupir' in a successful attempt to smother the inevitable feverish odours, she was possessed by the strange idea that the man striding insolently about the yard and digging in the garden exercised a bad influence over the whole household. A trifle light-headed, one evening she called Phoebe to find out if milk were consumed absolutely as the udders emitted it. Phoebe answered, no; it was strained, and was obliged, before Dorothy would settle down, to give a full account of the proceedings in the dairy after Easter had carried in the milk.

Lying still, Dorothy thought: 'Apart from anything else, his impudence is unbearable. He must go.'

She was really ill; the face that she watched in her hand glass bore a pale rose-coloured eruption on the chin. Her doctor said it was caused by nerves.

'You must be quiet and not worry.'

He looked at her with his head on one side, and, charmed by his voice, she wished she were married to him instead of Matt.

He sniffed the 'Dernier Soupir' contemptuously.

'Poof, what a fug!'

The ointment he gave her to put on the rash and the spots themselves lent her a feverish look.

Matt brought her books and flowers.

'Thank you,' she said flatly.

One day he bent over her and whispered: 'Do you want me to give you a smacking?' and she could not help smiling; it was an old tender reproof which they had used towards each other before they were married. She remembered the first occasion in a Cardiff street when she had cried 'Yes!' and he had flicked the back of her hand and suddenly tears came into her eyes, to think that husbands really did strike their wives and lovers and also their sweethearts. When it was growing dark she wrapped herself up and went to the window. How it rained! The lane was like a cart track with slimy ruts; the monkey tree shut out the mildewy last light.

She lay down again, cold and depressed. She heard Matt walk past her door.

'Matt!'

'Yes?' he answered, entering.

'Are you going out?'

'I was. What else is there to do?'

'Nothing... don't go.'

He stayed with her, relieved that her reserve was over, yet terribly depressed and jaded. He wanted to tell her that she was wrong to put a distance between them; very seriously wrong. That coldness did not draw him to her, but each time she let him feel it drove him farther from her, deeper, deeper, into a vague mental state where nothing held any significance.

'My blind island,' he called it to himself.

But he did not love her and he held his tongue. *She* took advantage of the moment.

'Matt, I want you to send Easter away.'

'Yes, I believe you're right. He must go.'

'Are you sorry?'

'In a way. I shan't sack him until the baby's born.'

'Is he a good groom?'

'Oh, not too bad.'

They did not discuss Easter farther on this occasion. Dorothy congratulated herself on gaining her point. In reality, Davis had gained it for her.

Matt hereafter often watched Easter, regretting he must part with him, yet aware of the uneasy malevolence which seemed to animate the man. Also he could not fail to observe his entire lack of respect.

'But why should anyone respect me?' he asked himself.

He fell into a sombre calm, and his thoughts were all sad: 'How is it people are happy in this world, or even at their ease?'

IV

One morning Mary opened the door to let the spring air
blow into the kitchen while she was cooking, and as she
did so she saw that a sapling which grew in the heart of
the wood pile was showing leaf. She began reckoning up
the time she had been at The Gallustree, wife to the
groom, living in two rooms above an old brewing house.

'It is *not* for ever,' she said, 'I'll kill myself rather than
go on always.'

As the days grew longer, Easter went out later each
evening; he was waiting for the dusk to conceal his
meetings with a woman. They used to wander about the
fields after dark. She was a limp, shuffling person, whose
nature was hardy and indifferent. She had a creased,
yellow face, her black hair hung over her forehead as far
as her wide-open shining eyes, which moved so swiftly
that they appeared to flash. A dirty merry little woman,

she walked with one hand thrust into the neck of her dress against her warm skin, and the other in the band of her apron. She was a charwoman.

She was always laughing and made him laugh too. She told him about the foul-mouthed old farmer who rented Matt's home farm, and his great, shouting, stingy wife and daughter who had a fine name for charity off their own acres. How Mrs Williams never let her have butter with her meals, gave her old mouldy cheese ends, and flew into a passion when she ate a cold potato; and how they abused each other, almost coming to blows, and Miss Margery went away to hunt for a husband. They were fond of entertaining; she had to wash up after the spreads, and sometimes she would be washing up by herself at midnight, afraid of the gloomy old kitchen where the mice ran over the range and played on the shelves. They gave a huge tennis party. The table was loaded – a whole salmon, meat pies, cakes, jellies, fruit piled up almost to the ceiling; cream stuck about like snow. While they were playing she nipped in and stole a banana. Then she heard their elephant footsteps, so she hid round the back of the house. They followed.

'Very angry they was, oh, they was vexed! They was going to take it from me, but the old man come up and he says, stamping his foot, "Let her 'ave it. I tell you she's to 'ave it, and if I 'ear any more talk she shall sit in my place to table. Now you knows!"'

'Don't you hate 'em?' Easter asked.

'Oh, ay,' she said, laughing. She made everything funny by the tone of her light-flowing voice, and she seemed to feel no lasting resentment. Taking her hand, all warm, from her bosom, she laid it on Easter's face, inviting him with her eyes.

She wore untidy shapeless blouses, a dark skirt that dipped at the back, cracked boots, and a soiled cotton or sacking apron. In her bundled, draggled hair she stuck a sham tortoiseshell comb, twinkling with coloured paste. She was furtive, yet joyous, looking like a woman who worked in the fields.

While he was in her company he would imagine himself in his youth, which had been passed among just such careless, fatalistic folk; often just after leaving her it would come back on him so strongly that the present seemed a dream.

She made him think of one woman in particular whom he had loved after his fashion. The first.... On a cloudy night in the beginning of May he left her behind the haystack where they had embraced, and made his way home through the fields. The river, full of dark water, ran bank high; everything was growing. What a fine thing it was to feel warm and well and to be able to look forward to the summer!

Easter, turning his face up to the sky to see if it would rain, observed a dim familiar constellation tilting in the southern sky. He stood still and watched it until the clouds hid it and it began softly to rain. He lit a cigarette and walked on, remembering...

He was lying on a shawl on the grass beside a rough stony road which went straight uphill and stopped dead at the top as though it had been shorn off at the horizon. Within a foot of his head a colt was grazing. It moved forward; he lay between its forelegs and then, without touching him, it walked right over him. He did not stir. Its belly was silky, almost white. This was the first thing he could remember; not very clearly, for he was hardly able to walk.

Then again it was summer dusk. He was naked, sitting on the bald ground; round him were a number of low shelters built of withies and tarred sacks. There were several fires on the ground and a crowd of people. He smelt the smoke and sat staring at a stream which ran between the camp and a cottage garden full of heavy pink flowers which clustered along the stem. He did not know what they were. In the garden a big brown and black dog lay beside a barrel; it kept getting up and turning round, and each time its long bright chain rattled against the barrel. Suddenly he heard a rustle, scarcely louder than a breath, in the long grass by the stream, and poking his head forward, he saw three beautiful water-rats run down the bank into the water and swim away out of sight – they were gone in a minute, those fascinating creatures, while he longed with all his heart for one more glimpse of them.... Now it was noon, blazing hot on a huge swerving field. He was kneeling on the edge of a shady spinney, pulling at the deep moss with both hands. The field was pink, but countless green lines ran across it converging in the distance; between these lines men and women were bending and hoeing. Among them was his mother, very far away, down in a hollow.

That year he was four. In the middle of November when the sugar-beet harvest was over, and she knew there would be no more work for her in the fields until spring, his mother moved into a town where they shared a room with the Fitzgeralds.

Easter's mother was small and sinewy. She wore a drab shawl over her head. Her face was rather manly.

Mrs Fitzgerald, a handsome, wild girl with yellowish-brown eyes, a tanned skin and a haughty manner, spent most of her time making pegs or going round the streets with a barrel organ. She always wore a voluminous plaid frock, quantities of jewellery, and, indoors or out, a black befeathered hat was perched on her plaited hair. She was odd: she hardly ever spoke, but sang and whistled and made a great deal of wooden noise by rattling her heels on the board floor while she spliced pegs and made mats and brooms.

Mr Fitzgerald was thin and stooping: his head hung forward, and his hands appeared to weigh his thin arms down close to his flanks. He seemed to be frail, but in reality he was very powerful. He was always in the street or sitting on the doorstep. He was eighteen; his wife sixteen.

Easter often helped Mrs Fitzgerald make the pegs. In return she would hang her necklaces round his neck and give him a ride now and then on their donkey which they kept in a shed up an alley. He also accompanied them into the town on Saturday nights, standing by his friend at the side of the road while she ground out the tunes.

He loved her, and when, in April, they went back to camp without her, he was almost stunned by grief.

However, he continually saw her in the fields, pea-picking, harvesting, and getting up the potatoes....

One day he saw her go into the shelter of a group of trees which stood back from a bushy hedge. She stooped her back in order to pass through a hole as smoothly as a supple weasel at play. Easter ran after her. She was standing with her back towards him, stark naked and flawless, holding her hat in her hand. When she heard him, she turned very slowly, lifting her chin as if she expected to see someone very much taller than herself.

Easter fled, puzzled by adult nakedness which had never been revealed to him before because the half-bred, hedge gypsies amongst whom he lived scarcely ever removed their clothes.

In the autumn his mother left the camp for good with what she had saved since Easter's birth. She took a two-roomed cottage near the summit of Riggs' Pitch, three miles south of Chepsford on the Salus road, at a low rent. Nobody else would live in it as, besides being very small, it was round and dismally overgrown, having been a toll house. It was a district of sharp hills, thick woods, and narrow lanes. In the garden was a well of drinking water which never dried in the driest summer, and quantities of old, half-wild roses, yellow and white. Easter's mother did away with the rats. She took in washing and went out charring.

When Easter was five years old he went to school at Petersthorn. There were three teachers at the school: an ignorant, insipid infants' mistress who was not capable of teaching the children to read; a blustering, raw young woman who had just taken her certificate, and was attempting to find her feet and keep discipline in the middle standards; and an indolent, neurasthenic, headmaster, whose one idea was to conceal his illness and incompetence from the school managers and the County Council inspectors.

After eighteen months with the infants, Easter went up to the first standard, not only unable to read, but desperately muddled in his head. His new teacher had nineteen children of all ages from seven to thirteen in her charge; the distracted master conducted his class of the big rude boys in the same room by striding about as though he were possessed by a fiend, knitting his heavy black brows above his furious, frightened eyes, and slashing the desks with his cane. Slash, slash, and the untouched boys bent back like standing corn in a gale.

At eight, Easter still was not able to read. One day a County Council inspector came, made himself extremely disagreeable to the terrified staff and intimated to the gruff assistant-teacher that she might expect her dismissal, which in the course of three weeks she duly received. She went, and soon after the other two followed. The County Council took over the school from the church.

Easter learnt to read. He could do nearly all his sums in his head and painted flowers in water-colours most wonderfully well, so well that one might have thought the blossoms had blown down on the paper. He was insolent, hating the boys because they were all taller than himself, and excited by the girls beneath whose pinafores he sought to discern the alarming nakedness of Mrs Fitzgerald. That memory became fearfully vivid as he grew older. He used to dream he was in the woods with her and awoke with a hot skin and a longing to drink. Then he would go out, often in the middle of the night, and light a fire under a hedge where he would sit until morning, or take an old bicycle which had been given to him in exchange for a stray pup and skim down the pitch without brakes or lights.

He began to display a cold cruelty. The schoolmaster adored birds. He taught the boys about them, and begged them with passion to refrain from tearing nests to pieces. After one of these lectures, Easter sought for nests. He found several, among them a goldfinch's, threw out the fledglings, stamped them to death and, arriving at school very early, laid the miserable shapeless carcasses on the master's desk.

He was never found out. The man looked once on his desk and those infinitely-delicate shattered bones and glistening trailing guts moved him to agonised tears. He asked no questions, merely ordered Easter to throw the fledglings away, and never spoke about birds again.

Petersthorn was named after one of the plentiful blackthorns supposed to have been generated from St Peter's staff, which were believed to burst into flower on Christmas Eve. People came from all over the country and even farther to mark the miracle.

The tree grew on a hilltop. One Christmas Eve, before it was dark, Easter left home and, shutting his eyes against the prickles, climbed into the thickest part of the thorn, where he was completely hidden. A pigeon flew out, buffeting its heavy wings. Opening his eyes, he regarded his bleeding hands and felt the long, sore scratches on his face. His coat was ripped, his legs red. For a long time nobody came. The tree was, indeed, in bud, but he was used to that – it had been for at least a week. The sky was a deep living blue, between the twigs the keen star points twinkled fiercely. He found his favourite cluster which he fancied resembled a terrier, and watched him slowly tilting up on his stiff hind legs.

Then he heard voices: a party of awe-stricken men and women were coming up out of the darkness, carrying lanterns which shone upon their legs, a fold of their clothes, their hands, faintly revealing their faces. Some touched the tree: 'Look, it really *is* in bloom!'

Easter, hidden, began to chant the legend as he had read it at school. He had taken the trouble to learn it off by heart, and, really, it did not sound ineffective in his clear voice.

He heard the exclamations, then a man's stern voice which he knew very well, having at times unwillingly listened to it in the pulpit, ordering him to descend instantly. He did not, but shook the branches tempestuously and sang.

The Rector, who hunted and had a just reputation for being a 'sportsman' and a man of tact, which he intended to retain at practically all costs, persuaded his party to retire. His attention was decidedly drawn towards Easter.

By all accounts the boy was solitary, reckless, and spiteful. With complacent conceit the Rector decided 'to take him in hand and make a man of him'. When Easter left school he offered him a place as stable-lad under his own competent groom. Easter accepted the job, but steadily refused to be confirmed or even to go to church.

The groom, far cleverer at his job than the Rector at his, at once perceived that he would never make a regular smart lad out of this sly, gypsyish creature.

He stayed two years. Meanwhile his mother died in Chepsford Poor Law Infirmary, of a bleeding cancer. Towards the end she was considered to be off her head because she was always declaring that if they would only let her out, she would cure herself with herbs; however, she was not emphatic, as were the rules and regulations which had so curiously closed on her independent, free little body, and she died, in pain.

Easter missed her.

The summer that he was sixteen he gave the astounded Rector notice, and went with the Fitzgeralds – whom he had seen working in the fields – down to South Leyfordshire in time for the pea-picking. That would be June.

Mrs Fitzgerald was now twenty-eight, splendidly graceful, and much more free and easy in her manners.

There were no children. The Fitzgeralds owned a yellow caravan which they did not keep very clean. It and two others were pitched beside a stream in meadow pocked with molehills, adjacent to the pea field where they were working. During the day the pea field shrilled with noise and swarmed with pickers, but at night it looked formidable, curving up to the sky, a rounded, dark hill leaning towards the caravans.

Years before a large tree had fallen across the stream; rain, frost, and floods stripped all the bark from it and left it smooth as satin, slippery and shining. Easter sat on it, smoking, hanging his hot, sore feet in the water. He was hidden by blackberry bushes. He was tired to death and sick with passion. The sun seemed to have scorched his back to the bone, his eyes ached and swam.

Mrs Fitzgerald appeared. Easter turned his head towards her. She sprang upon the tree trunk, balanced herself, and, treading crossways on her bare feet, reached his side. Stooping, she ran hands from his shoulders to his slack elbows.

'I know what's amiss with you!'

'What then?'

She laughed and held her face close to his.

'Let me kiss you...'

The pea field was at least twenty acres, and they worked in it for nearly a week. Two men were at the scales, a gentleman with a peppery moustache who was very popular, and a fat farm labourer in corduroys, who mocked Easter for his slowness.

The pickers were paid a shilling a pot; most of them picked seven or eight pots, and several experts like Mr Fitzgerald, ten. But Easter would not earn more than four or five shillings a day. His fingers were nimble enough, only he continually looked at Mrs Fitzgerald tearing off the pods and flinging the haulm behind her while her long necklace swung as she stooped.

The babies and children shrieked and squabbled under the hedge, dressing themselves up in sacks and decking their heads with poppies. It seemed strange to Easter that he was not among them, but working with people who were picking peas when he had capered in the shade. He remembered Mrs Fitzgerald making pegs and hanging her heavy jewellery on his neck. She was very different now.

Mr Fitzgerald, too, had changed from a narrow youth to a stout, shambling man with fat thighs and a gurgling tobacco cough. He passed the evenings in Salus, leaning against the market hall or sitting, half asleep, in a cinema; during his absence his wife goaded and indulged Easter's love for her.

One morning Mr Fitzgerald got up very early, made a fire, fried bacon, and ate a large meal. The others did the same. Then they harnessed their long-legged horses and trundled across the field towards the gate. Easter walked after them as a matter of course.

Mr Fitzgerald turned round, flourishing his arms and coughing so much that it was nearly impossible to distinguish what he said, shouted that they had done with him. Mrs Fitzgerald suddenly started towards him, flung her arms round his neck, kissed him, caressed his head and returned to her people.

This was too much for Mr Fitzgerald, who ran at Easter, seized him, heaved him nearly shoulder high and threw him to the ground; after this he kicked him, laying open his cheek.

As Mr Fitzgerald set off once more, Easter raised himself and hurled a lump of turf after him which hit him so hard between the shoulder blades that he stumbled forward. A loud shout from the pea field startled them all; it was the man in corduroys. He came running full tilt, both hands clapped to his pendulous stomach, and broke through the hedge, sweating and blown. By that time the gypsies were in the lane.

'Bist hurt?' he asked Easter.

He nodded, laid his hand to his face, stared ferociously at the blood and dirt on his fingers.

So it ended, his loving.

Mrs Fitzgerald had haunted his childhood with her nakedness, and she haunted his manhood also... he lusted after women from this time onwards, but his lonely and abandoned spirit dwelt in a wilderness where as yet none had ever penetrated. None. Never.

He grew into a man without ambition, without hope, and without compunction. He risked his jobs over and over again – and lost them. He had only one friend, but a great many enemies who pleased him much more. He disliked men, and longed in the bottom of his heart for a woman's tenderness. But he had not the least idea how to arouse it, and invariably went wrong from the beginning. The rest of his history until he became groom at The Gallustree is soon told.

He found work with a farmer who owned a great barn of a house with several hundred acres some five miles out of Salus.

It was wartime, and the farmer cherished a peculiar aversion for land-girls; the sight of a woman in breeches provoked him to such a degree that he was unfit to speak to a soul for a day afterwards. He was jealous, fiery and obstinate, but the kindest, the most generous husband, father and master that could possibly be imagined or desired. And he had genius. Easter passed four fat years with him and learned a great deal about cows, which knowledge he later turned to good account, displaying uncommon interest in them until the end of his life.

The farmer's son, a boy about Easter's age, extraordinarily handsome, used to drive a milk float in and out of Salus, with his huge mongrel sheepdog standing with its forepaws on the wings. Everybody admired them, and Easter among the rest.

The two were very good friends, wasting half the day in each other's company; often when they ought to have been working they would sit down in a snug, dark corner and play the concertina, which they both did abominably, and the farmer, instead of cursing or punishing them, only laughed. He came to regret this.

One day, when Easter was nearly twenty, they went out

with a high-spirited, valuable mare in the float, instead of the usual steady old cob. It was pure folly and bravado, which resulted in a bad accident. The mare ran away, attempted to leap a five-barred gate and threw them both out of the float. Easter escaped serious injury, but the other was flung upon a heap of stones, fracturing his skull. The mare had to be destroyed.

Easter was sacked. Later he heard his friend had married a carter's daughter and set up as a pork butcher in Manchester; he had always taken a great interest in pig killing. They occasionally wrote to each other, although for years they did not meet. Neither was fortunate in his disposition, neither prospered. Easter managed to get jobs, and good ones too, but he always lost them because of his insolence, his absurdity, or his women. Then came two years when nobody wanted him. Nobody seemed to be keeping horses... he shirked ordinary farm work....

He tried being a cheapjack and a stone-breaker; and lived in a crowded, filthy room in Mary Street, which is the Salus slum and a shameful one. When he could, he worked in the fields. He learnt a little caution; when Matt Kilminster advertised in the *Salus Times* for a groom handyman, he applied politely and speedily. Matt took him on at once, found him satisfactory, a little mysterious, and liked him.

* * *

Easter was still some way from The Gallustree when it began to rain heavily; he abandoned his thoughts and took to his heels. He ran up the steps two at a time.

Mary was taking her hair down and putting the pins carefully into her apron pocket. Everything looked clean and well ordered; a check cloth was spread at one end of the table with a place laid for him. A large basin with a white cloth over it stood in the centre. It contained dried apricots which were soaking, ready to be made into jam the next day. She told him this when he lifted the cloth, peered at the apricots and shook the basin. He pulled one out to try it. He was surprised at the full flavour of the withered, fleshy fruit.

She put a chop and a baked potato on a plate and handed it to him.

'You'd better take off your coat,' she observed. He threw it off and began to eat. She hung it over the back of a chair.

'Where have you been?' she asked, her back towards him.

'The Dog.'

He finished his meal, then swerved sideways in his chair so that he faced her as she sat with bowed head and folded hands.

'We might as well be without tongues for all we find to talk about!' he exclaimed.

'There's nothing to say.'

'I've plenty to say to other people... you never thought you'd come to marry a man like me, did you?'

She neither moved nor replied.

'This room seems little, eh?'

'Yes, it does.'

'Well, to me it's all right. I haven't lived so easy.'

'Have you been drinking?'

'No, but I do, you wait.'

He got up. 'I'm going to bed. It's late.'

She listened to his movements in the next room. He was soon quiet. She washed up the supper things, raked out the fire and fastened the door. When it was all done she sat down at the table, laid her head on it and thought that she could not bear her life.

'But perhaps I shall die...'

'Easter!' she called.

'Ay.'

'Mr Kilminster – the master – gave me a message for you. He's going otter-hunting tomorrow and you're to go with him. He came up here this evening.'

He turned over in bed but made no reply. In the midst of misery she suddenly wanted to go to sleep. She waited a little longer. Then she rose, blew out the lamp and walked heavily into the bedroom. The window was shut. She opened it, put her face outside, murmured: 'All be the same a hundred years hence.'

When she was lying beside her sleeping husband she found that, after all, she could not shut her eyes. A hundred years hence it would all be *different*, was bound to be. Dissecting the thought, she remained awake.

* * *

Easter did not go otter-hunting. He was expecting a cow to calve. About midday it began. The buildings, the whole yard echoed with the agonised cries. Mary turned very white. She was filled with dread. Her attention was so far withdrawn that she let the jam boil over, filling the kitchen

91

with a horrible burnt odour which made her so sick that she had to lift the pan off the fire and go to lie down.

Easter sent for the vet; in the end they had to drag the calf from the cow with a rope. For a while there was silence, then the vet, a big man with a handsome face and peculiarly watchful eyes, which always seemed as if they were calmly awaiting some dangerous crisis, stepped out of the cow-house with his hands on his hips and his forehead shining with sweat. Easter followed him, looking very exhausted and downcast. He was in his shirtsleeves, his hands and arms were bloodstained.

The vet, rolling in his walk, every movement expressing weariness, got into his car, nodded to Easter and drove away. Easter went to the pump.

'We've lost the calf,' he answered Mary when she inquired from the steps. He washed, rubbing his hands vigorously up and down his thin, coppery arms.

'Bring me some soap, will you?' he asked, without looking at her, still bowed over his hands. She brought the soap on a saucer, and a roller towel hung over her arm.

They heard a car drive up to the house; a moment later the children's loud voices carried to them. Dorothy had taken Rosamund and Philip to Chepsford, where they had spent the afternoon in a cinema. Rosamund rushed into the yard.

'Oh, Easter, is there a calf?'

'It's dead.'

'Oh, *Easter*!'

'Don't get in my way now,' he growled, and returned to the cow, carelessly flinging the towel on the wet ground.

Rosamund gave Mary a long, curious stare before she sped away with the bad news.

About seven o'clock Easter sat down and had a meal. Afterwards he pulled off his boots and leggings, filled his pipe and, stretching himself out in his chair, began absently to twist the ring on his finger, while an ironical disagreeable smile played over his mouth.

'How's the cow, Easter?'

'She's all right now.'

'Do they suffer much?'

'Ay, they do. As much as a woman.'

With an abrupt jerky movement he flung his head back and gazed up at her standing beside him. She was trembling and very pale. Immediately she removed her hand from the back of his chair and passed into the bedroom, where for several minutes she stood examining her haggard face in the white-painted mirror.

'Suppose I die?' she was thinking.

She was not afraid, but with all her soul she dreaded pain... she had never suffered.

She craved for comfort, or at least for a more exact knowledge of what lay before her. She felt so weak that she was obliged to sit down.

Presently she walked into the kitchen again.

'Easter, is there a parish nurse here?'

He was asleep, his head hanging on his chest. His overstrained arms trembled.

'Easter...' she tapped him on the shoulder.

'Eh – God damn you, let me sleep!'

'Is there a parish nurse?' she repeated.

'I don't know.'

'Does it never occur to you that someone will have to look after me?'

'We'll have the vet,' he said with his malicious smile.

She was shaken with rage and a spiteful longing to strike his face and see pain come into his mouth and his baffling eyes. He watched her as with sullen lips she set herself to tie down the jam.

The glass jars, full of dark golden fruit, were standing on a sticky newspaper. She wiped them with a damp cloth and put them on an enamel tray. Then she took a saucer of water and brushed over the glazed paper tops which she pressed down upon the jars. Her hands moved very slowly, the supple thumbs bent back. They were very beautiful.

'Who gave you that ring?' he demanded after some time.

She replied that it was nothing to do with him.

'Take it off, and I will give you mine,' he continued, suddenly troubled by the contemplation of her weak wrists.

'You took it away once, now you can keep it.'

'Is there arsenic in that stuff?'

'How many more ridiculous questions?'

He stretched again and tapped his pipe against the fender.

She descended into the yard and walked about in the evening sun. The cloudy scent of lilacs drifted across the laurel hedge and the unmown lawn was speckled with daisies. The sycamore leaves were small, almost transparently fresh and green.

On the left side of the yard were the stables and the cow-house, on the right a high blank brick wall with the tips of young apple trees waving above it. A narrow wooden gate led into the orchard beyond, which Matt himself had planted. Tulips, white and striped, grew at random in the long grass, mingled with silvery dandelion balls. She was looking over the gate when Matt and another man entered the yard. They were both wearing bright blue coats with red facings and gold buttons, and red stockings, having come straight from hunting. The strange man looked ruddy and energetic as if the sport had done him good, but the clear gay colour of his uniform showed up Matt's pallor and he moved languidly.

He lifted his cap to Mary.

'Good evening. The calf is dead they tell me?'

'Yes, sir.'

He looked at the ground absently and exclaimed without much feeling: 'What a pity. Where's Easter?' he added.

She did not quite know how to define her home, so she pointed and answered in a low voice, 'Up there.'

At this point Matt's friend started forward.

'How do you do,' he said, holding out his hand. She bowed, hesitated, looked into his face and finally took it.

She looked so haughty and so very ill that he was frightened and did not know what to do. She had met him on several occasions. His name was Harold Maidment and his parents were Miss Tressan's neighbours. He was shy and silent.

Matt thought: 'Good God, how awful!'

'It's a lovely evening. Why don't you go in the orchard? There's a path... it's too wet, perhaps?' he stammered.

'No, not too wet at all. I didn't know I could.'

'Of course. Any time. There's a lovely view.'

'Thank you, sir.'

'Easter!' Matt shouted.

'Where's this cow?' Harold demanded, 'I'll just have a look at her.'

He bustled across the yard, an ungainly person, horribly embarrassed. Matt followed him, and Easter, yawning, came down the steps, putting on his coat. It was not until the next day that Matt spoke to him privately.

'Easter, is your wife well?'

'Yes.'

'I don't like interfering, but has she seen a doctor?'

'No, sir, I don't think so. She was asking if there was a nurse hereabouts.'

'There is. Get her.'

He had never before spoken autocratically. He could not get Mary out of his mind.

V

An episode brought Easter before Matt in a new light.

The groom was walking back from Brelshope, a small village about a mile and a half from The Gallustree, on the opposite bank of the river. He had been sent with a message to the owner of a timber yard, one Samuel Collins, a pompous old pocket snob who hated Easter on the strength of his appearance.

It was afternoon and the middle of June; as he strode along the raised footpath he could see over the hedge. Meadows and fields of growing corn vibrated in the heat, the ruts in the lane were crumbling, and every now and then a sudden hot wind raised a powdery dust from the ground which made its way into his eyes. In spite of the heat his strides were as long as ever and he chewed a grass and looked about him with a bold, confident glance.

He was terribly untidy; his collar was crooked, his tie

flapping over his shoulder, his hair shaggy. Truly an odd person to be a gentleman's groom.

The lane took a turn and ran downhill, beneath thick tall trees which completely shut out the sun. In the cool shadow Easter stood still a moment, listening. He heard the blows of an axe, uneven, yet very powerful, and vague voices at the bottom of the hill. The property was Matt's; he knew no reason why axe should be laid to it nor person to wield it. He walked faster.

At the bottom of the hill a labourer, a woman, a youth, and a young girl stood watching a man who was hacking with a heavy bright axe at the thick holly hedge. He had made a sizable hole. Each time the axe fell, the onlookers blenched away, but the man himself did not appear to notice them. He was breathing in laboured sighs and sweat rolled down his high white forehead. The girl, in an extremity of morbid curiosity, kept on laughing and letting out hysterical screams, while the others wore the frown of impotent responsibility.

Easter joined them.

'What's up?' he demanded. The woman warned him: 'Don't go a step nearer. This chap's queer in the head.'

'Just look at him!'

'I'm frightened...'

He was an emaciated, frail man, craning his long neck forward between every two or three blows with the axe as he stared anxiously into the lower growth of the hedge. His hair was quite white, his large green eyes myopic, and his face was set in intense excitement. His clothes seemed to have been somebody else's, for the sleeves of his coat nearly hid his hands, and his trousers were rolled up at the bottom.

'We've sent for the police,' the youth told Easter.

He grinned contemptuously, spat out the grass, and, walking right up to the lunatic, closed his hand over his shoulder. The man paused, still holding the axe, and looked at Easter. His face was full of shining hope.

'Come away, you fool – he'll strike you stiff,' shouted the woman, hiding her eyes.

'What are you doing?' Easter asked in a peculiarly tender voice.

'My wife's in there, and my little girl. I must get them out.'

'Ah.'

'Look in here. You can see them... see my wife's bent arm... glimmering. Can't you?'

'I'll have a look.'

'Bend down.'

'Easter Probert, for God's sake come away!'

'Shut your racket,' answered Easter, as he stooped his head to the hole.

The woman and the girl screamed again as the lunatic shifted his hands on the axe that was so keen, so sharp, so dazzlingly bright like an unbroken sunbeam. But he made no attempt to strike Easter.

'Move. I must get them out soon,' he said.

Easter raised himself and looked seriously at the man who was preparing for another blow.

'I don't see them. They're not there. They must be at home.'

The man relaxed again as though pondering, but he shook his head.

'Oh, no, we don't live at home.'

In the circumstances there was such a suggestion of

tragedy in the reply that the labourer visibly shuddered.

'Well, then, why not come along with me?' said Easter.

'Can't you see her arm?'

'No; at first I thought I saw something, but 'twas only the sun on a root. Give me the axe and have another look yourself.'

The lunatic's face was hidden in glossy leaves. He stared and sighed himself back into a long accumulated grief. The joy left his face which now expressed such poignant hopeless affliction that he excited pity rather than terror. Without another word he gave up the axe to Easter, and with his eyes vaguely lifted to the arching boughs above them, walked away slowly by his side.

'Well...!' ejaculated the woman, folding her arms.

'Shouldn't 'ave thought it on 'im.'

'Some spunk,' said the young girl in the Salus Grammar School blazer. She was a keeper's daughter, at home with swollen glands.

'Maybe yer'll meet the police,' screamed the youth, who had rather more sense than the rest.

The labourer, with the reflection that if he put on a spurt he might reach The Dog before two o'clock, was the only silent one. He spat. The fun was over. Now he'd get a drink.

Easter and his companion met a couple of constables evidently walking up from the station. As they passed the church, the lunatic stopped and stood looking at his feet, panting like a sheep.

'Where's he from?'

'Gloucester Asylum. Got loose yesterday.'

'Dangerous?'

'So they say. Must have slept on the road. Where did you find him?'

Easter told them dryly. Then he looked once more at the lunatic with a singular expression. One might almost have thought he was in awe and dread, yet near to weeping. Indeed, emotion all but overcame him. The man had lifted his gaze once more; his head on its long, thin neck turned hopelessly from side to side in a kind of eternal blind quest.

Easter broke away from them all abruptly. The constables looked after him.

'A queer fish himself.'

Matt heard of the matter before he came home in the evening. He sought Easter, who had been hogging the mane of Phoebe's pony which was tied by a halter to the paddock gate.

After thanking him, he began to question him.

'Were you afraid?'

'No,' said Easter.

He knew few people, and the idea entered his mind that if 'Yes' and 'No' were the limit and extent of his vocabulary he would get along very well, since questions and orders represented the greater part of his intercourse.

His face was perfectly grave and reposeful as at times it could be, but Matt felt him thinking, 'You won't get anything out of me.' Matt stroked the pony's smooth coat with a hand which closed, tapered like a bird's wing. It was far too small to be capable, yet intelligent and very masculine. His lustreless eyes took in the groom's vigorous movements, his straight neck and balanced head, his enigmatical expression.

'The life seems to have drained out of me,' he thought, 'I can remember feeling very different. And the less I have, the more I watch for it in others. This chap's full of life. His wife, too, in her way.'

After dinner he left Dorothy to her coffee and sat in a little square room which quite recently he had taken to using. Long after it had grown dark he sat there, an unlighted lamp on the table before him, holding a box of matches in his hand.

At first his head was vacant and he was just thankful to be away from voices and high lights. Then nerves began to nag at him, stirred by the pregnant silence of the night.

He felt that his life at present resembled that dusky room... he knew that if he chose he could light a lamp that would throw its wild beams on the darkness. In his mind he fitted together an odd, stilted sentence which he found himself repeating out loud, while the thought behind them had grown cold.

'The contemplation of continued existence is almost too much.'

Yet his tired, enfeebled mind lacked the furious energy that prompts suicide. It did not occur to him to die.

Suddenly he struck a match and put it to the lamp. By the yellow glowing light he stupidly examined the oatmeal-coloured paper on the walls, the almost empty, carved bookcase and the crude frieze of unnatural fruits.

'It is so very ugly.'

His eyes were attracted to three cards fastened by drawing pins to the walls, simply because they were objects on an expanse. They made his thoughts meander towards Philip, who had taken an unreasonably excited dislike to the servant Gladys, although she was gentle and friendly, owing to her glass eye, under which the tears used to trickle. When he discovered she could paint roses in beautiful golden vases with long, flute-like necks, he was gradually attracted to her, and then loved her. The three cards were Philip's own work under her tuition; they were of red roses growing on trellis-work, and stiff, expanded butterflies; a birthday present to Matt.

'In the name of – affection, how many horrors must I put up with?'

The lamp was flaring. He gently turned the wick lower and deliberately began to think of Mary sensually.

It seemed as though strength rose up in him, and during the night he retreated before it, seeking to gain his old empty indifference. But the lamp was burning indeed… pulses beat in his neck and his arms.

'Dorothy!' he whispered, and touched her back, 'I can't sleep.'

She was asleep.

He longed to look at Mary, to appraise her, to marvel at her, to find in her thin severe face some potent charm or beauty. He asked himself: 'Why this one? What has aroused my feelings and when did they dawn? In what moment did I first behold something I loved?'

He found no answer to any of these aged questions, but he had a dream in which he saw her stepping over a candlestick on the floor.

He saw her twice during the next day. Her nostrils were pinched, and there was a shadow on her full lips, which were dry and cracked as if she had fallen into the habit of biting them. Since her marriage her face had become squarer, bonier; her expression was hard and her way of speaking lifeless. On the first occasion she said 'Good morning' from her doorway, on the second 'Good evening' in the yard. The last time, as she walked towards the steps, her head sank forward between her shoulders and her steps tottered. She touched the edge of the stone, leant on her arm and pressed one hand to her forehead. When Matt reached her side and looked into her face he saw that her eyes were shut. He asked her what was the matter.

'Oh, nothing... my head was buzzing. There, it's all right now.'

Her hand fell to her side.

'Are you really better?'

'Yes. It must be going to thunder,' she remarked, absently.

They lifted their eyes to the low bronze clouds. To his astonishment and pleasure she began to explain how she felt, very naturally, without attempting to call him 'sir'. He listened attentively to her voice which was already singular to him.

'Something like a telephone rings in my head, and then my neck seems to go numb, and though I always go on with what I'm doing, I haven't an idea what it is.... I have walked quite a long way and come to myself and wondered how I did it, for I couldn't remember a thing.'

She rubbed the back of her neck gently: 'When I was a child I thought the ringing was meant for a warning, and I used to say out loud, "Thank you, thank you... message received."'

She smiled, but Matt thought she was nervous.

'I believe you are frightened,' he said, 'why?'

'Look at me,' she exclaimed, 'you can't deny that I look ghastly?'

She did.

'Do you feel ill?'

'Desperately. All the time. You've children. Did *your* wife look like this before they were born?'

She turned her white, harassed face towards him: '*No!*' she continued before he could answer. 'She had a different sort of husband, different treatment...'

'Have you seen anybody?'

'Yes – the parish nurse!'

'Well?'

'She said I was to see a doctor.'

'And you haven't?'

'No.'

'Good lord! Listen, you must... tomorrow. I'll telephone.'

'You are kind,' she said in a formal voice.

'Oh, Mary... Mary,' he cried, his new love and his living sorrow like cruel stabs in his side. 'Mary, don't turn away from pity! People hate it and they're bitterly wrong. Of all emotions it's the greatest, the purest... don't be hard on me because I pity you!'

'It's myself I hate and loathe and scorn!' she said furiously, and he was silent, impotently watching her, searching her anger till she looked at him.

'But I'm not hard on you,' she added, far more gently.

'Let us go in here for a moment,' he almost whispered.

'Why?'

'I want to talk to you.'

She nodded, and her pouting lips parted. They regarded each other with dawning certainty, and emotion replaced their painful fatigue. It was too much for Matt; they had barely entered the brewing house and taken a few steps forward into the cobwebby dusk when he was aware of a fearful heat in his breast. He stuttered incoherently, threw one arm around her which instantly dropped, and the next moment was gone.

* * *

A little while before dinner he was returning from an aimless stroll which had taken him no farther than the church, where he had sat down on the mounting block. The threatening storm seemed to hang immobile in the branches of the yew above him; the lightning flashed in his brain, tearing the darkness with spasms of excitement. But he felt also a tenderness which restrained him. Having looked at his watch, he returned to The Gallustree, and paused with his hand on the gate.

'Matt!' screamed Dorothy.

'Yes,' said he.

'Come and help me.'

When he saw her he could not help laughing. She had climbed up the Danes' Mount to avoid a fat roan cow who, with drooping, pensive head, was breathing over her fallen umbrella.

'Why, it's only Emma!'

'It's a cow – that's enough. Doesn't matter what name you choose to give her. Drive her off, Matt, and help me down. It's disgraceful the way she's allowed to wander about.'

'It's only old Emma,' he repeated, giving her a whack.

106

She raised her heavy head with its wrinkled, pendulous dewlap, switched her tail and moved off, lumbering and stately.

Healthy and flourishing as Emma appeared, there had been a time when this good cow had wasted away to a magnificent skeleton. She would not eat anything. Finally her owner, a single, middle-aged woman with a passion for animals, screwed herself up to the point of having her destroyed. But on the morning appointed, Emma got out. She was discovered in a lane, eating. Later she lay down by the wayside and chewed the cud. The upshot was she recovered, regained her comely outlines, and (nobody quite knew why) received the freedom of the parish. She went where she listed, walked, and ate decorously, never molested man or beast. Nobody but Dorothy dreamed of fearing Emma, the mild and gracious.

Matt helped his wife down the steep grassy side of the Danes' Mount to the tune of 'dangerous cattle'... what might happen... pedestrians. He took her under the arms and set her on her feet. She wore high-heeled, snakeskin shoes which lent her an additional four inches, but the cubit she had contributed to her stature cost her something in grace of gait. She tottered, and yet in its way it was attractive, even fascinating, rather like a little, gay, artificial toy.

Matt wished she would do her hair another way, or else cut it really short. That mess of curls blurred her head.

He picked up her umbrella and hung her pink mackintosh over his arm. She went ahead, ran up the steps, waved to him cheerfully, and disappeared. Matt loitered.

Low-hanging clouds, lividly rose in colour, were rolling slowly before a sultry breeze, and more remote ones, bronze, indigo, greenish black, spanned the horizon. Above the house there still remained a ragged patch, calm and blue, through which the sun's rays struck on the roof and the tree tops.

Matt lingered for a moment watching the glorious ominous colours. The air was blighted, a peculiar unnatural dusk closed in, and minute by minute the atmosphere thickened. The breeze died. Momentarily he expected the darting lightning. He stood in a kind of torpor.

Dorothy, dressed for dinner in a long, flowered gown which flowed to the ground, came outside and shutting her hand on his wrist, gave him a minute squeeze. When she was in a good humour she habitually made love to him by trivial gestures and intonations. A waft of scent, spicy and passionate, positively assailed him. He turned his head aside, and the greedy caressing perfume followed.

They went in to dinner, Dorothy running her fingers up and down his arm. While they were sitting at the table it began to rain very heavily; a long, crackling peal of thunder brought Philip flying to his mother, more excited than afraid. Matt pulled up his little chair for him, peeled him an apple and fell back into his abstraction. The storm had surprised him, but in going over his conversation with Mary, he remembered she had said it would thunder. There was the dawning of a nervous smile on his face which Dorothy remarked as being unusual for those days. He sat back from the table, hardly moving, his heavy eyes far away.

Philip soon jumped up, dragging his mother to the window to watch the rain flattening the flowers outside. It was depressing, this broken, grey flood which beat and buffeted the fragile, velvety petals. Dorothy rubbed Philip's straight black hair.

'Matt, you really must tell Easter to get a scythe to this lawn. It's unbearable... he does nothing at all.'

'If you like,' he acquiesced, and added after a long vacant pause, 'I thought you liked it left long for the children.'

He had absolutely forgotten Easter, and now at his name he recalled him, startled. He pulled himself together. He was alert. Where was Easter? Could he have over-heard? Matt felt sharp distress and apprehension. He rose; he, too, gazed out of the window from which part of the yard could be seen. Like an obedient apparition, Easter appeared before him, mounting the steps, his head bent beneath the rain.

*   *   *

Easter had overheard.

While he was eating his evening meal he was quite sprightly with Mary. His lively speech was very much at odds with his balefully corrugated brow, his sullen, watching eyes. Mary hardly noticed him and replied only occasionally. She finished first. She got up to put the kettle down on the embers, and while it was boiling she took up some sewing.

Easter, still bantering, fetched a bottle of liniment from the bedroom. Uncorking it and sniffing the strong, stinging odour, he asked: 'Wouldn't you like to rub my arm now? I strained it yesterday.'

She shook her head.

'Come on,' he said, holding it out.

'No, I won't. I don't like the smell. You might do it in the harness room.'

'I'll go into the bedroom.'

He did, closing the door after him. The contents of the bottle were poured into the drawers where she kept her underclothes, and under her pillow. With the remaining spoonful he carefully soused her hairbrush.

Returning, he found her filling the teapot. He sat down morosely, and leant forward in his wooden kitchen chair, his bare arms crossed on the table, silent now with thoughts visible on his face like cloud shadows rushing across a field. She pushed a cup of tea over to him, resuming her sewing, but she lifted her head stealthily when he rose and stood in the doorway between her and the light.

With his back to her he rolled down his sleeves and put on his coat, then, raising both arms, he laid his hands flat on each side of the door, looking into the yard. He was outlined against drizzling, fine rain. The storm was passing off, but the day was closing prematurely; a heavy dusk was bringing on the night. Everything seemed gloomy and threatening. It thundered in the distance.

Mary, studying her husband's back, felt her dreariness threaded with something new, scarcely joy, but resembling it.

Easter strode forward, brought his legs together, poised, his head beautifully balanced, and leapt into the greenish dusk. She heard him strike the ground, sat with one hand raised and dangling thread... then he walked across the yard.

* * *

110

Cross the toll bridge which connects Gamus and Brelshope, continue your way for two or three hundred yards through the shadows of a pine avenue, turn to the left, and your road will bring you to the village where there is always something doing... brawls, dances, or revivalist meetings.

It is a small village, unusually compact for these parts. There is a short, curving street with The Dog at one end opposite a timber yard; the church, the cottage post office, and the shop are at the other. It is one of those places of which one can hardly have the roughest idea without detailed poking. The cottages are placed hugger-mugger fashion, and most of them are white with wooden porches. The shop which looks as if it had been built of child's bricks, and the church grotesquely copied from the Florentine style, are both supremely ugly.

No fewer than six roads radiate from Brelshope, and cottages extend for at least a mile on either side of the main village; they stand, sometimes one above another, on a high, steep bank under which it is thought the river once flowed. They have beautiful, simple gardens full of flowers and trees, and are approached by long flights of wood or sandstone steps. The Dog at the far end from the bridge is a spick-and-span white house whose twin bay windows look across a wide sweep of greyish gravel to the road and the timber yard beyond. The prospect is interrupted by a big elm which shades a bench beneath its branches. The timber yard goes back some distance into the gently rising meadows. Surrounded by piles of newly sawn timber, white planks, and lopped trunks, is a large, rusty steam engine slowly falling to pieces. The landlord of The Dog

111

was one Harry Lloyd, a Welshman, enormous in girth and ponderous in movement. He had played cricket for his county, but now he was too old and fat. This evening he was busy in the taproom. Now and then between serving he pushed his face outside the door to let the drizzle fall on his head, smalmed his hands over his hair, looked about and went back to work.

On one of these occasions he walked as far as the bench, where he could get a better view of the street, but there was no one in sight. He stood there, glad to be shut of the men for a bit.

He was a tall, pulpy man, very out of condition. His head was covered with rather long, wavy, blond hair, so fair, indeed, that it looked almost white, and his colourless appearance was heightened by a skin which resembled wet clay. His face was folded and creased, his bright, bulging eyes rolled from side to side. He was dressed in grey flannel slacks and a clean white shirt.

Presently he returned to the taproom. It was already pretty full. In his absence a dispute had broken out between two carters sitting in the window seat. They were arguing in loud shouts. He had heard it all before.

'We aren't getting 'alf enough wages. I want two pound... can't 'ave a drop o' beer or anything.'

'Go to blazes with you! We *got* to do on less, an' things be got a lot cheaper than they was.'

''Tis rates and rents as be dear...'

'But the foodstuff's down!'

'God damn it, man, bread's gone up tuppence!'

'I knows you be wrong,' cried the younger of the two, a thin-patched man sweated to a shadow.

The other grinned bitterly and fiercely, showing his long teeth.

'Well, I must be going. I be one of they chaps as fought in the war.'

He got to his feet, suddenly shook his empty mug in the young man's gaunt face. He also jumped up and grabbed his stick. Harry pushed between them.

'Now then, I won't have that. If you want to fight, out you goes.'

Both men began to curse venomously: 'I'll be damned if I'll ever come near the bloody 'ouse agen.'

'As you please. Come if you like or stay away,' said Harry, knowing his men. 'We're all free.'

He watched them off the premises. They went with filthy lips making menacing gestures, and bawled at each other till they were out of sight. Harry thought it was no business of his if they came to blows.

'What a life! Nothing but boozing and wrangling and sweating from morn till night...'

'World without end,' concluded an old man whose tanned face was misted over with white stubble. A rheumatic labourer joined in: 'I likes a bit o' fun. 'Tis only fun, 'Arry. When you've been working all day in a field... not a soul to speak to... well, beer's all right after. I coulda' wrung my shirt today.'

He passed the back of his hand across his mouth.

'I'll 'ave another pint thinking on it.'

He put three pennies down: 'There, it's all I got. You'll 'ave to trust me with a penny or draw a drop short.'

After he had served the labourer, Harry again went and stood at the door. The taproom behind him gave off a

113

warm, strong odour, the smell of wet sawdust blew across the road from the timber yard. The fields were darkening. A boy turning his bicycle in the street was the only creature in sight. Harry pressed his knuckles into his eyes, conscious of a sickening feeling that he was squinting. Even then, with the lids closed and his hand shutting out the light, he seemed to feel the aching pupils float over the eyeball and roll inwards. He was a ravenous reader; he used to read in bed at night by candlelight. Sometimes he read till three or four in the morning. Consequently he was always falling asleep in the daytime.

He groaned, still shielding his eyes. Beer and wrangling! He was a man who quarrelled with his bread and butter.

His wife was in the parlour. He felt he had something to say to her. He cast a last glance up and down the street which was still empty and turned back into the house.

Their parlour was fresh and well furnished. He himself had papered the walls with a curious orange and green paper. There were two leather armchairs, an upright piano of light wood, and slippery, polished linoleum on the floor. An expensive wireless whimpered; all the batteries were down. His wife stretched out her arm and turned it off. The action pulled her black cotton dress tight over her shoulders. She was a stumpy woman with freckles and a button mouth which was moist and full.

'Sammy not coming?' she asked.

'Not yet. That reminds me...'

(This was not true; he had been thinking about what he intended to say all the evening.)

'Listen, Ivy; if Easter Probert comes in here again we shall go losing custom. Sammy can't do with him.'

114

'I know that,' she said in her sad, remote voice, which was beautiful and unforgettable. English was a foreign language to her.

'Easter goes in the taproom along with the others. See?'

'Well, I'm sure I don't care,' she said listlessly.

'I'm only saying what I've said before. Now you pay attention, mind.'

He had seated himself on the arm of the chair which was the timber merchant's special place. The better-class customers, commercial travellers, men from the breweries who occasionally called on business, landlords of other pubs who came with their wives, farmers and tourists, were all entertained in the parlour. One armchair pertained in the old-fashioned way to Sammy Collins, the other to Matt's tenant farmer, both regular customers.

Harry's wife aggravated and puzzled him by having in the policeman, the butcher and Easter. To her earnest husband she seemed heedless; her game was not his. He did not understand her. She was from Trefor on the coast of Caernarvonshire, the daughter of a blind pilot; Harry hailed from industrious Glamorgan.

He got up and arranged his belt. Half in, half out of the door he observed her, blinking his inflamed eyelids. She sat against the table, leaning on her elbow. There was a bottle of iodine near her, a cup of warm water and some clean rag. That afternoon she had had her ears pierced by a jeweller in Salus, but already she had removed the gold sleepers and complained of the pain. She dipped the rag in the water and began to dab at the holes which were sore and bleeding.

Harry went back to the taproom, which was empty save

115

for the old man and two nervous, rosy-skinned boys who were chewing their fingers and blowing the dust off a couple of bronze figures on the mantelpiece. They asked for lemonade. A few minutes later two men came in, a carter and a hedger. They leant against the wall, stuffing their clay pipes with coarse yellow tobacco. A brisk little man in blue overalls entered next; a carpenter he was, always in a hurry, but usually he lingered longer than any.

''Ere, 'Arry, bring us a quart. I 'aven't got time to stop an' drink two pints.'

'Beer or cider?'

'I aren't 'avin' cider; I be gwine to 'ave beer. 'Aven't 'ad any fer a fortnight... dunno if I can drink it or no.'

'Oh, you can swallow down,' said the landlord, glancing at the two lolling fellows who were lighting up.

'Give us a pint, 'Arry,' said the hedger. The carter nodded and sucked his pipe. He felt depressingly tired.

'Beer or cider?'

'Cider.'

Money was short.

Harry served them. As he was bringing the drinks Sammy Collins appeared, leaning on his knotted stick.

He was a sour-looking pallid man with a spiky beard, reddish mingled with white, and saturnine eyes. He wore breeches, a tweed coat, and a slouch hat pulled over his forehead. He it was who, in a rhetorical mood, had described Easter as 'a prowling, preying panther, a dangerous, lustful, wild beast.'

He himself was a sanctimonious old drunkard who became abusive in his cups. He was followed wherever he went by a little tan, rough-haired bitch, very long in the

116

body, named Datty, who used to sit on his knee and lap out of his glass. They doted on each other. Sammy Collins was reputed to be rich, but nobody liked him for anything else.

He poked his old head through the door like an escaped goat, screwed up his eyes, nodded disdainfully, and passed on. His chair squeaked as he sank into it with a sort of peevish groan. The carter and the hedger also nodded to each other, as though each were acknowledging the truth of some unspoken remark. The carpenter expressed it after a silence: 'Old b—' said he.

The taproom filled up again. Four young chaps, strong creatures whose hefty limbs swung like hammers through the air, were playing darts. They drew back their arms and the darts flew. Harry had to fetch a lamp. Laughter burst out, raucous, jolly, obscene, the kind of sound that sends a pang of pure modesty through a sensitive woman. Talk as broad as the dialect, thick tobacco smoke rolling upwards like baudy incense, and from the carpenter a hoarse chant to the convivial mass.

Carpenter: I'll give me one-O.

Carter: What about your one-O?

Carpenter: When a man is dead an' gone 'e never more shall breathe O.

They continued then with various questions and answers until the carpenter, swinging his empty mug, reached twelve, when, with a scarlet face and wet forehead, he sang the whole thing backwards:

'Twelve the twelve apostles,
Eleven the 'leven Evangilists,
Ten the ten commanders,
Nine the nine bright shiners,

117

Eight to the eight Bulgian buoys,
Seven the seven stars in the sky,
Six the Simpsons in me buoys,
Five the five great walkers,
Four the gospel makers,
Three three the rifles,
Two two lily-white buoys all dressed in green O,
When a man is dead an' gone 'e never more shall breathe O.'

He was applauded by mocking laughter and smiles which twisted burnt faces into sardonic grimaces.

Some moments before, the company had become aware of Easter standing just within the doorway, with his arms crossed. He was without a coat and his drab shirt was open. His hair was wet, springing like a jet from his bold, broad brow. He advanced showing his teeth.

'That ain't a song!' said he, contemptuously.

'Ay? 'oo says? 'Twas a song afore ever *you* was born, Mr Loud-speaker.'

'Give us a better yerself!'

Easter tilted his head, rubbed his jaw and, moving his shoulders as if he were dancing, sang out in a gusty bass:

'Tell me, tell me, tell me, are you coming out tonight to dance by the light of the m-o-o-o-on.'

The carpenter interrupted him by jerking his elbow, springing back out of his reach when he moved as if he had been jerked by a cord.

'Old Tom-on-the-Tiles...'

Easter looked at the carter and then deliberately asked for beer. When Harry brought it he drained half off in one pull without greeting. He smacked his lips, and stretching out his arm, caught hold of the carter, pulling him round. Harry was busy.

'I'm an old tom cat? What the hell are you? Why didn't you give me a hand Wednesday with that chap that was setting on the hedge? All you b— seemed afraid of him.'

The carter retorted: 'Only fools meddle with blokes like that. Give thee a hand? Not likely... her'd give tha one with the chopper.'

Easter picked up the mug: 'None o' you aren't got no guts. Good job somebody can do summat.'

He finished the beer.

'Good evening to you. I'm going in with the gentleman.'

He turned round and walked towards the parlour. Behind his back the carpenter began to imitate his insolent stride, and the youths, lifting their lips with their fingers, tried to copy his face. Sammy Collins and Mrs Lloyd were both on their feet near the window. They had been talking, but hearing footsteps in the passage, they simultaneously shut their mouths, and Easter entered in a sudden empty silence. Their eyes still spoke, their lips were folded into an artificial tightness. They had broken off in the middle of a dispute about Easter. The timber merchant lifted his beer, carefully arranging his moustache before he drank; the landlady wished Easter good evening, while the bitch took two slow steps forward, snarling.

'Heel!' growled her master, regarding Easter under a narrow, ill-natured brow. He would have liked to have said, 'Set your teeth in him!'

Datty retired and crouched beside the chair.

The room was dull and dim as the two forms by the window obscured the remaining light which dribbled through the many raindrops now fast running down the pane.

Ivy wished to manoeuvre Easter out of the parlour before her husband discovered him. She stepped towards the door, beckoning him furtively, but he advanced and bent a discomposing glance on Collins.

The old man stared haughtily at him with his he-goat eyes. Drinking turned him livid. The stiff red and grizzled hairs of his beard, springing from the pallid, spongy flesh, disgusted Easter, and at the same time recalled to him Mary's beautiful red hair. He felt a thrill of rage, and he smiled the peculiar and knowing smile that Phoebe watched.

Collins coughed importantly: 'Well, Probert, so you tackled a lunatic down in Goose's Hollow... not bad that. Everybody's heard about it. How does it feel to be famous?'

Easter's answer to the spiteful patronage was swift, silent, and deadly offensive. He bent forward, threw Collins' hat off the chair that was his rightful seat as long as he was within The Dog, and sat down where he had no business to be, slapping his knees and glancing sidelong. Datty growled again, and her red-rimmed eyes were fixed on Easter's hands.

'Easter, get up; you're asking for trouble. Don't take heed of him, Mr Collins – he's had too much. Easter... Easter...' Ivy cried, distraught. It seemed wicked he should be troublesome when things were so wrong already.

The merchant swung his terrible face slowly over his shoulder and began a tremendous exhortation. Easter was to learn his place....

Easter laughed and reached out his arm and pulled the old man's coat at the back.

'Chaw-bacon,' he jeered. The merchant was a Gloucester man.

It was not the homely word, nor even the impertinence from an inferior, but the atrocious malice and the evil smile lying like a bad spell on Easter's mouth, which caused Collins to break into violent curses. He egged on Datty to bite; she leapt at Easter's knee, but he tossed her back, and Harry, hearing her howl and his wife scream, came rushing into the room: 'Hey, what's up? What, you, Easter, at it again? Out you go. Can't a man choose the company that's to sit in his own parlour? Why didn't you call me before, Ivy? What did I tell you?'

He was excited and kept clenching his fists.

'If you want me to go you must bloody well pull me out,' and as he spoke, Easter twisted his arms round the arms of the chair.

Harry looked at him, his eyes red with fury and then ran out into the passage.

'Hey, boys,' they heard him, 'who'll help me chuck Easter Probert into the road?'

'No, telephone the police,' shrieked Collins.

'We don't want any rough handling,' Ivy pleaded. Harry returned, his arms akimbo.

'Now then, will you go, or shall I send for the police?'

'Can't any of you laugh?' Easter sneered. He yelled, half rising from the chair. 'She's bitten me!'

Datty had sunk her teeth in his arm.

'You...!'

Collins snatched her from the floor before Easter had landed a terrific kick, and held her up, twisting and snapping. The place was in an uproar; Harry struggling with Easter, Ivy white and upset, exhorting her husband, Datty clawing to get free and fly at her enemy. The men

121

were standing in the doorway, watching the row.

'Come on, lend us a hand!' vociferated Collins, standing well back.

'Let's turf 'im out!'

'All right... 'ang on, 'Arry!'

Between them they hauled Easter into the passage. His boots scraped across the shiny tiles, leaving white nail scratches. From side to side the heaving group swayed and battled, crushing like one great awkward body against the wooden partition. A square youth of immense power finally ejected him, but not before he had dragged a dart from somebody's grasp and stuck it pretty deeply into the carpenter's hand.

He was hauled into the road with his own blood running down his arm and the carpenter's blotching his torn shirt. He limped to the bench and for ten minutes sat under the dripping tree, presenting to the curious eyes in The Dog windows a broad and obstinate back. Then he got up and walked away towards the bridge with his hands in his pockets. Before he was out of sight he suddenly stopped in the middle of the road. The watchers wondered why. It was this: after all, he had had the beer free.

Mrs Lloyd tried to soothe old Collins; she apologised with all the painful humility of those poor souls whose living depends on the good graces of capricious drunkards. The tears were in her eyes, but in heart she felt contempt for the old he-goat who stood in her parlour threatening her with the loss of his custom, and something resembling tenderness towards the bloody, unashamed groom out in the rain who had once or twice put his arm on her shoulders and asked her to drink with him – a small courtesy and grace which the under-bred skinflint merchant never displayed.

Harry was plainly infuriated. It made him feel ill.

'Mr Collins, I hope to God the time will soon come when that devil will be locked up,' he said, coming into the room for the iodine to patch up the carpenter.

'It's overdue now,' remarked the merchant, putting on the tweed hat and walking out. He crossed the road, entered his house and began to bully his daughter, who made a hard living for herself by taking in paying guests. She, however, possessed the same home temper, and before long they were screaming at each other. When they heard the guests returning they put on identical welcoming smiles, for to them profit meant even more than winning a battle.

As it grew dark the rain fell faster and the air freshened.

'Time,' said Harry.

He looked drawn, ill-humoured, 'fed up'. But he lingered a moment outside, cribbing with the carter who had witnessed the scene in Goose's Hollow and the carpenter. They spoke in the dry, thrashed-out way of people who are merely repeating what they have discussed before. It was all about Easter.

''E was never no good. Not sociable. A b— to 'is wife, they tell me. Wonder 'ow she likes living in a loft?'

The carpenter smiled: '"Shell's good enough for the chick."'

Then the carter also smiled.

''E got a bit o' mettle about 'im. I 'oodn't a touched that silly chap for an 'underd pound meself. Easter goes up to 'un an' 'andles 'un like a lamb. Could a done anything with 'un and there was we others lookin' like a lot o' fools.'

123

'It's my belief 'e's the same, that's why,' the carpenter explained. He seemed as if he would stay there all night while his bright eyes roved over everything.

Harry began yawning; from the back premises Ivy called.

'You're done,' the carpenter said, 'and I must be getting along or else the missus'll lock me out. Goodnight, 'Arry, goodnight, Price.'

He went.

The carter raised both arms wearily: 'Been out 'aying all day till past nine, up at four to fetch the 'orses in. Ah, I'm glad it's night.'

He, too, walked away with bent back and heavily swinging arms. Harry gazed after him indifferently for a second and then went in and shut the door.

* * *

Easter did not recross the bridge. Instead he walked straight on through the village following the road which ran parallel with the river. He was in his worst mood, absolutely yearning to work harm. As soon as he was well beyond the last cottages he stopped under the overhanging trees and, rolling back his sleeve, examined the bite in his arm.

It was an inch above the elbow, no more than a nip, but it had bled freely. He pulled a wet dock leaf from the roadside all dripping with rain, and tied it over the place with a yellow silk handkerchief. Then he looked about for a sheltered spot where he would be able to sit down without getting wet through. It was already night beneath the melancholy trees which dripped on the road; the fields and hedges were saturated and dreary. However, there was no wind and the rain fell straight.

The bank on his left looked gloomy and sinister; the tree trunks stood out against the shadows all green and blotched from the rain. His imagination plagued him with horrors; the trees towered above him. He could not stay there without giving way to vague thoughts which frightened him.

A broken gate on his right led into a field where there was an old haystack with hurdles round it to keep off animals. It was black and dishevelled, tipped on one side; rats, or something else, had eaten away the base so that it resembled a top-heavy timbered house. Easter thought it would afford him shelter. He crawled through the gate which was patched with wire, and established himself where no light from the road could expose him. His wet shirt made him miserable now that he was no longer walking, but he did not intend that to interfere with his object. He sat on stoically until the night was unrelievedly black, a brooding figure expressing vindictive determination in every invisible feature.

Hardly more than forty yards away the river ran; by the reddish colour of the water and the direct, unbroken flow, he had judged that it was rising. He watched it until it grew too dark to discern more than an eddying gleam here and there. His ears were filled with the flotant rush of the current.

Finally he spoke on a lonely note. Yet he did not move for several minutes – his body was more torpid than his brain. When he did, he sprang to his feet energetically. Before long the sound of his feet died away along the lane in the direction of Brelshope.

*　　*　　*

Two of the oldest cottages in the district were situated in Goose's Hollow, a long, patchily cultivated piece of ground intervening between them and the thick holly hedge which had been hacked by the lunatic.

The land lay very low, rising somewhat steeply on either side. It was, in fact, a typical example of what in Herefordshire are known as 'bottoms'. To one side of the cottages there was a melancholy-looking pond under a curtain of willows and brambles. The water, which seemed to be trying to burst its way out everywhere, here triumphed in a strong spring which never dried up; and the surrounding ground was also perpetually moist so that the inhabitants had contrived numerous narrow channels as a drainage system, bridged here and there by single planks or stone slabs.

Water flowers, rank grasses, rushes and peppermint flourished. There were a few cleared squares where runner beans, cabbages, onions and potatoes were grown, approximately half pertaining to each cottage. They were wrangling, quarrelsome, slapdash folk who were always fighting over the garden. The property was Matt's; he put up a wooden fence one year, told them off to keep to their own half, and hoped for the best... at least, the fence proved useful for drying clothes.

The cottages themselves turned their backs on each other with a dignified reserve which the occupants lacked. They were brick, timbered, with overhanging thatched roofs under which the small windows peered out suspiciously. Between the back walls there was a space of

126

about three feet which appeared to the tenants to be a marvellous dumping ground for tins and bottles, until Matt roused himself to put a stop to that. They were the sort of people whose activities must be curbed. Four years previously they had marched upon him in a body: four tough men and two attractive women.

'Well?'

'Build us sheds; we have nowhere to put our bicycles and our tools.'

'Our potatoes; our wood and washing.'

Matt put up a large weathertight, lean-to shed to each cottage.

The tenants thanked him, cleared out the dilapidated pigsties and took to rearing swine. On Christmas Day, by way of recompense, each family bestowed on him a nisquill. Matt knew enough about pigs and tenants to laugh.

In one cottage lived a family named Evans: they were strong, black-browed men, three brothers and one wife (it was said) among the lot of them. She had a dark son who resembled them, but the little girl, fair-skinned and sandy-haired, was trained to call her 'auntie', and once remarked abstractedly: 'That aren't my auntie, that's my mammie.'

It was probable.

These people Evans were sly as the devil, up to any knavery and full of cunning calculations. Tales of their prowess were common currency, even among those who had been done down by it. It was said that the single, middle-aged lady who owned Emma once publicly complained of there being a great quantity of thistles in her paddock. Thereupon an Evans presented himself, claiming to know of a cure.

127

'What is it?' the lady fires off bang-bang into the Evans' restless face.

'Donkey,' answers the Evans.

'Well, have you a donkey?'

'Yes, miss, that I have.'

'Well, bring it.'

Some weeks later the lady encounters the Evans and remarks that the thistles have in no way abated.

'Your donkey doesn't seem to like thistles, Evans.'

'Oh, miss, give 'un a chance! 'E aren't ate all the grass yet.'

The other cottage was occupied by a childless married couple by the name of Queary.

Tom Queary resembled a drunken, dissipated Punchinello. His red nose, thin grotesque face, puckered eyes and broken teeth, his long, shambling, ungainly figure, and neckerchief and flannel waistcoat made a figure at once amusing and sinister. He leered as a merry death's head might... a kind of smouldering ferocity lurked in his glance, and tangible horror in his starting bones and raking cough. The chest beneath that flannel waistcoat was nought but a bent cage for the wildest heart in the parish. And that was wild indeed. His wife Emily was Easter's field woman.

The Evanses and the Quearys all worked for Matt's tenant farmer: the men were farm hands, the women house drudges.

* * *

On this same night, Emily Queary was up plucking a fowl in the shed. She sat on a settle which had yielded up its

128

back to the burning the winter before, a hurricane lamp at her side throwing its whitish light in a broken circle over her limp figure, and repeating the same strange cubistic curves more palely among the slender beams which supported the roof.

She wore a white apron over her ordinary muddled dress, and held the fowl on her lap while she carefully stowed the feathers in a sack at her feet. The bits of red and green paste in her hair comb shone like glow-worms, her small hands were the same colour as the dead bird's stiff feet.

The shed stank – the hot, dusty, feather stink that gets to the throat. On the threshold it was met and vanquished by fresh peppermint exhaling on the wet air. Rain drops fell softly on the roof. It was past midnight, and Emily worked desultorily, yawning and blinking.

The door behind her opened and Easter inserted his face, a grim face distorted by a grin neither pretty nor pleasant, a ferocious smile below a corrosive brow. He was holding on to the latch inside the door, leaning his chin on his hand while he observed her. However, he was in no mood for continued passive contemplation: 'Emily!' he exclaimed abruptly, though in a low voice.

She started and clasped her hands.

'My Lord, how you frightened me!'

'Dost know it's nearly one o'clock?'

'Yes... more.'

'You ought to have been in your bed hours ago. Nothing's wrong now, though; if you miss the saints' hours you must carry on through the devil's. Since you're not asleep, here's summat for you to look at. See!'

'What bist?' She trembled, staring into his drawn face.

'What *bist*? Well, it *baint* in my eyes, young woman. It's under my arm.'

She saw that he had something under his arm, wrapped in a sack.

'You've been doing summat, Easter, you've never been poaching?'

'Never, Emily.'

'What is it, then, that you're 'iding?'

He had a flow of words behind his tongue that seemed to burst from him. It was incomprehensible to her.

'Tonight's my night... to take my pleasure. To have at them, to hurt them on their sores... that damned bastard, Kilminster! Emily, Datty won't go snarling at your heels any more. She's quieted. It's an old way to get even with a man through his animals. It's a gypsy's way. Look!'

He unrolled the corpse of Datty, old Collins' beloved bitch. She would not drink from her master's pint again.

Easter laid her on the settle. Her tongue lolled over her jaw, there was foam on it; her blue-glazed eyes were starting sharply from the sockets.

'It's a mean, sneaking, low-down hedge way,' Emily retorted, shrill enough to burst his eardrums, her eyes shooting light.

'Shut it! I said so.'

'Ah, poor little thing!'

'Rubbish, 'tis no worse than chucking a sackful of cats over the bridge.'

Emily began to burn.

'What if us *do* drown a cat now and then? It's got to be.'

He closed the door, picked Datty up by the hind legs and pitched her into the corner.

'She bit me,' he said, and seated himself beside Emily. Bending, he seized her apron to wipe his face. She dragged it from him, her fingers touched him. She went on with her plucking.

'Easter, it's late; you'd best go home. There won't be nothing tonight.'

He broke out savagely and suddenly: 'I told you I wasn't poaching! You dirty whore; a man can't look at you but you think he's out to get hold of you.'

'*You* never looked at me for no other reason...'

In some obscure way this man was again betrayed. He bounded to his feet and reached the door in one vital exhaustless spring. The pallid drawn look left his face. Those indefinable surgings which he sometimes experienced towards a sort of higher development invariably left their mark on him: a sign of suffering was a sign of grace. At his most animal he was magnificently unimpaired. That moment he radiated a physical joy fearfully brilliant to behold.

He rammed the bolt.

Emily, pushing away the fowl, gave a longing sigh. He enclosed her, kicking the lamp to the ground. It continued to burn on its side. He would have left it; at such a moment stars, moon, and noonday light were all one to him. But she was furtive and would not be still until he put it out.

Afterwards he lay face downwards on the ground, hiding his head in his arms. She heard how he had killed Datty, something of what had happened at The Dog. He spoke languidly, as if he were asleep.

'I crawled to the kennel... she barked... she was on a chain. Old Collins thought a fox was after the ducks... he

131

fired a shot from the window. I throttled her.'

'What're you going to do with 'er?'

'Heave her in the pond.'

'No, 'er'll rise.'

'I'll weight her, then,' he said drowsily.

'Get up; you can't sleep 'ere.'

They stood up in the dark. Easter relit the lantern. He prodded the half-plucked fowl.

'That there hen's a knowing old bird now.'

'Go on! Us couldn't teach *'er*.'

'Goodnight.'

Emily went to bed without undressing. In the morning she went to work at the farm all crumpled and creased. She was criticised for wearing a torn apron.

'That cock'ril's creels done it when I were twisting 'is neck.'

Miss Williams looked at the naked carcass on the enamel dish.

'It's a hen.'

''Twere a cock'ril as done it,' retorted Emily finally.

* * *

Easter returned home. He found the door open, a lamp burning on the table, and coals in the grate. Wet clothes were spread on a horse and hung across a line in the kitchen. He found Mary asleep in an odd attitude, or rather dozing, half-dressed on the bed. She was lying stretched on her side, her head lifted, her cheek on her hand. On a chair beside the bed stood a lighted candle and a large bronze bell.

132

As he entered she started up, uttering a single sharp groan. Her face, convulsed with pain and tense, stared up at him; her eyes were distended. She said something had happened to her earlier in the night when she was rinsing the clothes which he had ruined, and then she had suffered two awful attacks of pain. Then she spoke no more but, reaching out her arms, caught the iron edge of the bed under the mattress in a petrified grip.

Easter fled for help.

The same copy of the *Salus Times* which announced that Samuel Collins had lost a tan terrier bitch answering to the name of Datty, proclaimed also the birth of a son to Easter Probert and his wife Mary, prematurely.

For the first two days after its birth it was thought that the child would not live. The mother might. Matt paid for better aid than the parish afforded, and they both survived, although for nearly a week the boy did not open his eyes. He was kept alive on drops of brandy; in the night the vicar came to baptise him; it was done from a silver loving-cup belonging to Phoebe. They called him Shannon. He was amazingly small and still.

Six weeks in bed passed for Mary in a weak flow of night and day. Two events she remembered always: a night when she was still desperately ill and Easter came to her door, drunk, bawling and shouting that the child was not his.

'A bastard, and the son of a bastard.'

The parish nurse was sitting with her. She pushed him away, and when she came in, with her heart visibly heaving in her skinny bosom, she said to Mary.

'Remember that, I will.'

133

And her old friend Margaret Tressan lying across her bed, weeping: 'Mary, Mary... come back to me when you like, and you shall both live with me.'

Easter made up a bed for himself in the harness room. Every day now Dorothy urged her husband to give him notice. The topic was eternal, it nearly drove them all mad during July. Every single person in the house was affected by it. The sound of quarrelling travelled down the corridors; the opening of doors released shrill, abusive voices.

It was queer weather, with sharp showers, hot sunshine or whole days of grey stuffiness. Phoebe found a soothing occupation. She used to pump up soft water until her arms ached, or hide herself away to learn poetry. She learned the whole of the Rubaiyat. She loved it, but it depressed her, and for relief she kept a sort of diary, or rather a record of her vague, unhappy thoughts. Thus: 'Suppose there were no wine in Omar's jug – no companion in the wilderness?

'Your words are beautiful and I love you for that, but your philosophy, your creed is useless to console, harder than the Stoics! Hope of the *future* is everything for those who have nothing. You wrote for the happy. Today – the today you preached so exquisitely – is nothing.

'But the sheer music in that work of selfishness! Perfect as the Sermon on the Mount. Well, Phoebe, take your choice.'

She added that same night: 'My heart acknowledges Christ.'

The next day: 'There is much to do. Why do I stop to write? The house resounds with the awful clatter of dustpans – how I hate it! I feel rather like a cold potato, heavy and solid. I wish I knew what to do. There is a ton weight on me.'

One entry concerned Easter: 'I'm haunted...'

'There is a glorious moon in a streaky sky, so calm that I said my prayers looking at it for I felt God's very face might be behind it, so unutterably peaceful it is...'

'Yes, I'm haunted. Else why should strangers look at me with Easter's eyes?

'I do feel strange when he looks at me, so that I have to shut my eyes and feel my heart beating.

'When I came up to bed I found a bowl of yellow pansies. Mrs Wood had sent them in for me and they smell so sweet and pure and young as if they belonged to God. So what are they doing in my room?'

For some reason she felt violently ashamed when she had written these last words. She quickly tore out the page, put it in the grate and burnt it to ashes. The next day she destroyed the whole book.

VI

Nearly eight weeks after Shannon's birth in the middle of August, the weather turned hot again. It was three o'clock in the afternoon. Phoebe and Rosamund were going down to bathe.

They undressed by the river in an oval hollow in the meadow; a threshing machine was droning and they both felt sleepy and languid.

A watcher saw them standing on the bank, then sit down, and with upflung arms slide out of sight. A moment later they reappeared, wading through the shallows, Rosamund with eager limbs, Phoebe shading her eyes from the sun which flashed on the rippling water. When they were in the middle of the river they plunged. It was Dorothy who was watching them from the summerhouse where she was sitting with a basket of coloured wools on her lap, and a piece of canvas between her fingers. Near her, lying close to her feet on the warmed, wooden floor, Philip was playing with her pearl necklace.

The grass under the trees had been mown. Pale green apples hung glossy among the leaves. There were clumps of pink and yellow columbine growing near the summerhouse which was blistering in the sun. The ants ran over the steps.

'Don't do that, darling.'

'What, mummy?'

'Drag my pretty pearls across your teeth.'

He unclasped the pearls, wound them twice round her bare ankle above the strap of her thin sandal, and, in trying to fasten them, snapped the clasp.

'Can I get up?' he asked, looking at her slyly.

'Yes, if you'll promise not to run about in the sun. Does your mum's nose want powdering?'

'No.'

Dorothy raised her hands to her curls, stretched, lit a cigarette and rose. The pearls fell off when she moved. Philip saw them; he said nothing.

'Let's go down to the river and watch the girls swim.'

'Phib can't swim much, mummy.'

'No, but Rosamund can.'

They left the summerhouse and the pearls lying on the floor. Dorothy pick-a-backed Philip through the meadows and he tickled the back of her neck with a grass. He sang her a song, but all the time the pearls were at the back of his mind.

The river was low. They were able to sit on a little pebbly beach. Philip wanted to catch minnows, and then he wanted to bathe. Dorothy undressed him and he capered into the water with his tongue hanging out. He kept looking over his shoulder – he thought something queer lived in the sandmartins' holes, something like a large spider.

He was quite right; Phoebe was not even an average swimmer, although she forced herself to go into deep water.

Under the opposite bank a slowly turning pool curved into the red clay, overhung by fresh young alders thick with leaves whose dipping branches swept the water. Phoebe swam froggily into the pool with her neck strained, her mouth tight shut, her head far too high. Suddenly she saw a fishing line lying on the surface. It was Easter's; he was having a half day off and spending it fishing. His voice came through the green leaves flurrying Phoebe. She was dismayed.

'I'm sorry, I can't stop swimming,' she panted in answer to his request that she would throw the broken line ashore.

Her loose swimming suit frequently slipped off her breast. She felt terrified in that clean green water....

'He's smiling behind those leaves,' she thought, and put herself about.

'Let yourself go, miss; you'd enjoy it!' Easter called.

'Thank you; keep your advice. Miss Phoebe can swim,' cried Rosamund haughtily.

She had seen Easter all the time. What on earth did he hope to catch there? She was diving off a submerged rock into a narrow pool between two boulders. Each time the current brushed her softly against rocks. She had nerve, and a passionate love of flinging herself into water.

138

Directly after her aristocratic speech she hitched up her behind and disappeared.

Over them all the sun flashed and sparkled, caught by the broken current. The meadows were bathed in the full calm flood; the trees flung clear green shadows. Behind the alders, Easter slowly lit his pipe, gathered up line and bait, and strolled away.

Philip stayed in until he began to turn blue. Dorothy dragged him out. She dried him on his sisters' towels, gently butting her face into his thin body, hiding it in the folds.

'Eat you... eat you... with a big wooden spoon.'

He grasped her hair.

'Mammy, your pearls are broken.'

'What, what? Who broke them? You naughty boy! Where are they?'

'In the summerhouse. They came off.'

'Are you sure? Then come along at once.'

'Oh, you're cross...'

'A little. No – no, my darling.'

She kissed him again, heedlessly picked up the towel, wandered away with Philip leaning fondly against her.

Phoebe and Rosamund went and lay down in the yard on the hot cobbles. Rosamund rolled her bathing suit down to the waist, and Phoebe lay with her face turned up to the sky, her open hand pressed over her eyes. The yard was very quiet.

'We're ripening,' said Rosamund, who was in a good temper.

'Now we're the Modest Marys again,' she continued, while she tried to twist her hair into curls. The 'Modest

Marys' were two young ladies of their invention who loved to take off their clothes, particularly in public places. They made a habit of lying in the yard after swimming.

Several years ago, a grumpy old Methodist groom who had worked for Matt before Easter, raised objections to this and threatened punishment. Even now an unexpected footstep would make them jerk with involuntary wariness and turn their eyes instinctively towards the harness room which was their old refuge.

'Supposing Brant came now...' Rosamund murmured idly.

Phoebe smiled. She was happy, untroubled. Her piteous, puzzled brow was relaxed. She began humming to herself, but broke off as her sister asked: 'Why don't you always lie here like you used? This is the first time this summer.'

'Oh, I don't know.'

'That's a lie,' observed Rosamund.

Phoebe was ashamed.

'Well, then, I shan't answer the question.'

She lay still, assured that no Easter would appear. Presently she went in, dressed, and practised for two hours.

Matt did not have dinner with them that evening. Dorothy had quarrelled with him again. She began, as usual, to abuse him to the children: 'The fact is, your father is a thoroughly careless, indolent man. *Thoroughly*. He allows everybody far too much freedom. I told him I'd left my pearls in the summerhouse this afternoon, and when I went to get them they were gone. He took them out of his pocket: "Here they are; Mary picked them up," he said, as though that was quite an ordinary thing to happen.'

'Mary?' Phoebe exclaimed.

'That's Easter's wife apparently. I can't bear that couple. The idea of letting her sit in the summerhouse! Your father said he'd given her permission. Is nothing mine, I'd like to know? It's absurd, ridiculous. It's ridiculous. Eh? Disgraceful.'

She could not resist knocking on his door as she passed on her way to bed.

'I think you're disgraceful. It's humiliating to have to live with such a person; absolutely degrading.'

Matt did not reply. His eyes were on the book before him.

'Behold thou art fair, my love; behold, thou art fair; thou hast dove's eyes within thy locks.'

Dorothy, her long skirts gathered in one hand, her ear inclined towards the door, awaited some sound or retort from within. The unbroken, stony patience that Matt had shown towards her for the last few weeks enraged her.

She retired to her room, flung off her clothes in a heap on the floor, wrenched a strap off her shoe, patted herself all over with stinging perfume and jumped into bed, where she dragged the clothes close round her neck as if it were winter.

She was among those people who cannot hide their anger in their minds: rage shook her bodily and vented itself in violent action. She did not remain lying in the bed for more than a couple of minutes.

'He's drinking,' she exclaimed, sitting up. She sprang to the floor and ran impetuously down the passage.

'Matt, you're getting drunk in there by yourself. How disgusting!'

'Why; do you want to join me?'

'So you *are*.'

'No, I'm not. Worse perhaps,' he added to himself.

'You've locked the door. I *will* see what you're doing. Let me in,' she cried, shaking the panels.

He rose from the table: 'Very well.'

He unlocked the door. Dorothy leapt into the room like a toy termagant, her hair flying, her feet bare. Her eyes glanced here and there, flashing over Matt as if he were too contemptible to dwell on. He was standing by the uncurtained window. He moved and sat down at the table again, looking at her sideways.

'Do you know you're naked?'

Her nakedness roused him but not towards herself. She was soft and white with a fascinating angularity about the shoulders and hips, of which one was slightly more developed than the other. The strange charm of it used to delight him when they were first married. She abruptly dragged the curtain over the window, then, standing opposite him with the table between them, leant her two thin arms on it and sank her head between her shoulders. She stared into Matt's strained, bright eyes; she had reason to dread that stimulated brilliance.

'You've hidden it!'

She flew to the corner cupboard, flung it open and peered inside. It contained a tin of tobacco, an old calendar and a pair of broken spectacles.

She looked carefully around the bare room. Her face was flushed, so that she looked painted.

'There, now you've seen,' ejaculated Matt, suddenly rising, 'you've had a good look round, now go. Now leave me alone, for I've had enough. Do you hear me? Go!'

'You can't order me about. I don't care a twopenny damn for what you say. I won't go until it pleases me, and before I do you've got to promise me something...'

'Well?' he said with a sort of alarming restraint, striking his knee softly with his fist. 'Well, I can guess what that is.'

'Yes, because you know you ought to do it,' she shouted, quivering all over, 'because it's on your conscience that you haven't kept your word. Months ago you said you'd get rid of Easter. Now you must do it. Tomorrow.'

'Listen to me, Dorothy, and remember what I'm going to say, for I shall neither repeat it nor go back on it: I am not going to sack Easter – how *dare* you interrupt? Be quiet – he works satisfactorily, his wife has been ill, and they have a delicate baby. I won't have a decent man thrown out of work for your whim.'

He grasped her shoulders.

'Let go of me!' she spat.

'In a moment I'm going to put you out of the room and you'll run bleating to Phoebe. Do as you please, of course – what do I care what she or anybody else thinks of me?'

'Nothing, you never did,' she screamed bitterly, and began to sob, so that the tears dripped off her chin. Matt took his hands off her shoulders. She thought she could reproach him.

'If you were called by your right name it would be "coward"...'

'And "bully"...'

'And "brute".'

His face flamed so suddenly into fury that she fled,

143

banging the door after her, as the Bible flung by her husband crashed against it and fell open to the floor in a rustle of thin pages.

Trembling all over, he stooped and picked it up.

'Behold thou art fair, my love; thou hast dove's eyes.'

Matt shook as if he were moved to the very heart. There were deep furrows of pain in his face; he stood breathing in great sighs and his eyes were closed.

As a result, the next day he rode over to Davis' and remained a week, drinking persistently, although his carousals were even more spiritless than usual, and the memory of Mary, which haunted his senses, lay like a vision in the bottom of his cups. Mrs Davis was away with Marge; the two men kept to one room of the ill-kept old house, a room which was largely taken up with an incubator and smelt of straw. There was a grey pall of dust everywhere, and lumps of mud lay on the floor brought in by their boots. Davis' mongrel was always whining to get in or out, or lying in his basket, yawning like a crocodile and growling at Matt. Davis would pick him up; he would sit on his master's knee with his long snout pushed into Davis' ear, making the most horrible grunts while his eye rolled and glittered like a glass ball. Davis himself was not particularly lively, as he had taken a woman and kept lachrymosely wondering what his wife would say to it if she knew.

One evening he brought her in, a tall, stout, pale girl with dancing eyes, dirty hands, and ragged skin round her nails. She kissed Matt. He pushed her away, and Davis laughed, and they danced light-heartedly; but when she was gone he was more depressing than ever, and said he should give her up.

'I know I should take these things as they come,' he lamented, 'but I don't suppose Jean would like it, and for the life of me I can't help thinking what she'd say.'

At last, one night Matt went out and saddled his horse. There was a moon giving out a pale bluish light which made everything look hard and cold. It was just above the chimney stack and wavered like a reflection in rushing water as the invisible smoke shimmered across it.

Davis came running up.

'Why, where are you off to?'

'I'm going home.'

Davis remarked the shaking hand, the hag-ridden expression.

'Never – it's too late. Wait till the morning.'

'I *cannot* wait.'

Davis was startled by the fervent tone, and slightly offended.

''Ave you forgot summat you 'ad ought to 'ave remembered last week?'

Matt mounted unsteadily.

'"I have left undone those things which I ought to have done, and I have done those things which I ought not to have done, and there is no health in me." Goodnight, Davis; many thanks for the respite, although I've been in teeming hell.'

His horse moved, Matt swaying forward over its withers. He rode into his own yard at midnight. A lantern was burning in the saddle room; a thin line of amber light showed under the door and, where a board was broken, escaped in a single, soft ray across the cobbles. Matt called out: 'Hallo there – Easter!'

145

Easter emerged, looking wild with a glitter in his eyes. He strode up to the horse and, laying his left hand on Matt's knee, made a curious abrupt gesture with the right, almost as though he were pointing at him.

'What's the matter?'

'I think my wife's gone, sir.'

'Gone?'

'Run off.'

* * *

It was quite true. Ever since Shannon's birth Mary had made up her mind to leave Easter. Only weakness tied her to The Gallustree; directly she was strong enough to go she went.

Her plans were simple: in the bank she had forty pounds of her own which would enable her to live until she could find and undertake work. She would go to friends in Shrewsbury whom she vaguely hoped might help her. She knew she could easily be found, but she would refuse point blank to return, and if pushed to it, she would try to get a separation. In reality she had not recovered sufficiently to contemplate sustained work of any kind, but the fact was mind and body alike were temporarily undermined, and she was incapable of arranging details.

The effort proved abortive from the start. She put the baby into the pram and wheeled him to the Chepsford road where she intended to get on the first bus that overtook her.

It happened to be early closing day in Chepsford, and no bus appeared. At eight o'clock in the evening she was still pushing wearily, having been nearly an hour and three quarters on the road. She was almost done.

She decided to spend the night at the nearest roadside inn. Ten minutes later, when no house or building of any sight was within view, a wheel came off the pram. She drew one deep sigh of bitter exasperation and fatigue, lifted the baby in her arms and walked distractedly on. Very little farther there was a crossroads, or rather, a place where two narrow lanes branched off, and, lifting her jaded glance to the signpost, she read: Weir End; Gillow.

Afterwards considering the state she was in, her plight, and the time that had passed since she met him, she could never understand how her mind had leapt so quickly to William Dallett, whose gun-metal ring on her finger was the only sign of her wifehood to another man. She thought at once: 'I'll go to him.'

She walked back to the pram, opened a gate, and lifted it into a field, where it would not be seen from the road. Then once more, and with a long breath, she took up the child whom she had laid on the ground, and went on.

She went painfully slowly, for she was practically exhausted. All the time she saw Matt. She could not think of him ardently any more than she could have passionately clasped him, for she was too weak even to imagine action. Had he been near she would have gone to him and wound his arm about her, and leant upon him.

Lifting her head which hung almost upon the baby's breast, she moved him from one arm to the other. Two girls on bicycles were approaching her. They were laughing, shaking their machines all over, playing the fool. Their light dresses blew about and they held their hats in their hands.

'Can you tell me where William Dallett lives?' she asked as they passed.

'Next cottage.'

'Is it far?'

'Just round the corner.'

She saw it. That helped her.

The cottage was ugly, of grey stone, slate-roofed. There was a narrow flower bed under the front windows, and a green wooden fence dividing it from the road. A little girl in a red dress with a bandaged leg was standing on a pile of stones, dipping her hands into a corrugated-iron water butt. A little way behind the cottage was a small, dark spinney enclosed by wire.

'Does Mr Dallett live here?'

The child ducked her head and did not answer.

Mary pursued: 'Is he your father?'

The little girl sprang away and ran behind the house. Mary went up to the open door. It led straight into a littered kitchen. A flaming fire burned in the high grate; the table was spread with a blue cloth on which were plates, a loaf on a folded newspaper, and a pot of jam. Another girl, a little older than the first, was kneeling on a chair, vigorously flapping a cloth to keep off the flies. There was a smell of hotpot.

Mary repeated her question. This child, who considered herself quite grown up, answered her in a mincing, responsible little voice.

'Yes, Mr Dallett lives 'ere.'

'Can I speak to him?'

'No, because 'e aren't at home.'

Mary could hardly bear the pang of despair occasioned

by this self-possessed announcement.

She faltered: 'Where is he?'

This time the child hesitated, as if she were becoming embarrassed. She seldom spoke to strangers. At last she said her father must be at the pub.

'Is that far?'

Silence.

Mary would have tried to coax her, but she felt only impatience. Had she been aware that her eyes were fixed on the little girl with the same stare she was accustomed to meet with in an impetuous schoolteacher, she might have softened her tone. She repeated, was it far?

But the child had come to the end of her resources. She stopped, waving her arm over the jam pot, and her face turned red. There were steps outside. A thin girl with short, rough, brown curls and glittering eyes was approaching slowly, carrying a bucket of water. She was dragged sideways, one arm in the air, her teeth set. She appeared to be about fourteen years old. She was so very short-sighted that she had to go right up to Mary to find out what sort of a person this was.

'Did you want anything, ma'am?' she asked, setting down her burden on the doorstep.

'I want to speak to Mr Dallett.'

''E's down at the Three Magpies. It's only a step.'

'Thank you.'

She made a slow movement.

'Oh I can't carry the baby any farther!' she broke out. 'May I leave him here on the sofa? He'll be good. He never cries.'

The girl stared at her, biting her finger, then nodded.

149

'Yes, leave 'un, do. I'll mind 'un. Aren't 'e small? 'E won't be more than a few weeks old?'

'Two months. How shall I get to the Three Magpies?'

'Look 'ere, Alice'll fetch dad up. Sit down, ma'am.'

She fetched a chair, and as soon as Alice had run off after a whispered conversation behind the door, bent over Shannon and begged that she might be allowed to pick him up.

'Yes,' said Mary listlessly.

The flies were crawling all over the table, the heat was terrific. Dallett's daughter held Shannon, devouring him with her glittering, short-sighted eyes.

Alice stood under the deep wooden porch of the Three Magpies afraid to knock because of a little liver-coloured dog curled up on the mat. Above her head a faded sign swung from a hook. The dog barked lazily without moving. Presently the landlady came to the door.

'Well then, Alice, you seem in a hurry. What d'you want?'

'I want dad.'

'Bill, 'ere's a lady wants yer,' said the man on the bench nearest the door.

Dallett came forward, rubbing his flank. He was in a dirty magenta shirt, the sleeves rolled up above the elbows, corduroys, and a large flat, straw hat famous all over the parish.

'What's up?' he asked. But Alice had fits of silence when she would open her mouth for nobody, and she would not reply.

''Ere, missus, I'm off,' he said. 'Something's amiss perhaps.'

He nodded and walked away.

'Shall us drink up tha' pint, Bill?' shouted a voice from within.

'Ay, an' treat me another day.'

When they were close to the cottage, Alice found her tongue.

'There's a lady with a baby at 'ome,' she exclaimed, throwing her father into the most profound astonishment. He hurried on, leaving her behind.

So, more or less prepared for something extraordinary, he entered his kitchen with a dead cigarette in his mouth and saw Mary lying back on the old sofa, the baby beside her.

'Eh... you!' he exclaimed, 'you *be* in a way. Whatever's wrong?'

Involuntarily his eyes fell on her left hand. His ring was there. He pitched the cigarette in the fire and, going close to her, stooped and said: 'Now, mum, what can Bill Dallett do for you? Don't you be afraid to ask.'

She started up: 'Come out and I'll tell you.'

Dallett restrained her, and told the children to go outside. Mary wept.

'My husband's cruel to me... I've left him...' speaking in a breathless, disconnected way, she clasped his arm between her two hands and turned her worn, alluring face up to him. She wore the same expression that had so touched and charmed him months before when she told him of her marriage. He would do anything to please her. As she rose, one hand covering her eyes, he looked at her compassionately.

'Ah, I can see as you haven't done well for yourself! You'd best lean your weight on me. There now...'

151

He went on after a deep pause: 'My missus is dead an' my home aren't fit for you.'

'I'm going on.'

'No, no, that won't do. Why, look at the baby! You can't go on tonight, nor tomorrow either. When you've drunk a cup of tea I'll take you down to the Magpies. And mind, whatever they ask – say nowt. They won't get nothing out o' me.'

In a passion of gratitude, humbler than she had ever been in her life, she put her lips to his bare arm and kissed him.

*   *   *

The landlady of the Three Magpies ran about, waiting on Mary and Shannon, who lay upstairs in the big bedroom. She admired the picture while she absorbed the roughness of Mary's hands, her delicate, haughty speech, and the fine quality of her linen.

Nature had been very reserved over the landlady: nothing in her rather vacant, flat countenance, tied up in its morning glory of a pink cotton duster, betrayed her inquiring propensities. Dallett understood her, as he understood most people, and Mary did well to follow his directions. The landlady's mind ground on short commons; she was sour with the customers that day, inclined to flounce and snap. The big bedroom was a sensitive, moody room, where the light changed from hour to hour. In the morning a sun-ray, quivering on the low ceiling, took a peculiar shape like a bony arm and hand, weaving a long golden thread; the fingers moved, the wrist turned and the thread twisted. Towards midday it disappeared, the sun with it. Behind the lace curtains the room settled to shadowless afternoon.

Mary lay with her back to the child, her hair all twisted and wild. As the hours drew towards evening her mental pain increased. It was a simple, repeated agony of longing for Matt which she could have put into three words without any difficulty whatever.

At six o'clock she bathed Shannon in the basin. She had him at the breast when she heard a horse descending the pitch, disturbing the loose flints which had made walking so difficult for her the night before.

She went to the window and saw that it was Matt.

Such a nervous tremor of anticipation ran through her whole body that the child rejected her and burst into a suffering wail. From that moment there was no question of a continued flight. She put Shannon on the bed and began hastily to dress. She was only half clothed, standing in her petticoat, her hands in her hair, when, scarcely pausing to knock, he walked straight into the room and with one distraught glance at her, sprang forward and seized her in his arms. She felt his lips on her cheek, and desiring only to meet his mouth with her own, turned her head in a moment as violent as his advance, and her hand behind his neck, pressed his face down upon hers.

Two hours later he was riding back to The Gallustree in a triumph of love.

The evening was solemn; the hills lay like lions in the fields.

VII

Dorothy took Rosamund and Philip to Torquay for the first three weeks of September. It was cool, and in the hotel they were obliged to put on subdued behaviour. They were glad to return.

Dorothy had been well amused. At first she thought she would keep it to herself, but in the end she told Matt about her admirers at the hotel.

'Look,' she said, throwing herself back in her chair, blowing out her stomach, extending her legs and pointing her toes, 'he used to sit like that and say I was charming! Every minute I thought he'd fall asleep in the middle of a compliment. Oh!' she laughed, sprang up, and threw her arms in their elaborate sleeves round Matt's neck. Matt smiled. He was turning things over in his head, very far from heeding her adventures. Matters needed a little readjusting at The Gallustree. Between furtive transports it

154

was necessary to arrange the periodical absence of Easter in a natural, inevitable manner which could not be questioned.

Matt and Mary were not a frank, cold-blooded pair of lovers; they preferred to keep the relationship more or less spontaneous, and to discuss the disposal of Easter would have disgusted Mary, who was turning out surprisingly romantic. The whole of the responsibility therefore devolved on Matt. He rose to the occasion.

The stabling at The Gallustree consisted of five loose boxes and four horses were kept. Matt, with sudden extravagance which Dorothy bitterly upbraided, bought another hack and two more hunters.

At the conclusion of a long, angry conversation, she ran out of the room. However, she was no sooner out of the door than she returned, for she had really made up her mind to try to be more patient. Matt had not moved. She sat down again and lit a cigarette.

'What on earth are you going to do with so many horses?'

'Well, you've done away with the hounds, so I shall keep horses instead. Have you any objection?'

'Oh, none, if you can afford it.'

'Thank you so much. That's kind.'

There she sat, pulling at the end of her hair and sending out sickly fumes of Turkish tobacco. His violent, hidden happiness kept bursting like breakers; the room was dark, she could not see the transformation.

'But where are you going to keep them?'

'Well, at first I thought of Davis'. But that's too tumble-down. In fact, it wouldn't do at all. So I've arranged to have them over at Sidney Jones', Pendoig.'

'Pendoig, Matt! That's five miles away!' she said, amazed.

'True, oh Queen! You're always complaining that our Easter has too little to do. Now he'll have plenty.'

'I *don't* complain that he has too little to do; my complaint is that he should have anything – here.'

'Then you've changed your song.'

'You are disagreeable. You used to make yourself pleasant to me sometimes.'

'The fault's not altogether mine,' he said gloomily.

They were silent until a charred log fell flaming to the hearth and the bitter smoke found its way into their eyes. Matt lifted it into its place. He remained leaning forward, his profile exposed in the red light.

Dorothy continued: 'You'll have to get another man. More expense. Really...'

'Nothing of the sort. It's quite simple. I shall get a boy. Cyril Price wants to work up here. He asked me for a job months ago. Mondays, Tuesdays, and Wednesdays you'll have to put up with the presence of your old friend Easter. Thursdays, Fridays, Saturdays, and Sundays he'll be over at Pendoig and I shall do the work here with Cyril.'

His face glowed.

'It seems a funny arrangement,' said Dorothy uncertainly. 'Why?'

'Just at this time... so much added and unnecessary expense.'

'You must curtail your clothes and cinemas.'

Dorothy flew into long-suppressed vixenish abuse.

'All right, all right,' said he, sardonically, soothing. 'Go on with your little amusements. But I don't see why I shouldn't have mine as well. And I'm going to.'

Dorothy looked anxiously at her husband.

'You do such dreadful things: drinking, gambling...' she began, throwing away her cigarette and sighing.

'And going into strange women.'

'Matt, don't talk like that! If I ever find out you've been unfaithful it will kill me,' she exclaimed hysterically.

He broke into a loud laugh.

'Oh, nonsense, you'd survive.'

'I'm not so sure.'

'Then if my footsteps ever deviate I must take pains to conceal them.'

He rose, lit a cigarette, and sauntered towards the door.

'Come back,' said Dorothy slowly, modulating her high-pitched voice, 'I want to talk to you.'

He returned, unwillingly, and stood with his arm on the mantelpiece, looking soberly at her.

'Do you know you have a very remarkable daughter?' she began portentously.

'Yes,' he replied, 'I knew it long ago.'

'Phoebe.'

'Exactly... Phoebe, you said it, lady. God damn it, Dolly, I'm not blind or deaf; nobody's died, either, that I know of, and you're not in church. For heaven's sake, don't pull such a long face. What is it?'

She sat up, extended her thin, graceful arms, and felt in his pockets while she talked.

'Give me a cigarette, and don't bluster. Shall we have the lamps?'

'No, I'm going in a minute. Do tell me what all this is about.'

'Mother wants Phoebe to go and live with her in

157

Clystowe. She says a school in Salus isn't good enough for her, and she wants her to have proper music lessons. She says Phoebe's playing and singing are really remarkable.'

'How old is Phib exactly?'

'She was fifteen last February.'

'If she has a voice she shouldn't *begin* to use it before she's seventeen or eighteen.'

'Rubbish! What do you know about it?'

'I've heard your mother say so herself.'

'Yes, but, Matt, she wants Phoebe to *live* with her.'

'Well, what does Phoebe say?'

'I haven't asked her, and she hasn't mentioned it.'

'Then I'll ask her tonight.'

'Shall you let her go?'

'By all means.'

He looked across the room with a strange, preoccupied stare: 'for we aren't good enough for her either,' he added.

* * *

Phoebe described the adventures of Calpurnia and Cleopatra every night when Philip went to bed. Rosamund also adored to listen; the tears sometimes came into her eyes just thinking of the little animals walking on their hind legs, giving concerts and going shopping. For this reason she sat on the floor, her head bent over her knees. Phoebe lay across the bed, twisting her hands and playing with her plaits while her invention ran on: 'Calpurnia sneered as she drove past. "Aren't you getting wet walking about in the rain, Miss Cleopatra?" So next day, as it was still raining, Cleopatra took out her new umbrella...'

'Oh, Phib, where did she get it?'

Phoebe laughed and said: 'Out of a cracker. You see, Philip Kilminster had a birthday party on the lawn, with crackers, and this tiny, tiny umbrella dropped out of one and Cleopatra found it.'

'Yes, but how did she hold it? Cleo-pat-ra hasn't any hands.'

'She had a subservient sparrow-servant who walked behind and carried it in one claw.'

'A subservient sparrow!' cried Rosamund.

'A froggy an' a snail and a sparrow with an umbrella!' screamed Philip.

They all burst out laughing.

Matt stood outside, watching them through the open door. Presently Phoebe turned down the lamp and took away the hot water bottle. Matt followed her and questioned her.

'Do you want to go, Phib?'

'Yes,' she said in her low, mature voice, as if she had made up her mind long before.

In the beginning of October she went. At the same time Matt put his plans into execution. Life at The Gallustree was changed, less gloomy, less high-strung, because Matt himself was active, healthy, and stirring. Mary was none the less fascinating for being easily accessible... besides, she knew instinctively how to draw a fine inner line which kept Matt continually interested. They were violently in love with each other.

Easter drank more, but for a long time it passed unnoticed, like so many of his subterranean activities. It pleased him to think of himself as a mole, silently destructive beneath the green, smooth surface. He grew haggard, lost a great deal of his former malicious gaiety. There was usually a brooding morose look on his face.

He did not want to live at Jones' farm in Pendoig. The farmer was ostentatiously religious, and Easter was a blatant scoffer. They would never have agreed. So Matt bought a small cottage, one up and two down, which, owing to its mouldy condition and dreary situation, was going very cheap. He had the roof and spouting put in order, the windows made weather-tight and stopped up the rat holes in the floor. The place was full of rubbish, a broken wooden bedstead, a couple of rotting potato baskets, and a heap of smashed china. The rubbish was carted away to be tipped in the river, but Easter retained the bed, which he slept on the whole time he was there. It was low and wide, and mended with wire netting which sagged beneath the mattress. The rude, obscene figures of men and women had been burnt into the headboard with a hot poker and some power. They were grotesque, but not amusing. Most of them were erotic in character, but one represented two undertakers pushing a child into a coffin. A woman stood by with her arms flung out in an attitude of the most abandoned grief.

With a little money that he had in hand, Easter bought a few bits of furniture at a cottage sale, all rather weird. He had a bamboo tripod, holding a cactus in a red pot, a wooden gramophone, a rocking chair, one or two cups and saucers belonging to a really beautiful old tea set, three china plates adorned with flowers and birds, a steel fender, a milking stool, a pair of large wooden candlesticks, and an engraving in a fretwork frame called 'Parted'. Easter liked this engraving which represented a fair, large-eyed woman leaning on a stone wall, perusing a letter while a tear flowed down her cheek. Behind her appeared a suggestion of melancholy, windswept distance; the noble trees in the foreground were represented as rocking in an autumn gale, which, however, did not disturb one sculptured fold of the maiden's colourless robe.

The gypsy in him recognised no necessity for carpets or curtains. His bed was made up of old horse rugs and blankets; the rocking chair was uncushioned. He usually sat on the milking stool close to the high, old-fashioned grate and partly screened from the roaring draught between door and window by a projecting cupboard.

Inside the cottage looked bare, utterly comfortless, slovenly and pathetic; outside it merely seemed uninhabited.

It was a bare quarter-mile from Pendoig village, right on the main road, having no more than a few feet of loose gravel between the door and the tarred surface. Heavy traffic shook it so that even the spiders did not spin their webs among the beams, and in summer dust coated the windows until it became impossible to see in or out. The raving south-easterly storms tilted full at them; the rain was dashed under the door. At all seasons it was infested with flies and midges, active or torpid. It was a plain whitewashed cottage, built of large, irregular stone blocks and with a bluish slate roof. The garden – such as it was – was to one side. A yard from the rear wall sprang a rocky precipice, casting its cold shadow over the cottage and half the road. In the crannies of the sandstone, which was piled in long, powerful, sloping layers, grew enormous, wet green ferns, oddly and repulsively luxuriant. The deep bed of rich red marl which the blasting of the rock had temporarily exposed, was now hidden by a weltering mass of crawling vegetation; it had killed the hedge and used the dried sticks to support its own exuberant life. It was like a great green wave breaking over the precipice, crested in autumn with silvery diaphanous old man's beard. In wet weather, surplus water used to pour down behind the cottage, trickling through the garden into the road. One might have almost supposed that this seedy dwelling place had been constructed by a savage misanthrope, who, bearing a general grudge against human comfort, and a furious contempt for life, health, or joy, had calculated on torturing its future inhabitants with rheumatism, and sending them either twisted and crippled to their premature coffins, or driving them sore and stricken to some drier situation. Its history lent colour to the idea. I will add that anyone beholding Easter's goings and comings, or seeing him through those same bleary panes as he sat absorbed in his reflections, with his brow knitted, his strange eyes fixed on the back of the fireplace, that person might have thought the influence persisted and gone away, thanking his stars that *he* was not that man and not his friend.

That which the door failed to exclude, as it did the rain, was the washing sound of the river. The road was an intermediary step between it and the crag, divided from it solely by a steep willow-fringed bank and some rusty iron railings. Occasionally the floods rose nearly to the brim; very exceptionally the road was under water right up to the doorstep. The cottage windows then afforded a heartening and invigorating view of reddish, livid waters swirling over the opposite flat meadows, with spiky thorn hedges very sparse and starved sticking up through the desolation encompassing them.

In other weathers, sheep of much the same sulky hue wandered about, picking at the brown grass, limping on three legs and coughing up their lungs like sickly tramps under a haystack at night.

The cottage and its site were altogether cheerful and picturesque. Easter never said anything. He chose to live there rather than at Pendoig. He seemed happy.

The cottage was called 'The Hollow'. He usually referred to it as the 'Louse Pit'.

At any rate, there he lived for two years, every blessed Thursday, Friday, Saturday, and Sunday.

* * *

Emily Queary being too far away for his immediate casual needs, Easter sought the acquaintance of various young women. The first was a Russian, about thirty years old, who lived with her aunt and grandmother. The latter did not approve of her connection with the groom on the grounds that she had noble blood in her veins. But Katya declared that all the English were swine, anyway, and a groom would do just as well for a lover as a certain widowed Colonel Aston, who wished her to go and live with him.

Katya was ugly-beautiful and very strange. She had a broad, straight nose flattened into her brown face, and eyes and eyebrows that slanted towards the temples. Her clothes were like sacks flopping from her shoulders; her voice had a nasal drag. She seemed to be everlastingly

163

boiling fish in a large kettle, washing up, or roaming the fields with a book in her hand. Easter met her one autumn day standing in a shower of golden hazel leaves, staring at the red and white signs which marked a jump.

'What are those?'

He told her. She had thought they were a kind of trap; without adding a word to her abrupt question, she scrambled through the hedge and, looking after her, he saw her squat, strong figure crossing the swell of ploughed meadow beyond, a blue blot against the dry red furrows.

She invited him to her home. He went only once. It was a small, ivy-covered house in Pendoig village. The aunt and grandmother were entertaining a crowd of casual, smiling visitors in the living room. Easter caught a glimpse of their grey, lace-covered heads as they sat at a little round table facing their visitors. He did not wish to go in, so Katya put him in her bedroom while she finished the washing up; he entertained himself by examining the Russian books which were lying in heaps on the bed and floor, and counting the dirty cups and saucers stacked on the washstand.

When finally she said farewell to Easter a few months later, Katya told him that she would have felt really affectionate towards him if, on that day, he had helped her with the washing up. When she had finished, they went for a walk in the woods. It was a cold, fresh, autumn day. A rainbow against the black clouds formed a complete and vivid arch. They passed a pond under an elm tree where a vast sow lay wallowing. The lazy creature seemed dead.... Katya laughed; the wind blew her draggled hair away from her forehead.

As they reached the outskirts of the wood it began to hail. They sheltered, and the stones bounced off their heads and rolled down their necks. Katya said: 'I'm thirsty, Easter.'

He held out his hands to catch the hailstones, and she licked them from his palms. Then he wanted to make love to her, but she began stooping and gathering up an armload of rotten twigs. She would not stop, for the twigs positively fascinated her and she could not leave them alone. The Russians were very poor; they had to pick up wood for their fires.

When this had gone on too long for his patience, he snatched the twigs from her and threw them down. This made her furious. She ran away, and for a month would have nothing more to do with him.

But one night she came to the Louse Pit and told him she wanted him. She would not go in, so that time they went to an isolated barn. Easter was never under a roof in a gale afterwards without thinking of it. It was calm, then suddenly they heard the wind advancing like a frenzied army along the field; it struck the barn in a frantic, sustained assault, blowing through the slits in the walls until the hay rose in eddies.

Not very long afterwards the Russians moved to London and Easter heard no more of them. Katya was the one person who enjoyed the ridiculous side of Easter's character. He had only to be absurd and she would lie back helpless with laughter, and when it was over, sit up and wipe her eyes and beg him never to look gloomy again.

When Katya was gone he found a successor in a solemnly immoral young woman who talked too much.

Though handsome, she possessed too many drawbacks, and he could not subdue her. He saw her pulling up roots in a field when he was exercising the horses, a tall, strong creature with a large bosom, a ruddy face, and firm, straight legs. It had been raining, and she stood squarely with a leg in each corner of her skirt, ankle-deep in soil. She wore an overall of clear, watery green over a big coat, and a deeper green woollen cap which glowed in the fine drizzle like a jewel.

The woman, the wet field, the green plants, and her sulky face peering at him over her bent shoulder, made a vivid impression on him. There was nobody else in the field. Solitary, unamiable, she went on with her work. Easter smiled, his white teeth flashed; she scowled, he rode on.

The next day he rode that way again. She was still there, a little farther on, standing resting, her hands on her hips, puffing and blowing at a Woodbine. Easter sniffed: 'Them cigarettes are dear at the price,' he shouted impudently, 'have one o' mine?'

She grimaced. He chucked one over the hedge and she caught it. They talked until the Woodbine and the Player were both smoked out.

Her name was Lucy, and she lived at Mostone, a nearby village. She had an illegitimate son by a married man. She fairly jumped at Easter, but to hear her talk one would have thought her excessively refined and prudish. For all 'unpleasant' words or circumstances she invented genteel names, and all the time she spent with Easter she never shut her mouth. He simply could not understand what it was all about. Great names were mixed up in it, and favours done to Lucy, all for artless admiration presumably.

They quarrelled and parted over the fleas in Easter's bed. All night long Lucy used to be up and down trying to catch them. She declared she could hear them singing in the mattress, that not only was she ravenously devoured, but they danced on her back and ran deliberately, malicious, all the way up from her toes to her head. She would lie as still as she could for about ten minutes, just twitching and shuddering impressibly now and again; then, having finished as bait, up she would leap, drag off the top rugs and wetting her finger, turn huntress. She caught them as they fled beneath the pillow, as they wildly burrowed for safety; she made Easter hold the candle and burnt them under his nose. In the morning her body would be covered with great purplish blotches. He grew to hate the sight of her, and took his revenge in his own way. One night, when she allowed him no opportunity to come near her, he suddenly jumped out of bed, snatched up a girth and strapped her down among her enemies. Lucy, abandoning her affected vocabulary, lay on her back, cursing from her heart's depths. It was the end.

The woman who came nearest to occupying a like position to Mrs Emily Queary was a virgin when he met her, and she became very fond of him. Physically, she was the least attractive woman in his life, being undergrown and slightly crooked, but the delicacy and docility she displayed towards him, endeared her to Easter. He was never quite so rough with her as with the others.

Her name was Ann Vey. Her father was a farm labourer, a widower with only one child. He was selfish, affectionate, and tyrannical in his wish that she should not marry.

Easter told her he was a single man. A week later she found out the truth, but she said outright that she was too fond of him to give him up. Night after night she returned home late. She used to hang up her old coat, clean and polish downstairs until her father ordered her to go to bed. He hit her, threatened and coaxed her. It was all the same.

Returning once at one in the morning, she found the door locked. Then she was in a helpless to-do, standing in the porch trying to break in with a hairpin. Her father spoke to her out of the window: 'You be grown up – you be free. I've spoke to you time an' agen – now you can go.'

She went away and slept in a cart, covering herself with sacks and pea-straw. Nobody saw her the next day or night. Easter did not know where she was. A sergeant visited the cottage and while he was speaking to Vey in the kitchen, Ann walked in, dirty, pale, and in tears. The sergeant listened to the story.

'Don't be a fool,' he counselled her.

It made no difference. She went her way. She had a child, but it died. Easter was as unpopular in Pendoig as he had been in Gamus and Brelshope. Stories of his doings and his strange marriage began to go about. He remained indifferent. Instead of drinking at the Pendoig Arms he kept a barrel of cider in the cottage, or if he felt like beer and spirits, rode his bicycle into Salus.

On one of these expeditions he believed he saw an apparition. He began to be tortured by outlandish nightmares, and for hours afterwards he would lie awake, afraid to close his eyes lest it should invite a repetition of the visions, pondering over sights which he was afraid he might one day meet in reality.

VIII

One Sunday evening, towards the close of October, two years after Mary's flight, Matt was leaning over a stable door at Pendoig, gazing into the loose box beyond. There was the sound of a horse munching, and vague soft movements.

Easter led out a bay cob, saddled, and stood waiting for Matt to mount. He straightened himself, rubbing his hands as though they were cold, then, drawing a long breath, turned and looked at the impassive figure of the groom. Easter was looking at him; the eyes of the two men met in a long, hostile stare, and into Matt's face came a curious tensity as though he had been insulted. The groom's face, yellower and thinner than it used to be, with a perpetually sullen and gloomy expression, changed not at all, only his eyes intent yet restless played over Matt.

The latter moved forward and gathered up the reins.

The groom stepped back.

'How long has she been off her feed?'

Easter shifted his gaze.

'Two or three days, maybe.'

Matt mounted.

'You take no interest in your work.'

Easter gave a short insolent laugh.

'I need a change.'

Matt broke into an imprecation.

Easter watched him ride out of the yard. He lit a cigarette, spat and put on his coat. The air was raw. From the pigsty came the heavy grunting of a prize sow. Easter laughed again while he twisted the ring on his finger. He locked up and strode through the yard with all his old graceful ease. The buildings behind him, with their narrow black, slit windows and deep sandstone walls of a mottled pink, were sturdy and threatening, like fortresses. The yard was snug and clean, deep in fresh straw, settling to the night. At the gate a thick-stemmed Spanish chestnut had scattered its leaves in the mud, and one of the men, in a faded jersey, torn breeches and puttees, was sweeping them into a glistening green and yellow heap. He wiped his spongy nose and shook his fingers in Easter's direction. He was Billy Vey.

The sky in the west was clear and brassy, shedding a metallic light over the fields and buildings which were still wet from midday's rain. The pond across the lane behind a wooden railing, a big square sheet of water, was trembling in greenish ripples. The horses had just drunk and churned up the mud.

Easter stood against the railings, inhaling smoke and

watching the ducks scramble ashore, where a young boy with a pan and a hazel switch in his hand waited to drive them into the duck pen.

'Lord, what a din!' he thought, listening to the raucous voice. The boy waited until they were all ashore, then swished the stick and drove them before him, waddling pendulously and shaking their tails.

The farmer's wife, hatless, peering, and stout, ran down the garden path, looked over the wall, and flinging her voice in front of her as she returned, screeched: 'Here comes dad, and the kettle not on!'

Jones would not turn his eyes in Easter's direction. He felt a great contempt for him, and righteous indignation against his way of living. The farmer was a Plymouth Brother, known as Slimy Sid. He shut his heavy front door with a clang upon the lewd man bare-headed in the lane, who smoked and stared across the fields.

At length, Easter moved off. He avoided Pendoig village, and made his way to the cottage by a field path which ran along the edge of a small, abandoned quarry. Passing it, he peered into the red hollow filling with darkness, and chucked his cigarette end into the shadows.

Entering the cottage, he kindled a fire and ate some bread and cheese. Then he drew a jug of cider which he stood on the hob to warm. He removed his boots and leggings. By rights he ought to have gone up to the stables again at eight o'clock, to take a final look round, but he did not intend to do it. He sat down before the fire, put on a log, and reached for the jug. He thought he would get drunk.

It was quite dark; it poured with rain, which ceased after a while, and the lights of passing cars stencilled the lines of the window frames on the walls in rapid transitory shapes. The shadow of Easter's head, with its stiff, tufty hair and harsh features, his bowed shoulders, and the hand holding the jug, was flung by the quivering firelight on the corner of the ceiling and the wall. There was no lamp in the room. Hours passed. A man came striding down the road past the cottage and on up the pitch to Pendoig.

It was between nine and ten, a night of cloudy moonlight, a pale, shifty luminosity which seemed to emanate from the wind rather than the sky. The man turned into the Pendoig Arms. Coming into the light, he was seen to be a great, swinging chap with bold, full eyes under an overhanging brow, a longish nose and a saucy mouth. His chin was pressed against his neck; his hands were in his pockets. His age was about thirty-five. He wore a shabby overcoat of some fuzzy material, no hat, and carried a small suitcase.

The only other person in the bar was a pale, refined man in smooth, dark clothes, whose black moustache was twirled into points. He looked at the stranger flatly, then turned away his eyes as though he was not interested. After a second he looked again. The stranger was brilliantly handsome. The top of his head was flat, covered thickly with damp, auburn hair, and the jaw just beginning to thicken, still perceptibly ran up to the ears in a delicate sharp curve.

'Good evening,' said the pale man in a careful voice.

'Good evening,' replied the handsome one.

'Dark night.'

'Blowing up for more rain.'

The pale man thought before he acted. He leant forward, his hands on his knees.

'Excuse me, haven't we met before?'

'Not that I know,' the stranger answered, hanging his coat over the settle. The pale man persisted. He actually took out a pair of spectacles, perched them on his nose and leant still closer.

'I'm sure I know your face.'

'I have three sons. Maybe you're mistaking me for one.'

'Really...' exclaimed the pale man, sarcastically, 'how old are they?'

'Forty-four, forty-five and forty-six,' said the stranger very quickly. He exploded into laughter, turned crimson, and spat into the fire.

The pale man sat back offended. He took off his spectacles and began to polish them in a finicky way with a bit of red silk. The other's laugh roared round the room and expired in a glorious exhibition of regular white teeth.

Suddenly the pale man moved in his seat: 'Rasp!' he shouted, as if he were calling a dog.

'Eh?' said the other, starting, 'are you mad?'

'I was only calling your dog.'

'I haven't a dog,' said the stranger, with a mischievous glance.

'My wife has, though,' he added, 'does that help you? It's one of them little snapping yappers. It's useful, though. What d'you think I do when my feet get cold? I put 'em in the dog basket and the dog lies on 'em.'

'You had a dog,' said the pale man; 'how you jumped!'

'Anybody would've.'

The pale man again donned his spectacles. He was incessantly playing with them.

'I've placed you now,' he announced.

173

'Allelujah,' shouted the stranger.

The landlord walked into the room, exposing a gold front tooth in a ready smile.

'Did yer shout?' he inquired, his head poked forward.

'This gentleman did.'

'Bring me a pint o' beer, a packet o' clubs and a box of England's Glory,' said the stranger in no strange dialect.

The landlord did so.

'Quiet for a Sunday,' said the handsome man, paying.

The landlord looked at him. He winked.

'Playin' skittles.'

'Bloody heathen.'

The landlord grinned, showing another gold tooth, and went away. The pale man nodded, as if to himself: 'Well done, bravo, for a stranger. He showed a couple – when it's three you stands a pint. Rare, you understand?'

'Aren't you going to tell me my name?' asked the stranger, stretching his long legs to the fire.

'John Lewis.'

'That's right,' said Lewis. He drank. 'I – I – what a memory you must have! Don't go shouting it about, though.'

'Have you been up to something?'

'No. I came down here to see one man and I don't want anybody else. See?'

'All right.'

'Who're you?'

'Name's Trefor. You wouldn't know me; your dad did.'

Lewis was smoking. He pushed the packet of cigarettes across the table.

'No, thanks,' said Trefor, 'I'll have a pipe.'

Lewis stared at his knees.

174

'Old Rasp died years and years ago. I left 'un down here with Tom Williams.'

'He's dead, too. Left the farm to his brother, who sold it five years back to Sidney Jones.'

'Ah, did 'e?'

Lewis occasionally lapsed into dialect and then his speech lost its vulgarity.

'I come to see Rasp once. The bones was stickin' through 'is 'ide and 'is coat – you know what a coat 'e 'ad?'

'Like a mat.'

'Ay. Well, he was all over sores. I took 'un out and shot 'un.'

He fingered his empty mug.

'Have one with me?'

Trefor shook his head again.

'You're not very companiable.' He shouted, and ordered another beer. After a pause, during which he gulped and puffed and examined the room from the bacon rack to the skirting board and set his watch by the brass-faced clock, he remarked that the place was changed. This led to a narrative of his unbridled senseless youth, and he recounted how one night they had drunk the previous landlord stupid, put him to sleep on the settle and served themselves. The landlady came downstairs at two in the morning, found her husband snoring and Lewis in the cellar.

'This very settle,' said he. He kept calling for more beer and tipping it down without showing any difference. He grew white when he was drunk, crimson when he was laughing.

'I can guess who was with you that night,' observed the pale man, whose cold, grey eyes were fixed on Lewis with

175

a kind of severity.

'You're a bloody clever chap,' said Lewis. 'Who then?'

'Easter Probert. He that's groom to Mr Kilminster.'

'You're right. And he's the man I want to see. Can you tell me where he lives?'

'Nothing like coming sixty miles to see the devil,' Trefor muttered. 'Yes, he lives in that white cottage bottom of the pitch.'

'I must've passed it. Oy, more beer!'

'That went down quick,' said Trefor.

'They do with me.'

The landlord brought another pint. He looked at the clock. It was ten.

'Put 'un down quick, case the copper comes.'

'He's round these parts,' Trefor observed, getting up. He turned a check muffler, very neat and clean, around his neck; having finally doffed the spectacles, he put them gingerly in his pocket and slowly blew his nose. Lewis also put on his coat and the two went out together. It was not raining. They stood a moment talking.

'You still in the same business?' Trefor asked.

'Oh, yes. Had a bit of a dairy for a while, but I went back to the old line. More used to it. Has Easter been long with that Kilminster?'

'Five or six years.'

'Long time for him. Must be doing well...'

'Well, I don't know. People talk. But we don't know much about him. He's given up coming here. Not sociable, you understand. That was a queer marriage of his.'

Lewis exclaimed. He seemed greatly taken aback.

'Married, is he? Never told me. Who did he marry?'

'Stranger. She was brought up among the gentry or something. It didn't turn out too well. That's only talk, though.'

'Well, I shall see for myself,' muttered Lewis, swinging the suitcase.

'Oh, she's not down there; she's over at Kilminster's. Probert's half the week there, half here.'

'Well, that's bloody queer...'

'Ah.'

'Ah.'

'Well, goodnight to you.'

'Goodnight.'

The two men walked away in opposite directions, dogged by their pale shadows.

The sky was obscure, broken, yet curiously symmetrical; clouds radiated from the moon like rays of darkness. Descending the steep pitch, Lewis could hear the river washing among the branches of a fallen willow. From the village behind him came the measured howls of the dogs baying to the moon. A woman would have been afraid out here alone in this mysterious night, or she would have felt unhappy, restless, disturbed. An imaginative man might have paused on the brow of that hill – Lewis was not so made.

He possessed plenty of animation, charm, a sort of blowsy vigour, a destructive dreaminess which undermined all the practical side of living, and a wild, wanton humour. But his visions were all solid and selfish, they did not arise like ghosts from immaterial, intangible beauty, they never evoked melancholy, mild fear or maddening panic; they arose like aldermen, mayors, and corporations. Thus John Lewis saw himself a highly successful, wealthy man. The reflection was

177

enough; he was satisfied; reality might go to the devil. In short, he was at least mentally ambitious. He and Easter had few characteristics in common, and here lay the first great difference: Easter had no ambition of any sort whatever, only a primitive longing to see that he obtained an eye for an eye and a tooth for a tooth. Easter's imagination was purely visionary and unconnected with cupidity. Lewis loved, worked, revelled, ate, and slept without noticing where; from earliest childhood Easter had moments when he was arrested by moving wonder at a vast earth and scarcely comprehended sky. Therefore, when he might have lingered, Lewis descended the hill briskly, and, having paused a moment only to light a cigarette, knocked on the cottage door.

Easter opened it, staggering slightly, one hand raised to his ear which was ringing like a chapel bell. He was half drunk, with haggard, brilliant eyes which could make nothing of the dark form in an overcoat.

'What d'you want?'

His tone was rude and harsh.

'Get a light and 'ave a look at me,' Lewis replied, holding the cigarette away from his face.

'I don't want to look at yer damned mug,' shouted the groom, preparing to shut the door.

Lewis came forward.

'Easter, yer old b—'

'God, it's Jack!'

Lewis burst out laughing.

'Ay, that it is,' he exclaimed, grabbing Easter by the arm and shaking him gently.

'Strike me lucky, who'd a thought o' seein' you! Come on in.'

They fell immediately into their old way of talking: Lewis in his loud, boisterous voice, with its flat town intonation, Easter in his swaying, pliant bass, blind by drink.

'I bin over to Gamus and they told me I should find you 'ere. There weren't no buses, so I had to walk; that accounts for me bein' so late. You're out o' favour there, Easter, or summat's up. That Kilminster spoke to me death without mercy...'

Easter's only answer was to mutter unintelligible curses, during which his friend continued to pour out whole unheeded sentences and unbutton his coat.

'Well, come on in, and don't stand on the b— doorstep,' broke in Easter, impatiently.

'Why, what's up with you?'

'Nothing,' he replied, holding fast to the door; 'come on in, 'case you wear an 'ole through to Australia.'

The two men entered the kitchen, Lewis towering over Easter.

''Ere,' said the former, taking the groom by the shoulders, ''ere, aren't you got a light? I want to see yer beautiful face.'

'No, there aren't no b— light, and my face is all eaten up by worms.'

Lewis struck a match and held it up to Easter's face. He stared wild and sullen, his mouth lifted, the pupils of his glowing eyes contracted, the sockets like pits.

Lewis started back: 'God, you look pretty!'

During the years they had not met, Easter's expression of malicious playfulness had changed and deepened into one of downright ferocity. He was in shirt and breeches, shoeless, with torn cuffs and an open neck. Entirely the kind of man that Lilian, his wife, would have called a lousy tramp. Lewis looked round the gruesome little room, which was hot and smelt of cider, and his eye fell on the two wooden candlesticks holding thick dusty ends of wax candles, unlighted since Easter bought them. He put a match to them, pulled off his coat and threw himself down in the rocking chair.

'Queer old things,' he remarked, pointing at the candlesticks. Easter nodded: 'Made out of altar railings. From Pendoig Church.' He went out and drew more cider. A jug three-quarters full was standing on the hob.

''Ave some cider?'

'I don't mind just a tot. Is it any good? 'Ave it got any mettle in it.'

''Taint so bad. Couple o' tots'll warm yer. What made you come down 'ere?'

Lewis drank, wiped his mouth, and set his hands on his knees.

'Thought I'd come down to see you. Fact is, I 'ad a bit of a brainwave.'

Then he thought he was going on too fast, so he broke off and began to relate how he had met Trefor in the pub. Easter sat silent, still with his hand to his ear, and Lewis studied his features closely.

'How the hell have you been getting on lately?' he ended, as he felt the jug with the back of his hand.

'Not so bad.'

'Doing well?'

'Not so bad. But I say, 'ave some more o' this cider.'

Lewis held out his china mug. The firelight exposed his

butcher's hands, large, spongy, and puffy with frequent dipping into water. Easter's were dirty, narrow, and callous. The silver ring shone.

Lewis rocked the chair.

'Come on, Easter! Tot it out,' he cried exuberantly. 'Let's 'ave another drop. We don't meet every day...'

'Come on, then, swallow it down. You drink so slow, a person mid think you'd summat in yer throat.'

He again refilled the jug, and the two of them drank faster. Lewis was not quite sure what it was he wanted to say. He kept jerking out questions.

'Got married, I've heard?'

'Ay, couple o' years back.'

'Well, what d'you think of it?'

The groom glanced stealthily at his only friend.

'I'd as lief be over 'ere on me own,' he said with infinite reserve.

'Go on, all yer troubles are over when you're married.'

He began to rock the chair violently. To and fro he swayed, a mad grin on his face, his cider slopping over:

'I'm always glad I was married,

Oh, I'm always glad I was married,

My Lilian's a treasure,

A – and a pleasure!'

'Got any youngsters?'

'One boy,' said Easter, staring between his knees, his mug trembling in his fist.

'I got a girl an' two boys. You never told me you was married. Dammit, you never said nothing.'

'Go on, pull into that cider – you're slow, aren't you? 'Tis getting flat.'

181

'I baint used to that, mate. Had none for years since I been up in Manchester. Might upset me...'

'Oh, she wore a belt...'

He was singing loudly.

'Go on,' said Easter in a throaty mutter, 'get it back – it won't 'urt tha. Come on with it, 'taint every day we kills a pig.'

Lewis' confusion was increasing. He sang songs muddled up with an account of his life in Manchester, his shop which he had just had painted, his wife who was going to have another child soon, even his squabbles and how he got the best of them all.

Easter got up reeling and went into the back kitchen, a cold, stony place where he kept the barrel of cider. He now had to tip it. It was streaming with rain again; a regular depressing drip-drip came though a weak spot in the roof, forming a puddle in a broken flagstone.

The candles were flaring, while grease poured over the rim. Lewis was rocking again. Crazy shadows swayed on the ceiling, the chair creaked:

'Oh she wore a belt
Whenever she felt
A pain in her tiddly push...'

'Who did yer marry, Easter. Anybody I know?'

'No, you wouldn't know 'er.'

'Well, you 'aven't moved, so you must a met somebody round this district. Come on, out with it! I bet you got round Kilminster's bloody cook.'

Easter growled like a baited dog. He filled his mug, spilling cider on the ashes.

'Come on,' he said, his fierce eyes on Lewis, 'drink

hearty and never mind about that piece.'

Lewis put his trembling lips to his mug, but persisted: 'Well, tell us, who didst tha marry, old 'un?'

Easter's throat swelled, but he made no movement and no answer.

'Come on, out with it. Was it that girl, Doris Watts, that wouldn't kiss tha...?'

'Oh, curse you, curse you. Can't you leave me be? What d'you want to know for? What the hell's it to you? You be no doctor. Don't ask me no questions. For God's sake, don't. What d'you come down here for, poking and prying? Want to find out all I been doing... Christ, what's it to you?'

His strident outcry bewildered Lewis, who sat staring with watery eyes.

'Surely we can know who one another married – we've always been pals. 'Er isn't as bad as all that?'

'I haven't no pals; I haven't no wife. Now bloody well shut your rattle or get outside,' Easter vociferated, staggering to his feet.

'I'll bloody well close your trap,' shouted Lewis, beginning to peel off his coat; 'I'll clump you one,' he roared, the garment dangling from one arm as he became entangled in the sleeve. 'That's yer tune, is it? Come on outside if you're a better man than me. We'll soon settle this lot. Got yer bloody hasty on you, I should think.'

He stumbled and fell into his chair as Easter's fist swept downwards across his face and the blood began to trickle from his nose. An arm of the chair crackled clean away and was left hanging. He wrenched at it and, with a jerk that nearly made him sick, pulled it clear, a horrible weapon with a nail on the end.

But the groom also had fallen back and lay with a ghastly livid face and twitching, gaping nostrils. Lewis held on to the mantelpiece, and the bit of wood fell from his hand. For several minutes he felt too ill to move, but, recovering a little, went and stooped over Easter. His eyes were open and he was moving his shoulders. A drop of bright blood fell on his face as Lewis pulled him up.

'Come on, Easter; you don't want to be like that. We don't want to fight. You be takin' me the wrong way. Up with you.'

Easter sat again on his stool, his head bent. There was a long silence. Lewis' drunken eyes were heavy and swimming.

At length Easter spoke, sullenly: 'I'm not so struck on marriage, Jack. I don't want to talk about that lot. 'Taint me she wants.'

'You want a woman like mine,' said Lewis.

'God, no! I don't want no woman at all.'

The row died down as suddenly as it had broken out. Lewis went on talking drowsily, and Easter continued to be quite silent. He was not drinking now, but he heard very little of his friend's murmurs, which developed now and again into song.

An hour later, maybe, Lewis went to fill the jug, stumbled over the chair and sat down on the floor, where he sat, gulping from the jug and squalling,

'She took quin*ine*
and chloride o' lime
to cure the pippity-pop
Until she came
a what's 'er name
a travelling doctor's shop.'

184

'That was a day we had that smash up. Remember?'

Receiving no answer but a heavy nod, he unbuttoned his waistcoat and continued: 'We was only youngsters then, not quite so steady as we are now. Hell, it *was* a smash up. Our dad didn't 'alf cuss. 'Ad to 'ave the float done up... smashed the float... poor old mare...'

He emptied the jug: 'Well, that was all right. Easter, goin' to 'ave some more cider? 'Ave to be up in the mornings now?'

'All right... all right.'

Lewis pushed the hair away from his temple. His eyes were running terribly: his cheeks were of a bluish pallor.

'My head, too... look, you can still see the mark. I'll tell you what I come for. Well! Be damned if I can remember. I bin an' got too much of this cider. I'll 'ave to see you in the morning.'

Easter lifted his head.

'Ah, that's it. Leave it till morning, and 'ave some more cider. 'Ave some bread an' monkey's elbows.'

Lewis, however, had fallen asleep. Easter lay down on the floor with his head on his friend's legs. The fire had gone out.

At first he lay like a log, stupefied, dead, for all his pulsing heart. And then, after an hour or two his brain began to work all out of gear, causing great drops of sweat to break out on his forehead. His disconnected dreams were so horrible, so gloomy and terrifying that they half woke him, and he started up on his elbow to stare around him, pressing his unavailing eyes against the thick, cold darkness, groping with his fingers along the stone floor. He did not know where he was, nor what he was doing;

185

only that there was a horrible flavour in his mouth, that he was a living thing – somewhere, that his last ghastly vision of a white, sculptured head was torturing him. He *saw* it again, trembling; the marble smile, the quick expression on the beautiful face, the white and sparkling brow, an effigy of a murderer on a great stone tomb.

His extended hand touched Lewis and it seemed that he had put his finger on the core of dread; his very heart paused and then leapt back to living in vehement bangs against his chest.

In the midst, sleep broke over him again like a vast breaker. He was buried, not in the black vacancy of deep water, but in the flying, stinging, outside spray of unconsciousness, and in this restless, tormented sleep he burst into a violent passion of weeping and woke himself by his own convulsive sobbing. His mouth was shaking, his lips salt, but this time he was broad awake, and he stood up, trying to recollect where he had put the lantern. He did not really want to light it lest he should come face to face with the shame of crying like a youngster in the dark. Now he was quite a man, hard, unbelieving, and proud – himself entirely who had no grief.

He opened the door and stepped into the road. It was night no longer. The moon had gone down, and in no quarter of the sky was light visible, yet he could make out the grey, torn shapes of clouds whose rents revealed the stars were failing, and the solider chain of hills behind which the sun would rise. The earth and air were fresh as though all human breath had blown away, nor was there one human sound. He walked a few solitary paces along the road as though he were the only man alive. A quick, cold wind ran through his hair, a sudden shower of drops from an elm fell on his upturned face. Then a cock crew, haughtier than a trumpet, imperious as an archangel's summons. It was four o'clock. He returned to find that Lewis had been awakened by the air blowing through the door. He was sitting up and passing his cold hand over his head, while he cleared his throat and feebly moved his legs. The two of them were very stiff from lying so long on the stones. Easter lit the lantern. They badly wanted cider, but they found it was all drunk, and cursed before the empty barrel which yielded no more than half a pint, even when they tipped it steeply.

'If I don't want a livener this morning...' said Lewis fretfully. He thought of his usual arising from a feather bed, and the pleasant way Lilian had of making tea.

They stripped and pumped on each other's necks, Lewis white and clean all over, Easter tanned and dirty. Then they rekindled the fire on the ashes, brought out the ham and ate a few mouthfuls. Lewis lit a cigarette and told Easter the reason for his visit. He spoke in a hoarse voice, rubbing his rough chin and looking across the table with dissipated eyes.

He had a plan. He wanted to return to Salus and set up as a pork butcher; there was a business going, but he needed a little money to put to his own. It struck him Easter might have money after all this time. As he talked, the colour came back to his face. He was very ardent and persuasive. Easter sat, clasping one foot on his knee, his dusky eyelids dropped.

Well, had Easter any money?

The groom answered directly: yes, a little.

187

How much?

Two hundred pounds. His eyes were still lowered, his head inclined towards his shoulder as if in deep reflection. He knocked the ash off his cigarette against his callous foot.

Two hundred pounds! By God, that would do it! How did he get it?

Saved it.

Would Easter think it over?

Yes, and let him know within the month.

Lewis was more than satisfied. The groom repeated his words of the night before: he needed a change.

'You're bloody mysterious,' observed Lewis, leaning on the table. He had taken a little comb from the suitcase and was combing his auburn hair. Still without raising his eyes, Easter smiled. The position in which he was sitting, his immobility, and the rays of the lantern striking upwards, revealed how deeply bitten were the lines on his forehead, how sunken the flesh.

As soon as it was beginning to get light, the friends parted, Lewis returning to Salus, Easter going off to the stables.

Lewis stopped and looked back at the cottage.

'Two hundred pounds!' he exclaimed, amazed.

He went over his shabby friend's appearance, his way of living, his unpopularity, even Matt's curtness the night before.

'My word, I'd like to know more about him!'

He caught sight of Easter for a moment, striding along the edge of the quarry, arms swinging, easy and graceful.

Lewis had lost most of his former geniality and warmheartedness in petty calculation, but now for a brief space he wished he knew more about Easter as a man. He walked on, puzzled and, for some reason, vaguely sorry.

The day turned out stormy and cold. Rain fell in lashing showers, dead leaves whirled. Women kept running in and out of their doors, fetching and putting out washing which, in the fine intervals, blew from the lines till Pendoig seemed to be in the midst of a white gala. The sharp, heavy flapping of sheets was heard on every side.

Easter rode by Vey's cottage. He saw Ann outside, standing on the muddy path, disentangling a long roller-towel from a clothes' prop. Her fine brown hair was all over her face, her hands and half-bare arms were red and soapy.

'A bad washing day,' shouted Easter.

'Yes,' she screamed, as a wet shirt flapped in her face.

In the middle of the morning, when Easter was preparing to take himself off to The Gallustree, the boy who worked for Matt rode into the yard on his low, red bicycle. He held the shiny handlebars in the middle and wore his cap back to front. He was a fair, thick-skinned youth of twenty-one, short, cheerful, with wide shoulders, a skinny waist and a bull neck.

'Hullo, Easter.'

Easter answered in some fashion.

'Old Kilminster come off yesterday.'

'He did! Where?'

'Rigg's Pitch. Mare went down clean – slipped on them flints. He went over her head: 'twas funny.'

'Hurt?'

'Nah... right as rain. Scraped his hand a bit. The mare stood still like she was saying "Anything wrong?" I laughed, but it do make you afraid.'

'The roads are awful. Well, so long, Cyril... keep your eye on this 'un. Off her feed.'

'So long,' said Cyril, and began to whistle.

IX

Phoebe was having a music lesson.

It was past four, getting dusk, and her master had just lighted a lamp. His old house looked out on a churchyard; the branches of the tall, silver birches brushed the window. The heavy curtains were undrawn. The room was long. In one corner an electric stove gave out a dry exhausting heat. The furniture comprised an armchair, a couple of music stands, a low-fronted chest of drawers on which lay a violin, and the Blüthner Grand, at which Phoebe was sitting. The board floor was bare.

The master stood behind her, looking over her shoulder. She stopped. The piano hummed like a choir of supernatural voices ascending to heaven. She took her foot off the pedal and there was dead silence.

'I knew you couldn't,' said the master. He had a thick, Jew voice. 'I told you you couldn't play Chopin and, what's more, you never will.'

'Why not?' cried Phoebe passionately.

'You are too serious! It wasn't badly *done*, you understand... but Chopin... he is laughing all – the – time. I've told you fifty times and – you – will – not – listen, you are so headstrong. Now you've had your way, you've failed, you see you – cannot – play – Chopin. Remember that: you – cannot – play – Chopin. Say it after me: one, two, three. I – cannot – play – Chopin.' She was silent.

'Ah, you're obstinate...' said the Jew balefully. He was a withered little man with a dark skin and a tangle of unshorn grey curls. He spluttered when he talked, wore canvas trousers, and frequently soliloquised. The townspeople thought him almost disreputable, but Phoebe's grandmother knew what she was doing when she sent Phoebe to him. He had quarrelled with the organist of Saint Mary's Church, whom he had utterly routed in a battle of correspondence through the *Clystowe Times*, and when he wished to be particularly unpleasant or harsh, imitated the organist's hiccuppy way of talking and walked about the room on his toes, twisting his hands and blowing through his teeth.

'I will play Chopin,' said Phoebe suddenly. She had grown even more obstinate.

'Ah...!' he made an impatient gesture.

'Now get up. Listen to me.'

He sat down to the piano.

'I know I cannot play the piano; I am a violinist. But I can do better than that. Now listen.'

He pursed his irascible mouth and began. His hands were brown and supple with rather large joints and short, flawless nails. It was true that he did not seem to be able to play very well, but with all his faults he contrived to get at the quick of what he was playing. His method was unfinished, strong, domineering. Under his hands the music took on a kind of mournful, subtle humour.

He turned to her.

'You see?'

Phoebe nodded unwillingly.

'But how can you *prove* he was laughing?' she asked triumphantly a moment later. The Jew was used to the expression on her face at that moment. He jumped up exasperated.

'Miss Kilminster, you are like a little child, asking "Why does two and two make four?" I cannot prove it; there's no need. I know! In theory you can prove anything. We, too, have our grammar, our multiplication table, but there is a time when all that is past – we enter a new region where there's no *proof*, only understanding – sympathy?'

He added the last word doubtfully as though he were aware of its poverty, then resumed as he saw she was about to speak.

'Bah!' he burst out violently, 'there are no words. You may know your grammar. Good. You can sit down and write out verbs. But you cannot write a living book...'

She waited until the tirade was over, her clear, somewhat melancholy eyes fixed on the Jew's animated face. He always threw her mind into a chaos. Then he suddenly became tranquil and, touching the back of her hand with his forefinger, spoke a few words which she remembered.

'You are obstinate. That is a good thing to be. But think

sometimes, "There – are – some – things – I – cannot – do" and you will go farther. You will not waste so much time. Because you have not all natures you cannot be all things; because you cannot be good, bad, selfish, self-denying, religious, blasphemous and so on, you cannot *do* all things.'

'I can be all those things.'

'For a little while; not consistently.'

'Then I may have a mood when I can play Chopin.'

He shrugged his shoulders: 'Perhaps; I think not. You are not cynical. It isn't your direction. There – are – some – things – you – cannot – do! And plenty of very good ones that you can. Stick to those. Remember. What a lecture! There is Leyden.'

Someone was knocking at the door. Phoebe gathered up her music and put on her gloves. The Jew was dragging the curtain across the window.

'I've given you too long,' said he briskly; in a totally different, more everyday, and less arrestingly sincere tone. 'Hurry up. Come in, Leyden.'

There entered a tall spectacled boy of nineteen in a blue, tight-waisted overcoat. He was carrying a violin case and looking at the ground as though overcome by shyness. He brought with him a faint odour of eucalyptus.

'Please, Mr Cohen, I want to ask you a favour. Will you give me my lesson another time.' He was a Dutch boy, speaking English correctly, but in a stiff, toneless voice. He was blushing; the Jew looked at him in amusement, for it was the first time Leyden had ever asserted himself in that room.

'All right,' he said, 'I'll give you an hour tonight – nine to ten.'

'Thank you so much – I am greatly obliged.'

He stood, painfully embarrassed by a belated idea. Ought he to have greeted Phoebe? They had spoken several times. He felt he had been rude. The old man was looking at him sardonically.... With a great effort he opened the door for her. It was difficult to speak with Mr Cohen listening, so obviously listening.

'You are going home, Miss Kilminster?'

'Yes. Goodbye,' she said, confused.

'May I walk with you?'

'Oh, yes, of course!'

Mr Cohen was positively laughing.

'Goodbye,' they all cried at once. Leyden shut the door with a bang. He had to open it again to free a corner of his coat. He stood with Phoebe at the head of the bare, draughty stairs which wound down into darkness between cold, blue walls. She gave him a shy glance, arranged her glove, and led the way. Leyden watched her fair plaits swing against her shoulders.

When they were outside he gently took possession of her music case.

'I shouldn't like to live in a churchyard,' she began as they descended the steps. These were no more than nervous words meaning nothing, for she loved the elegant town-house, and its row of sedate neighbours, which looked across the green turf to the church.

'Oh yes, I would like to live here. It seems to me to be beautiful and nobody is buried here now.'

It was slightly misty. She raised her eyes to the tall spire going up, up into the sky, still smouldering from a fiery sunset. They walked in silence for some minutes,

Leyden carrying the music case. Her face was happy. How did she guess the boy had put off his music lesson in order to walk with her? She knew it. And so did the master, but luckily Leyden was not aware of this, or he would have smarted with humiliation.

It was not far to Phoebe's home. He realised that he must speak at once.

'So you are going to Paris, Miss Kilminster?'

'Yes; after Christmas; my grandmother is taking me.'

'You have left school?'

'Oh yes. We – my grandmother and I – don't believe in schools for old people.'

'Oh... oh,' Leyden laughed. His cheeks were rosy from the cold and his spectacles were dim. Phoebe noticed that the mist had already damped his thick rough hair. He wore no hat.

'But you tell – *told* me that you do not speak French very well. What will you do?'

'I shall say "yes" or "no".'

'And suppose that you wish to buy something?'

'I shall draw a little picture of it.'

'Bravo,' exclaimed he, laughing again. They were very near the grandmother's house.

'You would do better to carry a dictionary, mademoiselle. *Regardez!*'

On his open hand, extended towards her, lay two tiny red volumes, smaller than a match box. 'Look at them,' he said hoarsely. He cleared his throat. 'They are for you.'

Phoebe was so startled, so acutely embarrassed, and so delighted, that she was absolutely dumb. Look what began to happen when you were seventeen!

'*Oh monsieur c'est trop! Vous êtes vraiment trop bon,*' was all she could utter in her confusion, while Leyden dropped the music case and one dictionary.

'Thank you very much,' Phoebe continued enthusiastically.

'It is nothing. It makes me very pleased.'

Then he handed her both dictionaries, and made her a bow. Their two bright laughing faces were curiously childish and expectant. They were soon at the grand-mother's steps. Phoebe took her case and turned on the bottom step to say goodbye. He had laid one hand in its woollen glove on the narrow iron railing, and so, he looked up at her.

'*Au revoir*, Miss Kilminster. I shall see you perhaps, next Monday?'

'Yes...' she replied uncertainly, 'yes, yes. Goodbye,' and she ran up the stairs trembling.

'Thank you,' she called again as she opened the door. Leyden smiled and walked away with a manly stride.

Phoebe rushed upstairs to her room, tore off her hat with some of Dorothy's impetuosity and flung herself into a chair, her elbows on the windowsill. The garden below was full of dead leaves. There was a bare fig tree, and one frosty red rosebud hanging heavily from the bush.

'He is too young,' she thought wildly, and all the time she was smiling a lovely, absent smile. Her expression suddenly changed, but before it was clearly defined her eye fell on the clock. It was nearly five, and she would be late for tea. She went to the mirror, took off her coat, and combed the top of her head. There she stood in a narrow dark dress, a tall figure which promised grace.

*　*　*

Phoebe's grandmother was sixty-seven years old. She was the widow of a Cardiff doctor who had had a large practice, worked indefatigably, and managed to leave her very comfortably off. Her father had been a Welsh farmer, yet love of luxury and delight in all beautiful things was born in her. From her, Phoebe inherited her lovely voice, though it would never be as fine as the grandmother's had been in its prime.

The doctor, who was passionately devoted to music, had trained his wife to sing. In his youth he taught in a Sunday school, and at a picnic party of his pupils he noticed a newcomer, a little wild girl in a red frock, who was dancing and shouting like a creature possessed. He watched her; presently she joined in a singing round game, always making more noise than all the others put together. He pointed at her: 'You, little girl in red, stop shouting and sing properly.'

Afterwards he caught hold of her as she was running past him.

'What is your name?' he asked, looking at her earnestly.

'Eirian Thomas.'

'Well, Eirian, how old are you?'

'Twelve.'

She was a small child. He had not guessed she was so old.

'Listen to me. Eirian, and stand still while I speak to you. There's plenty of time for play. You can sing very well, so do not shout so much. Go and learn a song.'

She ran off laughing.

198

The young doctor noted her comings and goings until she was fifteen years old. One day he went quite a long way to her father's farm on purpose to ask her if she would sing in a competition next day. He thought she had grown more serious; she was studying, a table was littered with her books.

He was surprised when she actually turned up at the competition. She was just the same fascinating, laughing girl, always moving, her curly hair standing out all round her head.

The accompanist did not take her seriously. He refused to play for her.

'Go away. You can't sing,' said he with a frown.

'I'll play for you,' said the doctor.

She sang four bars of an old religious song and then broke down in tears. The competition was won; she possessed a rare contralto.

The doctor began to teach her, but there came an interlude in their relationship, a long interlude, when the doctor was forgotten, and the voice unused. This bit of romantic history, both fantastic and pathetic, did not lead to marriage, and when it was over, remained absolutely secret and unguessed by people who knew her really well. She never alluded to it. It developed her cultured tastes and deepened her naturally quick observation. She became a singularly loving and sympathetic woman whose marked virtues of charity and human kindliness were tinged by impatience. At the age of twenty-four she married her doctor. He taught her much besides singing. After her marriage she refused to give concerts and could hardly be prevailed upon to use her voice in public at all. To a very few she was known as the Welsh Nightingale. When the doctor died she gave it up altogether. At her present age she was still a vital impulsive person who was happy in her own company. Phoebe was the only grandchild in whom she took any interest. Even she had no idea of Eirian's astonishing past. Her only confidant died with the doctor.

* * *

When Phoebe entered the drawing room she found her grandmother entertaining a visitor. This was a lady verging on middle age, wearing a fur coat which was pushed back from her shoulders, and talking in a plaintive voice while she held her tea cup close to her face.

'All those monstrous bungalows on our beautiful road,' she was saying as if concluding a long speech: 'a group of splendid old elms are to come down next. There's no end to it.'

Eirian nodded and gazed at the woman's arched eyelids, and dolefully drooping mouth. Phoebe advanced, shook hands, and taking some bread and butter, sat down on a stool.

When the visitor had gone, Eirian opened the glass door leading into the garden and called the dog. There was a smell of dead leaves mingling with wood burning on the hearth. The room was papered in dull old gold, the carpet was like soft golden moss, the furniture, of which there was little, was solid and old. There were no pictures and few ornaments save a large Buddha, the size of a small child, in gilded wood sitting tranquilly on a chest.

Eirian shut the door.

'If he wants to come in now he can go through the kitchen,' she said, smiling at Phoebe. She took up a book. She was a very small woman, whose tiny, tintless face was thin and seamed. The eye sockets were peculiarly deep and age did not seem to have affected her charming blue eyes... her hair was still bushy. After all she was the little girl in the red dress who danced so wildly.

Eirian rang the bell. The tea things were removed by a morose-looking parlour maid with a fringe, whose cap was askew.

Eirian took a letter off the mantelpiece and passed it to Phoebe remarking: 'From your mother. Something wrong, as usual. You'd better read it, I think.'

She went back to her book. Phoebe opened the letter which was very long and rather untidily written.

'MY DEAR MOTHER,

Please send Phoebe home at once. I don't see why I should be expected to bear everything alone, and really, she has had an easy time for two years, while I have had to put up with it all by myself. Matt's conduct has been most annoying, although until lately he has not drunk nearly so much. Now it's beginning all over again, for never, in all our *unhappy* married life has he been so inconsiderate and sharp tempered as he has during the last three weeks. He drinks again, and shuts himself up alone. Really, he looks ghastly, and I'm quite prepared to admit that it may be due to illness but it isn't my fault, and I don't see why I should have to put up with it any longer by myself. Phoebe ought to come back and see if she can do anything.

'Yesterday, after sulking all day on something, and looking like a corpse, there was an insane outburst when he went for Philip and Rosamund and me, until both of them were crying and I hit him with the hearth brush. Then he stalked out of the room and sat in the hall with his head in his hands. By that time I was crying myself. I went to him and asked him what on earth was the matter. He said, "nothing, Dolly," and when I begged him to tell me, absolutely screamed at me and ran upstairs shouting, "Leave me alone, or I'll get out of all this for good"; who could stand such treatment from their husband? Do you think he could have been threatening *suicide*?

'Today he has not left the little room he has upstairs; the door is locked and he has had no food, although I carried up a tray myself. I'm sure he is drinking. It isn't fair on me and the children.

'To tell you the absolute truth, I sometimes wonder if he isn't going out of his mind. It sounds dreadful, but, if you had been through some of the scenes I have, you would probably believe me.

'The other night he came into my bedroom at two o'clock in the morning and woke me up. He was fully dressed and sat on the end of my bed. He was holding his head, and without a doubt he had been drinking. I remember what he said, because it seemed so irrelevant and ridiculous: "Don't you think it is easier to bear going without something all your life than if you find it and lose it?"

'I said, "What do you mean?" He repeated the words. I may not have given them exactly as he spoke them, but almost. It was very involved, and he spoke as though he were talking in his sleep. I was very tired. I sat up and tried to get him to say something reasonable. I asked him if this business of Easter were worrying him and he answered, "Good God, no! Why should you think that?" Then he got up and went to the window for air. He said he felt as though great stones were falling on his head. All this at two in the morning! At last he went out.

'I haven't told you what happened here last week. As though we haven't enough trouble of our own, Easter must go and have an appalling row with his wife, which resulted in her formally suing for a separation or something of that sort. I think she is a very foolish, weak-minded, hysterical woman – just the sort of person to make trouble wherever she goes. I imagined Matt might be upset in case he has to be a witness, as he saw her directly afterwards. It is so annoying to be mixed up in servants' affairs. All terribly unpleasant. The summons was served on Easter the day before yesterday in *our* yard. Matt said he saw the constable talking to Easter and handing him the summons. Easter tore it up and cursed and swore he would not go, but afterwards he seems to have told Matt he would. The case will come off next week.

'I tried to make Matt tell me what he saw the night of the row and he said he had heard a woman scream, and gone downstairs and found Easter's wife in the pantry, crying with her child in her arms and half her hair cut off. He gave her some brandy. Then he looked at me and said: "but you'll know all about it soon enough." Certainly I shall; I mean to go to the police court next week and hear everything. This isn't all. It appears that in addition to being a rotten servant, this man Easter is a perfectly terrible licentious brute. He's been carrying on with women at Pendoig, and here, in our own village. There's a farm labourer whose wife has just had a baby he swears is Easter's, and if ever he has a chance to get at him he'll kill him. One thing, he oughtn't to be hanged for doing it.

'This is a dreadful letter. I tell you, mother, I wish I'd never been born, except for dear, dear Philip who is, thank heaven, very well. But even he spends his time playing with Easter's odious little boy Shannon, a horrible foxy-haired little brat who is to be found all over the house, even in the drawing room. I thought I'd break that up, anyway, so I ordered Phil to have nothing more to do with him, and Phil wouldn't kiss me, wouldn't come near me, even began to jeer at me, until, on Matt's advice, I gave way, like a fool. Then I got a governess for Phil. He actually refused point-blank to do any work unless the child was there too. So imagine it, there he sits with his dirty little hands in a box of letters all the morning. And Miss Mason doesn't object at all.

'I tell you, we shall be well rid of that brood, for I forgot to say Easter took himself off after receiving the summons and hasn't come back. Good riddance! I always told Matt to sack him, then all this would never have happened.

'So please send Phoebe back to cope with her father. I can't. She can go back later. After all, she's seventeen. With love.

'DOROTHY.'

Phoebe folded up this letter carefully and restored it to the envelope. She sat fingering it for a long time. She had turned very white; her face was liable to sudden changes, which seemed almost to transform her features so that one would hardly have recognised the young girl who had been laughing with Leyden in the street.

'Well?' said Eirian.

Phoebe passed her the letter and began to thread her fingers in and out of her long plaits.

'I must go home,' she said.

Eirian marked her place in the book with her handkerchief, and laid it down on her knees. She watched Phoebe steadily.

'Do you really think it's necessary? Can you do anything?'

'I don't think I can, Grannie, but I'd better go.'

'You evidently take it more seriously than I do.'

'It is serious.'

'Of course... if your father really is ill. Your mother won't be of the smallest use – in fact, she'll make everything ten times worse. But this business of the servants seems to me quite unimportant. Sooner or later one always experiences these things. Your grandfather had a coachman very like this man, who used to get drunk and beat his wife. Your grandfather once got out of the carriage and thrashed him. I was there, and it didn't upset me. Dorothy has lost her head. Who is this Easter?'

'Father's groom. He's a very strange man, Grannie. I... hate him.'

'You are looking worried, Phoebe. If I were you I should feel inclined to go home for a few days and find out exactly what is wrong. After all, it may be nothing new.'

They discussed it for a while, and then Phoebe wrote a letter to her mother. She took it to the post herself. When she returned she went close to her grandmother, who was dozing in her chair.

'Grannie...' she said.

Eirian moved her head, but did not open her eyes.

'Put some coal on the fire, dear. It's cold.'

Phoebe did so, and for the first time tears came into her eyes. Her grandmother's fair share of troubles were over... let her be. Phoebe went away.

For over two years she had tried to stifle a nauseous memory: she was fully aware that Matt and Mary were, or had been, lovers. She had seen them kiss, and she had never dreamed that two people could be so savage... she had heard them arrange to pass a night together and she had never imagined that two faces could be so pinched and agonised with momentarily frustrated love. It had made her sick, this dreadful inadvertent discovery which in the end had compelled her to go and live with her grandmother. Even then, she had been pursued by an unsigned letter which informed her that Easter also knew everything. That he himself had written it she never doubted. It was hideous, mocking, like his smile. She was escaping and he could not prevent her, but she should not get away without a final pang.

Could she have done anything to prevent the imminent explosion of which her mother was so completely unconscious? Dorothy was going to the police court; that in itself made little difference, save for the horror of public discovery, for, as Matt had bitterly remarked, she would know all about it soon enough. But there before a crowd, before a Bench who knew them, there Easter would surely blow the Kilminster household to jagged scraps unless something could stop his wicked mouth.

'I'll tell mother myself rather than that.'

She lay awake tearing at her mind.

The next morning she started for The Gallustree. Seeing the little dictionaries on the dressing table she put them aside as indifferently as if they had been Philip's toys.

That same afternoon Dorothy and Matt were together in their drawing room. The weather was wet, the rain falling heavy and fast with a drumming roar. They could hear the conservatory door banging in the draught.

Dorothy was sitting by the window on a green lacquer chair, in front of a lacquer chest of drawers, holding up a long strip of Chinese embroidery on satin. From the open drawer bright silks spilt over her knees – purple, sheeny blue, dull rose, and greenish yellow. The floor was littered with bits of brocade and lace. Her head was turned away from Matt, who was lying back in his chair, apparently asleep.

Gladys brought in the tea. Her somewhat noisy arrangements roused Matt and he sat up, his hands clasped before him, staring blankly across the room. His face was bloodless: he appeared like a man who has had a terrible shock from which he has had no time to recover.

'Tea's ready,' Gladys announced, as she went out.

Dorothy was rummaging with her back turned.

'Where are Philip and Rosamund?' she asked.

'I don't know.'

'Having their tea in the kitchen, I suppose.' She came to the tea table, lifted the teapot and set it down again without pouring out any tea.

'Matt!'

'Yes, Dolly?'

'Have you a headache?'

'No.'

She rose and sat down again on the arm of his chair, in a coquettish attitude, laying two fingers on his hair.

'Darling...' she said after a pause. He drew a deep breath and bent his head.

'If I met you today for the first time I should fall in love with you all over again. There, what a compliment! Make me a bow. Or kiss me... yes, kiss me, Matt....'

'Don't, Dolly.'

She kissed him.

'What's the matter, sweetheart?'

He could not answer her. He leant back against her arm, his face smothered in her hair, and he longed to push her away. She excited him. He smelled smoke, and 'Dernier Soupir', and a far older subtler perfume, something like sandalwood which clung to her fingers from the silks she had been handling.

'What *is* it? Tell me... don't pretend any longer. There's something I'm sure. I won't be angry. I'll keep my temper. I'll help you.'

She clasped his face between her hands. He plucked at the arms of the chair.

'Will you?'

'Yes. If it isn't too bad. But you'd never be really bad, would you? Because I couldn't bear it.'

'What a help you are! What a support you have always been! A tower of strength to me,' he whispered, vibrating with bitter emotion. He raised his arm, closed his hand over hers, which still lay on his hair, and passed it smoothly over his brow.

'I've seen you do that to your canaries – smooth them

with your finger, I've heard you petting them and cursing them, like you do me. You fool... you fool of a woman, what use to a man have you ever been?'

He was still passing her hand regularly over his forehead, and his voice was rising almost to a pitch of hysteria. Dorothy dragged her hand away.

'I'll never try again!'

He continued disjointedly: 'What do I care for anything? I'm done. Let them say what they like.'

'You *shut up*,' screamed Dorothy, vixenish. She sprang to her feet and stamped, her face creasing with temper. 'I don't know what you're talking about. I think you're off your head.'

'So do I,' he remarked, going towards the door.

He looked at her.

'I hope to God I'll be free one day,' she shouted. Whether it was some actual pang that passed over his face, or whether he turned paler she could not tell, only something like a white flash transformed every feature. He left her. She snatched a biscuit, nibbled it, threw it in the fire, muttered '*Impossible*,' and looked at the clock. Phoebe would arrive any minute now. Matt went through the dining room, pushed up a window, and stepping out into the rain, followed a stone path round to the back premises. Passing the kitchen door which was slightly open, he heard the servants scolding and the children's laughter. Philip was chasing Gladys round the table with a dripping spoonful of jam.... Custom only muffled Matt's footsteps. He noticed as he went along by the wall how the water butt was overflowing across the path, and how rich and spongy the thick moss on the laundry roof looked.

Farther on, almost hidden behind laurels and junipers there was another door, painted dark green. He pushed up the latch and walked straight in. The door led into a large stone room, with slate shelves on three sides which were crowded with dishes, and wire meat-safes. Crockery was piled up untidily. A small lamp burned. It was the larder.

A flight of wooden steps with a hand-rail led up to a baize door. Matt mounted the steps and entered the room beyond. It was large, carpeted and thoroughly warmed by a hot fire in a high grate. The walls were distempered yellow, long curtains were drawn.

Standing by the fire in outdoor clothes, a black coat open and hanging straight from the shoulders, a béret pushed off her forehead, was Mary. She had evidently been stripping off her gloves when Matt's entrance disturbed her. And disturbed she seemed. Her pose expressed arrested action, and a kind of grim defensiveness heightened by the line of her mouth and the desperate sparkle of her eyes.

The fire gave out the only light in the room. It was enough for him to see all this. He walked to within a few paces of her and then stood still, his eyes on hers. She spoke first: 'What's the use of my trying to keep you out of this business if you come walking in here at all hours of the day? I've told you to keep away. You must be mad.'

'I am,' he exclaimed energetically. 'I've all the feelings a mad person has. Just now I could have killed. Are you afraid?'

She made a sullen movement.

'Don't come near me, please.'

He trod in her very footsteps until she reached the wall. There she allowed him to enfold her.

'Do you still tell me to keep away?'

'I do.'

He dropped his head on her breast.

'Still?'

'Yes,' she gasped.

She freed herself, and in another moment was standing in the shadow at the far end of the room. She spoke, and there was a ring of dominant obstinacy in her voice which Miss Tressan would have recognised more easily than Matt.

'There's only one thing I want to do now, and that is get away with Shannon. I ought to have done it long ago – I *should* have done it if you hadn't followed me. I hate you for it! You can't alter my resolution this time, but for the sake of your past kindness to me I'll try to keep your name out of it. But if your name must appear to secure my freedom, I'll use it without scruple. I'll use every device a woman can think of... throw myself on the mercy of the magistrates, implore them to help me to get Shannon away from his father. After all, it doesn't matter what I reveal; he'll see that it's all made public.'

Matt regarded her in a turmoil of anguish and passion. Then once more he went to her and took her by force into his arms. She felt his words bursting against her throat.

'I'll do anything I can to get you away from Easter, by God I will, if it means pulling my life with Dorothy to ruins! I don't care for that, my dearest love, you know I don't. When every touch of her makes me mad for you... But Mary, Mary, not to drive you away from *me*? How can you dream of it – how could we bear it? It's you that's mad, not me.' His hands were opening and closing against her back, his whole frame trembled. She felt her own

211

passions rising irresistibly, but her will was inviolate. He cried out that he wanted her.

'If you take me now you won't alter my resolution by a shade, nor my opinion of you. You made a contract with him for my body – I'll never forgive you. Do you know what he said?'

He shuddered.

'Don't speak of him. He isn't here... Mary, you *do* love me... I can feel it.'

Their lips met more than once.

'Yes, I do, but I despise you too, and that will conquer. Let me go, please.'

He would not release her.

'The old game of the cup and the ball,' he said, with wild dreaminess, as he closed his hand on her breast. She took him by the wrist and pulled his arm away.

'Matt! I shan't change; if I give way, I swear I shan't change. This is wicked, my heart's not in it,' she wailed.

They struggled.

'Let me go, or I'll call the servants. They're near. Matt, we shall come to loathe each other. It's ruination...'

He released her. She stepped back and looked at him with uncontrollable emotion. They were apart a moment only. It was she who embraced him, holding him so strongly that he was breathless, and reeled against the wall. Clasping her with one arm he stripped off her coat and threw her cap on the floor.

'I must lie,' she whispered, 'lie on oath to speak the truth.'

'I'd lie before God for you, let alone a Bench of magistrates,' Matt gasped.

'It is before God.'

They walked into the inner room and locked the door.

*   *   *

Phoebe missed a connection, and as a result was forced to sit two hours in a waiting room, reading what she could find on a station bookstall. She was a fool when travelling.

At seven o'clock she arrived at The Gallustree, with blue hands and a pinched face. At first Dorothy thought she had grown decidedly plainer, but it proved to be only the effect of the elements and lack of food, and soon wore off. Dorothy gave her a tearful and affectionate welcome. She was in the relaxed state which usually followed a dispute with Matt.

She told Rosamund to leave them alone. Rosamund went after an argument and Phoebe, wan and jaded, prepared to listen to her mother's troubles. Dorothy paced about in irregular bursts of movement, or sat on the bed running her fingers through her hair. She was dressed for dinner, in green velvet pyjamas, very expensive and peculiar, which tended to over-emphasise her slightness. She repeated all she had written, while frowning. Presently she interrupted her disjointed account by exclaiming: 'Why aren't you more interested in clothes?' She opened the trunks, throwing out tissue paper and sliding her hands between the folds.

'Ah – not so bad. Put this on, quick, before the gong goes.'

'I don't want to dress,' Phoebe expostulated. 'Yes, I will,' she added, feeling that she ought to please her

213

mother. She went close to her and kissed her hand. Dorothy smiled absently. There was very little spontaneous affection between them now.

Phoebe dressed herself as her mother wished, even putting on silver shoes and using powder.

Dorothy looked at her: 'You're quite good looking. Why don't you cut off your hair and put on lipstick? Wide mouths are fashionable....'

She smoked all through dinner, but ate hardly anything. Matt was not there.

'Ah, you haven't seen your father yet. I hope you don't get a shock.'

'He looks beastly,' said Rosamund, in her heavy voice. She was growing fat and uncouth. Then Dorothy began to describe her quarrel with Matt that afternoon, and Rosamund shrugged her shoulders. Phoebe heard in every word a confirmation of all she feared; she felt an awakening of something like awe at her sister's solid power. A child, no more than a dozen years old, she had learned to stand square, a block, to the family until they interfered with her, and then she struck out with all her force. Dorothy might adore Philip, might use Phoebe, it was clear that she respected Rosamund, who, having made the coffee, wished them an indifferent goodnight, and, grabbing a handful of biscuits for the dog, departed to amuse herself. On went the recitation, on, on, painful, inexpressibly grievous to the mute listener who was completing it in her mind, measuring what she heard against what she already knew, and finding proof in every sentence that her suspicions did not fall short of reality. Dorothy spoke in a muffled voice, her features distorted by emotion. At last she paused, crossed the room and closed a window. She remained there, standing with her back to the room, one hand holding her embroidery.

For a moment Phoebe sank into pure misery, and covered her face with her hands. She shrank from meeting her father, she felt herself recoiling from his very name. Her heart was so heavy... 'What can I do?' she thought. She remembered 'There – are – some – things – you – cannot – do.' She looked up, humble, terribly unhappy. The room was chilly; she felt her cheeks were drawn and her eyes heavy. A sudden icy sensation, like a draught up her spine, warned her. She ducked her head between her knees; she had been close to fainting.

'How dull it is!' Dorothy exclaimed drearily. 'I'd like to throw all the vases on the floor and smash them to *bits*. Shall we go out, Phoebe? Shall we catch the nine-twenty, stay the night in Chepsford and enjoy ourselves tomorrow? Eh, wouldn't that be fun?'

'We can't get to the station. There's nobody to take us.'

'Neither there is. Damn that Easter. Do you know, Phoebe, I think he was a bad influence on your father. Do you think that's possible?'

'Yes, I do. Quite.'

'I'm glad he's gone.'

'Where has he gone?'

'Gladys said something about him being at Pendoig. Living at the pub.'

'There are two. Which?'

'Oh, I don't know.'

She sat down and resumed her embroidery.

'The last time we had any fun was on Guy Fawkes day,' she began. 'Phil had fireworks on the lawn – just out there. They shot up... it was quite dark... they were like fiery flowers. We had a Guy too, made of straw. Such a ridiculous figure with a painted face and huge, flapping ears. Matt was there and all the servants. I did so enjoy it. That was the night Easter had such a row with his wife.'

'Tell me about it,' said Phoebe.

'I don't know anything. You must ask your father.'

'Where is he?'

'Upstairs probably.'

She started to sing.

'There's a tune running in my head. Did Grannie ever teach you to sing "ffarwel fy nghariad"?'

Phoebe repeated the words slowly.

'What does that mean? Sing it.'

'"Farewell, my love." She used to sing it to us. I'm going to say goodnight to Philip.'

She went out humming.

Phoebe sat quite still. The occasional tread of a servant in the passage and the fall of the ash on the hearth, were the only sounds. Half an hour passed and Dorothy did not return.

At length Phoebe stood up. She went to her bedroom, unlocked a letter case, and took from it a paper. She glanced over it. While she was reading she heard her mother's voice, shrill, trembling with anger: '...and I hope she'll be able to deal with you better than I can. You'll drive me mad.' A door slammed. Dorothy came running towards Phoebe, her face scarlet; she paused, holding her hand to her side quite breathless, then rushed away without saying anything. Phoebe proceeded to her father's sitting room and knocked. He asked who was there.

'Phoebe. May I come in?'

'Yes.'

She entered. Matt was standing by the window. He turned round. He was wearing a prune-coloured dressing gown which threw his livid pallor into relief. She never forgot his appearance as he stood with his head thrown slightly backwards, the light catching the point of his chin. Beyond lay the dark night, behind the uncurtained windows which shone like black ice. He extended his arm. With fear she took his hand and pressed it.

'I want to speak to you, father.'

'All right. How are you?'

'Very well. I want to show you something.'

He did not look at her.

'Why have you come home, Phoebe?'

'Mother asked me. And I wanted to... you're ill, aren't you?'

'No, I'm not ill. There's something on my mind... Listen, Phoebe: I don't want to talk to you here. Go downstairs. I'll come later, but leave me alone for a minute or two.'

She looked into his desperate eyes.

'Father, I'm not going.'

'This is monstrous,' Matt uttered under his breath, neither to himself nor to her.

She thought she had to deal with a man who was for the present, at any rate, out of his senses. It seemed madness to press him, and yet there was so little time. She held out the folded paper then, as he did not attempt to take it, opened it and put it into his hand. She was obliged to shut his fingers on it.

He suddenly smiled: 'What is it?' he asked, having evidently brought his mind to bear upon her at last.

'Please read it.'

Matt read it, first with no attention, then carefully, a third time with shocked intensity. Presently he lifted his eyes.

'Who wrote this?'

'I'm not certain...'

'Easter?'

'I think so.'

'Yes. I know it. What a – demon! How long ago?'

'Two years.'

'Then all that time you have been aware of what was going on?'

'Yes.'

'When did Easter write to you?' he continued painfully.

'About three weeks after I went away.'

They were standing within a yard of each other, still as granite.

'Then how did *you* find out?'

'I saw you.'

Matt reeled on his feet. Phoebe rushed to him and put her arm around him. He steadied himself, tore the letter across. She felt herself being pushed towards the door, and clinging to him with all her strength, cried: 'Father, don't put me out!'

'By God, you must go,' he said. 'I hate to have you under the same roof, but you can keep away from me. If you breathe the same air I think you'll strangle.'

He lifted her in his arms and set her down outside the door. Still clasping him and turning her face towards him, she held fast to the jamb of the door. He wrenched himself free, stepped back, and slammed it hard. He did not hear her shriek. She put her injured fingers to her mouth, then wrapped them in her frock, and with her shoulders bent, her mouth hard with pain, walked slowly away.

Rosamund was dozing off towards deep sleep when she became aware of a light in the room. It was Phoebe in her nightdress, wrapped in an eiderdown and carrying a flashlight. She was shuddering, her jaw was quite out of control; her face was greenish-white. She came close to the bed, and huddled over the pillow.

'Oh, give me your hand, Rosamund!'

She knelt beside the bed, pushing her arm under the clothes along her sister's side.

'It's silly to be like this, but I must just touch you.'

Rosamund felt annoyed and foolish. The best thing was to go to sleep.

*   *   *

The next day Matt was seen by nobody, and Phoebe was too sick to do anything. Towards evening she left her bed and went down to the kitchen to question Gladys, who was able to tell her that Easter was living at the Pendoig Arms. Her one bright eye raised to Phoebe was in strange contrast to the fixed downward gaze of the glass orb. Phoebe returned to her bed, depressed and terrified by the curiosity this one crippled gaze expressed.

The following morning she walked as far as the Salus road, where she caught a bus, which put her down at the door of the Pendoig Arms. It was a cold, windy morning.

The Pendoig Arms resembled an E with the middle left out. It was of stone, whitewashed, and had an air of cleanliness and order. Phoebe waited outside to speak to a man who had run out in his shirtsleeves and was standing talking to the driver of the bus. As it drove off he flourished his arms in ironical farewell. She approached him.

'Does Easter Probert live here?'

'Well, miss, I don't by rights belong to the place, you'd best step inside and ask,' he replied, still following the bus with preoccupied eyes. She pushed open the door which led straight into the taproom. The stone floor was swimming with steaming water, a large zinc bucket stood in a corner with an upright broom in it; holding the handle of the broom, supporting it in a discoloured fist, was an elderly grey-faced woman who had long prominent teeth and inflamed eyelids. Nevertheless, she looked pleasant.

Phoebe repeated her question in a docile voice. The woman nodded her white head.

'Yes, he lives here,' she answered, leaning on her broom.

'I'd like to see him.'

'He's out, I think, but I'll just inquire.'

She opened an inner door and called out: 'Sheppy, is Easter anywhere about?'

'Gone to Salus,' answered a man in a kind of rusty distant bellow.

She repeated the information. Was it anything urgent?

'Yes,' said Phoebe, considering. 'Do you know when he is likely to be back?' she added.

'Nobody can't say that, but I'd say he'd certain sure be here by six o'clock. Can you leave a message?'

'I'm afraid not. I must see him.'

220

'Well, miss, if you're here by seven you're pretty sure to catch him.'

The water in the bucket was getting cold and from the back premises a child began to scream. 'Oh Gran, Polly's bit me finger!'

'Then you shouldn't put your fingers in the cage,' Gran retorted, as she let her broom fall with a clatter against the wall and ran from the room.

Scarcely ten minutes later a bus going towards Salus overtook Phoebe. She stopped it. She passed a strange solitary day in the town. As it grew dusk she walked in the grounds which overlooked the centre of the river. The meadows in the twilight were of a soft brownish colour, the swelling uplands towards her home melted into the low-hanging clouds. Owen Cross was a constellation of mellow lights. She stood close by the iron railings; the sandstone cliff dropped to the shining main road below where traffic was humming.

Walking up and down she made up her mind that rather than permit her mother to hear the truth in court, or to find out that such a truth had there been revealed, she would tell it herself; yet – surely it would be almost better that she should have her eyes opened by strangers than by her daughter. Phoebe walked to and fro with numbed feet. Her head was beginning to ache, she felt absolutely forlorn and helpless. She came very near being locked in the grounds for the night and caught her bus by a minute. However, she arrived safely at the Pendoig Arms by six o'clock, shaking all over from nerves.

'What time do you return?' she asked the conductor as she descended.

'Seven-thirty – nine-thirty. Goodnight, miss.' The bell rang, and the bus moved off, a strip of lights and wooden profiles sliding past her. She turned slowly towards the pub. A pile of bicycles were propped up against the wall already, a lantern hung from a hook at the side of a porch.

She entered the warm bar. Four men were sitting at a long deal table playing cards.

'Can we do anything for you, miss?' a bright-eyed little man, with a broken nose, inquired. She stammered and bungled over her reply. Three more pairs of brooding eyes were raised from the cards to stare at her. Fortunately the woman whom she had seen in the morning came in; she slapped a crumpled newspaper on the table, picked up an empty tankard and said: 'Easter Probert's here if you want to see him, miss. I seen him come into the yard wheeling his bicycle half an hour ago. If you don't mind waiting here, I'll go and find him. He won't come for no shouts. I'm sorry I can't show you into the parlour, but we're having it papered, and it's in a mess.'

Phoebe thanked her. While the woman was gone she looked at the large parrot cage covered with an old curtain which was standing on the floor. She stooped and lifted a corner of the curtain; the parrot opened one brilliant eye and moved its grey feet along the perch. The men behind her continued to play cards in silence except for the one who had spoken to her; he kept exclaiming under his breath while running his fingers along the sides of the table. Presently the woman returned and told her that Easter refused to stir. She was almost ashamed to ask a young lady into his quarters, but it seemed to be the only way. She regarded Phoebe doubtfully: 'You see, he don't live in the house. It suits us all better that he shouldn't. Will you please to follow me?'

She led the way through a back kitchen where she took a lantern from a shelf. They stepped outside. When they had gone a few paces she turned round whispering: 'Excuse me, miss, but you're very young and that Easter isn't a nice man. I'll just leave the door ajar, and if you're in any difficulty give a shout; we shall hear.'

'Thank you.'

They went on, the lantern shedding a circle of light about their feet. Phoebe saw that they were traversing a garden by a straight box-edged path. The smooth trunks of young fruit trees were subtle strokes on the blackness. They took a sharp turn behind a tin-roofed pigsty and arrived at a row of wooden sheds. A lamp was shining in a cobwebby window. They stopped before a plank door, which had recently been mended with a strip of flashing white wood.

'Here you are,' said Phoebe's guide, 'I'll leave the lantern.'

She set it on the ground, regarded Phoebe earnestly, and turned away. When she was out of sight Phoebe stepped softly to the window, which was rather high, and tried to look through it. She fancied she saw Easter, but he was no more than a huddled shadow. She went and knocked at the door with a hand which visibly trembled. All her muscles were locked and strained in an effort to be calm.

Her hand had scarcely fallen to her side when the door was hauled open. She saw Easter as a dark shape, standing right athwart the threshold. It flashed through her mind that she had waited all day to speak to him, and now she had only to ask and he would refuse. No matter what she said...

223

'Will you let me come in?' she asked.

He moved sullenly aside, and she entered. Herself she shut the door.

This dwelling place was no more than a common draughty shed. The plank walls were roughly nailed and tarred. There was a fire in a rusty stove, and the smoke escaped through an iron pipe which pierced the roof. The floor was hard earth. The furniture consisted of a camp bed, a bench, and a green-painted table.

Easter was about to eat his supper; on the table were a teapot, milk jug, a loaf, a tin of treacle, and a ham with a gash in it.

Easter looked filthy and vicious. He was at his very worst, although instead of the usual leering smile he stood regarding her with a sullen and menacing gravity.

'You've got some reason for coming here, I suppose?' he growled.

She approached him.

'Easter – is there anything I can do to persuade you to leave my father's name out of the proceedings next Friday?'

He did not speak. She went on urgently: 'Must you do us all so much harm?'

He went close to the table.

'Look you,' he said, lifting the loaf with his dirty hand, then banging it down with so much violence that she heard the china plate crack...'Look you, Miss Phoebe – bread-and-butter – Kilminster... I'm not your father's groom now, and you'll get no respect from me... if I was starving and you came up mincing so pretty and said to me: "Can't I persuade you to leave that loaf alone?" d'you think you'd stand a chance of keeping me off it? Eh, what could you say with that milky little trap of yours that would keep me from devouring the loaf?'

'I'd tell you it was poisoned; that you'd be worse off afterwards.'

'Ah, would you? That's bloody silly talk. Well, I'd eat it – in great bites – and die quick and satisfied. But the loaf *isn't* poisoned. It's sweet and sound. Maybe I'll feel better for it. Better when I hear 'em tattling that your father took his groom's wife and made a whore of her in his own house where he lives with his own wife and kids.'

She would have interrupted him, but her voice was overwhelmed in the rush of his vehement speech.

'You're a lady, though your mother isn't. I'll say that for you. I like to see you change when you look at me – you know what I think you're good for. And I don't particular dislike you. I've seen worse girls and ones with less spirit. But you got to get it with the rest. When a man's driving a flock of sheep he don't choose one out for special tender treatment. I'm not going to change my ways because you comes and lifts your face, all pure and pleasant, and says: "Please, Easter". Please be damned – why should I please you? Why shouldn't I give your father what he bloody well richly asked for?'

'But it's you – it's you that will be harmed!' she cried incoherently.

'I reckon I can look after myself.'

He put one foot on the bench, laid his elbow on his knee, and cupped his chin, while he stared at her with eyes which she could not meet without a spasm of shame and something besides, something sharp and acute which stirred her so deeply that she began to shake. He desired Phoebe ardently, had done so for a long time, almost unaware; even as he sneered at the purity of her face it fascinated him. He experienced once more the voluptuous and painful craving for unsought caresses. The furious rancour which he had fostered for the last two years was beginning to give way before a sense of isolation which at times sapped his manhood and caused wild outbreaks of unconscious weeping at night. He was discovering that no creature of seven skins can be an outcast without suffering at least intermittent grief and yearning.

Phoebe was silent.

'There's no sense in your staying,' he resumed obstinately, 'why, God blast it all, you innocent toy, you don't know what you're asking of a man! It's my nature to be revengeful; you're asking me to change my nature... you mid as well say "hop out of your skin, Easter, you'd be handsomer in a new one".'

'I *do* believe you have a cleaner one underneath.' For the first time he was moved a little beyond his predatory senses. She heard him sigh.

'Perhaps,' he went on, 'but you wouldn't touch it! You don't even offer me anything. You'd make me a new man if you could, but you won't take the new man near you and keep him against harm. You're Miss Kilminster and I'm a groom, and that's enough.'

He broke off, watching her. Her heart was beating so hard that he could see the throbs shaking her breast. Had he been aware to what extent she was fighting her own rising instincts he might have gone forward and taken his revenge on Matt without leaving the shed.

226

'The Salvation Army offers more. There you gets plenty of music and a pi reputation. Jesus Christ, Miss Phoebe, you're mean!'

'I wasn't bargaining, I was asking a favour,' she said.

'Don't you ask no favours from this quarter, see? I'm going to get my own back – I got some of it already. I never thought it 'ud be so good. I thought she'd chuck him that was all, when she heard he'd paid me two pounds a week for the lend of her. But up she goes, like dynamite, and before I knew what I was doing, I'd got my hands on her. Then off she goes to lay information, and whether she tells on Kilminster or not, out it'll all come beautiful, that you may be sure! *I* don't care for the bloody beaks – never did. I been before them for boozing and breaking in a door, and assaulting a copper, but, God, this ought to be a sight worth seeing – a parafenaria.'

During this last speech he became wildly animated and he concluded it by slapping his knees and going off into a fit of uncontrolled laughter.

Phoebe turned away defeated. As she walked slowly towards the door, she let fall a glove and a handkerchief, without perceiving that she had done so. Easter followed her: 'You b— off and expect the worst.'

She went out quietly, without making any reply, picked up the lantern, and walked rapidly out of his sight. He looked after her, because he fancied she was in tears. The branches of the loftier trees sighed in a passing current of air, and a flock of dead leaves fell rustling. He re-entered; as he shut the door he noticed Phoebe's scattered belongings. He picked them up, examining them as minutely as he had Mary's clothes on the night of their

227

wedding, handling them more carefully, with wonder. Their cleanliness, the freshness and delicacy which emanated from them, pleased him exceedingly. The white handkerchief was scarcely crumpled – unscented. He rolled back the glove, exposing the fur lining, which he brushed across the back of his hand. Then he put them on the table, stoked the fire, ate his supper, all the time pondering on the interview which had just passed. He sat in his favourite attitude, his head drooping, his arms crossed before him, eating lazily with his fingers.

He was troubled; the image of Phoebe pleaded more potently when she was gone than when present, her features recalled the existence of her father. Solitary she would always have power over him, when his mind had time to single her out and dwell on her.

He took the glove again in his hand and, opening a drawer in the table, pulled out a piece of brown paper and a ball of string. Having made it into a neat parcel he pushed it into the drawer with the string, got up, pulled on a coat and, yawning, walked towards the door. Suddenly the lamp, which had been gradually growing dimmer and dimmer, went out altogether. Left in the dark Easter paused, his breath whistling between his teeth. Then he turned, reached out his hand and grabbed the handkerchief, which he stuffed carelessly into his pocket. This time he really quitted the shed.

When he returned, after ten, he was quite drunk. He tugged open the stove door muttering and fuming vague obscenities. There were only a few embers red at the heart. He flung the handkerchief in, rolled to the bed and fell across it. He slept like a log till morning, and awakening, went to kindle the fire; the handkerchief, black, filthy, scorched all over, as sordid a tag as ever blew in a gutter wind, was, nevertheless, intact. The initials were grimed. He pored over them, stretching the shred of material between his thumbs. Then half smiling, so that his upper lip took on its peculiar curve, he gravely tied it round his wrist. From the drawer he took the small parcel which he untied. All this was done slowly, with many pauses, as if his mind were wavering, but at this point he began to move rapidly, even excitedly. He searched for a pencil and a bit of paper, scrawled a line or two, retied the parcel, and immediately went out and posted it. He had at last decided.

X

The following Friday Mary was dressing herself in the room where Matt had last visited her. She stooped and kissed Shannon as he sat on the floor trying to button his shoes. He was shouting.

'Be quiet. I'll take you downstairs in a minute, and you can play all the morning in the kitchen. You'll be a good boy, won't you?' When she had put on her hat and coat she looked anxiously in the mirror, and the eyes on the reflected face probed deeper than vanity. She had a look of stony-cold resolution.

She carried Shannon downstairs to the kitchen, where the cook was reading the paper to Gladys as she washed up. Clouds of sour-smelling steam rolled out of the scullery, water slopped, crockery rattled as if carelessly handled. The reading stopped as the cook flung away the paper, holding out her arms to Shannon.

'Here he is, the little rascal,' she said, taking him from Mary and immediately beginning to play with his reddish curls.

'Thank you ever so much,' said Mary hurriedly.

'That's nothing... I'm used to children. You needn't to hurry, you've plenty of time. Good luck,' said the cook, waving Shannon's arm up and down.

Gladys also wished Mary well, but she was a little in awe of her and did not express her feelings by anything more than a wide smile, while she stood wiping a steaming plate. Mary hesitated a moment in the doorway, looked at her watch, and walked rapidly away. At the station she was greeted by a thin sharp-faced young woman with patchily red cheeks, who came out of the waiting room. She was dressed in the uniform of a parish nurse. She clasped Mary's hand.

'I thought you were going to miss it.'

They had not long to wait. When the train arrived they got into an empty carriage and sat all the way to Salus without saying a word.

On the same train were Matt and Phoebe, in separate compartments. Matt was travelling from Chepsford, where he had spent the night, Phoebe jumped into the train just as it was beginning to move. She was alone; other and newer projects for amusement prevented Dorothy from accompanying her to the police court. It was the one stroke of luck that had been dealt to her.

She did not know the way. Having inquired she was directed to the police station. It seemed very quiet – there were no sightseers treading the neat yellow gravel entrance. Hearing voices, she knocked on an unofficial-looking green door, which was opened by a woman in a coloured pinafore, who continued to turn a mangle with her right hand while she held the door knob with her left. She directed Phoebe to the police court, which was in quite a different quarter of the town. Afraid that she would be late, Phoebe ran all the way.

The building resembled a chapel outside. The walls were of grey stone, the door yellow and varnished. A line of cars was drawn up by the kerb.

'Is this the police court?' she asked an errand boy.

'Yes, miss.'

She waited until her panting had subsided, then pushed open the door. It led into a narrow lobby, which was penetrated by a sequence of orderly voices. She dare not enter until an old man, whose hideously scarred features and huge diseased nose made her flinch, pushed his way phlegmatically through the inner door, as if he had paid for a ticket to witness this entertainment. Confused and self-conscious she followed him to find herself confronted by a bare-headed policeman who looked at her inquiringly.

'I want to watch,' she whispered.

'Come in.'

She moved forward. The place was crowded so that for the first few moments she could make out no more than the backs of the standing people. She received a vague impression of grey shoulders, craned necks, and a line of policemen, who all looked strange through being without helmets. It was a foggy morning and the lights were on.

She could hear balanced voices, but she could not see the speakers. When she had recovered from the solitary plunge among so many strangers, she made her way very quietly towards a window from whence she was able to see clear across the court. It was a long room; the roof was supported by slender beams, the windows were pointed, each containing a circle of rose-coloured glass. In front of the magistrates' circular desk were two green baize-covered tables spread with papers; at one sat the magistrates' clerk, and his clerk who was taking notes, at the other a newspaper reporter, a lawyer, and the chief constable. Two thin ranks of bare-headed policemen stood against the wall. The dock and witness box were on the right and left of the magistrates' desk. A woman was stepping into the witness box. The first distinct words Phoebe heard were the oath: 'I swear by Almighty God to speak the truth, the whole truth, and nothing but the truth, so help me God.'

They were followed by the sound of a kiss.

The next moment she saw Matt's head on the opposite side. He was pale, his eyes were cast down. Phoebe locked her cold hands together. She smelled a warm odour and remembered that there were breweries in the street behind the police court.

Six magistrates were on the bench this morning, including one intent woman who sat with folded arms drawing a grey glove through her fingers. The chairman spoke authoritatively, fixing his eyes on the shiny pewter inkpot at his side, or raising them in a sudden fierce arrogant stare. These were men as lords of creation, quiet and proud, altogether different from themselves, as they usually appeared. A woman could not but respect and detest them. The young constable who had spoken to her stepped softly to her side, bent forward and whispered:

'Why don't you go and sit down, miss? There's an empty chair.'

He pointed. She softly went and sat down between two women just in front of the red cord which divided the court. The crowd was now behind her and she came into the magistrates' full view. She could not help thinking that they stared at her inquisitively. At the same time Matt perceived her. He started, and drew farther back, dreading her melancholy eyes. He was like a man in a vacuum. Phoebe was in torment.

The magistrates retired. She looked across the empty desk. Above the chairman's seat the royal arms hung suspended on a dark shield; below them there was a greenish patch on the grey wall which looked like mildew. She thought it resembled a ship.

Behind her a hum broke out such as one hears when passing under a council school windows. It blotted out the monotonous rasping of a saw. The air was growing close.

The constables were standing against the wall with their hands behind them, and the magistrates' clerk had risen and was talking earnestly. The man who was standing in the dock moved his feet, as though he were impatient, and sighed deeply. He mumbled something, and gripped the railing. When the magistrates re-entered, the court rose in sharply cut silence and the chairman delivered the verdict, while his arrogant eyes travelled scornfully over the assembly. This man, who was well known to Phoebe, was the impersonation of public code, and therefore her greatest dread. He possessed a loud voice and a bullying manner, which were perfectly in keeping with his appearance: a narrow skull, a bony face, curved nose, small mouth, flat aristocratic ears.... She thanked God Dorothy was not present. On his left sat the lady in grey, and a burly man of sallow complexion, whose enormous black eyebrows spanned his waxen forehead; on his right a stout small man with crinkly hair and a curled moustache who was playing with a pencil, a white-haired sickly man who sat holding his chin in his hands, and, lastly, an olive-skinned man who wore gold-rimmed spectacles.

Afterwards they would talk...

'A queer case today. You know, Kilminster.' And so on. Disgraceful.

Not two yards from her a reporter to the *Chepsford Times* sat taking notes in shorthand.

'Easter Probert!'

Phoebe started so convulsively that the woman sitting next to her drew away. She stared spitefully, jerked her chin, and opening her expensive bag, took out a lace handkerchief and buried her red nose in it.

Easter clove the crowd from the very back of the court. He was dressed in a seedy blue coat and waistcoat, a filthy white flannel shirt with the band wrenched off, and rusty canvas trousers. He wore neither collar nor tie, but a black and white spotted handkerchief, tied round his neck in an untidy knot under the ear. His broad leather belt, loose and low on his hips, was secured by a silver buckle of intricate pattern. He carried his head low, almost hanging, and yet his wide-open eyes looked up. He was smiling defiantly, and to Phoebe he seemed incarnate malice.

She prayed.

'Easter Probert, you are charged with persistent cruelty to your wife. Are you guilty or not?'

'Guilty,' he replied without a shade of change upon his face.

Phoebe's lips were moving. He bent his enigmatical gaze upon her head.

The chairman called: 'Is Mrs Probert there?' and tapped his pointed fingers.

Mary, dressed entirely in black, her face set, took her place in the witness box. She repeated the oath after the constable, and Phoebe noticed something significant which seemed to escape the attention of all present.

'I swear by Almighty God,' the constable intoned.

'I swear by Almighty God...'

'That the evidence I shall give,'

'That the evidence I shall give...'

'Shall be the truth,'

'Shall be the truth...'

'The whole truth,'

'The whole truth...'

'And nothing but the truth,'

'So help me God,' she concluded rapidly without repeating the last phrase as it left the constable's lips. In the silence Phoebe heard her kiss. She moved her head slightly, took a pace forward and looked intently at the magistrates. Easter gazed at her obliquely across the reporter's head. Phoebe could no longer bear to watch – she had no hope.

'Just tell the magistrates what you have to say,' said the magistrates' clerk, loudly and encouragingly.

She began inaudibly.

'Speak up, magistrates can't hear.'

She cleared her throat and began once more in a firmer voice.

The crowd gaped at the elegant woman in her long coat, who with her hands joined, was speaking deliberately, and then at her husband, that ragged man in the dock, whose teeth were bared as though he would bite. That was no husband for a lady. Listen!

'I beg that you will allow me to say a few words before I tell you the circumstances which have brought me here to plead for a separation from my husband *at any cost.*'

There was an infinitesimal pause before she continued: 'I know that I'm not an innocent supplicant – in my own mind I am convinced that in much I am as guilty as he...'

'If you are guilty you should be in the dock yourself,' observed the chairman with a grim smile, casting his eyes around to see what effect his humour had on his listeners. There was laughter, and the olive-skinned magistrate scowled: he found it difficult to concentrate.

'Silence.'

'If I could attain my object I would stand there gladly,' Mary cried passionately. She resumed more quietly: 'I have to reveal matters which will implicate me deeply. Even if I wished I doubt if I could rouse much sympathy for myself in anyone present. But please remember that there is one other than my husband and myself to be considered – in fact, the only one, my child. I bitterly resent the brutal treatment that has been inflicted on me since my marriage,' she went on, her eyes flashing into rage in spite of herself, and looking no supplicant indeed, but a fierce resentful woman.

The magistrate with the thick eyebrows leant towards the chairman. He nodded sideways and requested that she would come to the point.

'It is the point, the very heart of it, the only reason why I am here to throw mud in my own face!' she retorted energetically.

'That may be so, but at least, there's no point in losing your temper and answering rudely,' said the chairman sharply. Mary flushed, took out her handkerchief, and wiped her lips.

'I am sorry.'

'Go on.'

'But as I am on oath, so I swear that I am pleading for my son, not for myself. Just to get him away... that's all, if you will remember when you hear...'

She swallowed. Her face tilted back so that the exposed throat, curved outwards against her high collar, had turned livid.

'Speak up.'

'I was married two years ago last February and my child was born at the end of the following June.'

'Did you marry your husband because you were expecting this child?'

'Yes, I did.'

'Is he the father of this child?'

'Yes. He is.'

'Go on.'

'Excuse me if I go into details but I wish my husband's attitude to me to be clear from the very beginning. On the morning of our wedding he arrived at the church without a ring, and he boasted to me afterwards that he wouldn't dream of buying one. We were married with one which he always wore himself – it is on his hand now.'

The magistrates glanced carelessly at Easter's dirty

238

hands. He did not move a muscle.

'Directly after we were married he took the ring away again. He pinched my arm and when I shrank away he told me to go home by myself. He pushed me down on the road. After that he took a bus into Salus and left me.'

'And how long had you been married?' inquired the chairman.

'About half an hour.'

The chairman again glanced around.

'He made an early beginning.'

There was more tittering. Mary resumed.

'Between our wedding day and the birth of our child, he ill-treated me on several occasions and habitually used filthy language to me. Often he was just malicious and incredibly spiteful; sometimes he was utterly brutal, especially towards a woman in my condition. Once I went for a walk with him; he said he wished to take a thorn out of his hand and told me to walk on slowly. I offered to do it for him and he refused. When I was about twenty yards in front of him he started to throw stones at me, picking them from a heap of flints by the road. Several struck me, and one cut open the side of my hand. He used to come in very late at night and wake me by pulling my hair, and then he would play an old gramophone until it nearly drove me mad. I was almost off my head... there was no peace, always blows and curses.'

The woman magistrate had been whispering. The chairman put another question: 'Mrs Probert, did you ever, to your knowledge, wilfully aggravate your husband?'

'Never.'

'All right. Go on.'

239

'Once he pushed a dead and rotten rat into my neck when I was in bed, and followed it up by dragging me across the floor and pouring a jug of cold water over my head and shoulders. I was very ill afterwards; he thought I should have a miscarriage and from that time until the premature birth of my child he did not physically ill-treat me. But he continued to plague me in every way he could imagine – he poured liniment among my clothes. When my child was born I nearly died and three days afterwards, when I was still in danger of my life, he stood outside my door for a quarter of an hour shouting that the child was not his and he would strangle it if he got in. He kept banging on the door and kicking it. I am convinced that had the baby or myself died then he would have been directly responsible. The nurse who was with me agreed and advised me to get away if possible.'

Mary drew a deep breath and wiped her forehead which was shining with perspiration.

'As soon as I was strong enough to walk, which was not until three months later, I ran away with the child. I intended to find work but I miscalculated my strength, and all my plans failed. I was benighted and forced to spend the night at the Three Magpies. The next morning, Mr Kilminster rode over and persuaded me to return to my husband.'

Phoebe looked at Easter. The terrible smile, ferocious yet mocking, was playing over his mouth. Mary was turning her head from side to side like a person in extreme agony, who finds relief in the monotony of movement.

'Your husband is groom to Mr Kilminster?'

'Yes.'

'Go on.'

'I can't... for a minute. Oh God!'

She suddenly covered her face with her hands.

The woman magistrate turned crimson. Phoebe heard a murmur of sympathy behind her.

'Try to continue,' said the magistrates' clerk gently, after a pause which revealed that Mary sobbed. She controlled herself, standing rigid, her uncovered face revealing the shining channels left by tears.

'I went back... my husband was not always at home... I had a lover. We were happy.'

A word was passed to the chairman from the woman magistrate. He nodded: 'Can you tell us the name of this man?'

'I would rather not.'

The chairman deliberated.

'Very well.'

The woman magistrate appeared to insist.

'Will you write it down?'

The magistrates' clerk rose, and approached the desk. The chairman leant forward and they whispered.

'You need not reveal the name,' the chairman proclaimed, sitting back.

Easter burst out laughing.

'Silence!'

A kind of spasm shook the lady in grey. She opened her mouth astonished, and again her cheeks flushed a deep bluish crimson.

'Go on with your tale,' said the chairman.

'Brute,' muttered a voice behind Phoebe. Her neighbour turned, glared and then leant forward eagerly.

'I was not aware that my husband knew about this,' Mary continued.

'You thought you were deceiving him successfully?'

'Yes.'

'How long did this affair continue?'

'Until last November the fifth. That day I had been watching the fireworks on the lawn. The servants were invited,' she said deliberately. 'My husband was there. I went up to our rooms about nine o'clock and went straight to bed. My husband came in about eleven and wakened me. He was half drunk. He said "Wake up, I've some news for you."

'I said, "What is it?"

'He said, "We're going away."

'I said I should not go with him. He replied that I would like it, that we had both worked hard, and now we should have our fun. I asked him what he was going to do if he threw up his job, and he told me he had put his money into a pork business – a shop. I said: "What do you mean? You haven't any money to spare."

'Then he put his arm round my neck and said he had plenty of money. I could not make out where it came from, and I asked him how he earned it. He said: "I have not earned it, you have. But as your body is my property, the money was paid over to me for the loan of it. Your friend gave me two pound a week for you, and I've saved it all up." He was quite quiet until he had finished speaking, and then he suddenly seemed as if he had gone mad. He said he would teach me, and hit my ears until I fell down on the floor. I screamed. He stuffed his handkerchief in my mouth and said he would strangle me if I moved. I ran to

242

the door, but he had locked it. The key was hanging on the nail but I couldn't get near it. He chased me round the table. At last he dived under it, catching me by the ankle. I fell down and he carried me to the bed. He held me. He kept saying that if I woke the baby he would knock me out, but if the child slept I'd be all right. The child was crying all the time, in the next room. I thought he was mad. Presently he left go of me, took a pair of scissors from his pocket and cut off one side of my hair close to my scalp, saying that he wished he had a red hot poker to make a mark on my back. He threw the hair out of the window. I dared not struggle with him, and at last I fainted. When I came round he had gone, and the door was locked outside. I broke it open with a skewer, rushed into the next room and found the child sitting up crying. I must have been beside myself, for I rushed downstairs carrying Shannon in my nightdress. I remember trying to get out of the door into the garden and shouting for help. I was terrified he would come back. Mr Kilminster found me clinging to the stairs. He took me to the library and gave me brandy. The next morning I laid information against my husband.'

She ceased.

'Is that all?'

'Yes.'

The chairman conferred with the magistrates' clerk, who requested that Mary would remove her hat. She did so. The man with the crinkly hair tickled his face abstractedly with a pencil, as he looked at the outline of her head.

'Not much damage done *there*,' he reflected.

The reporter thought it was a plum of a case. They

243

were usually so boring, one knew everything beforehand. He did not think everything had come out.

'Has anything occurred between you and your lover since that date?'

'No, nothing.'

'Your motive in seeking this separation is to get away from both men with your child?'

'Yes, and begin again if possible.'

The magistrates' clerk turned towards Easter: 'Do you want to ask any questions?'

'Yes,' he said. He flung his voice at Mary: 'When we went for a walk and I chucked stones at you, had you been saying to me before, all along the road, that you wished to God you'd never married me because I was only a groom?'

'Yes.'

'Did you refuse to rub that liniment on my arm when I poured it in the drawer among your clothes?'

'Yes.'

'Is that all you want to ask?' the clerk inquired, as Easter drew himself up.

'No,' he replied. He leant forward again, speaking very slowly.

'Is it true you haven't seen that bloke – your lover – since November the fifth?'

'I have seen him – yes.'

'Is that all?'

'Yes.'

'A damned lie,' he remarked. 'That's all.'

'You must be careful what you say here,' exclaimed the magistrates' clerk.

'Ay,' said Easter laconically, 'that's a fact.'

Phoebe's eyes, full of despair and pain, met his. He looked away.

Mary was asked if she had any witnesses. She had. Elaine Marshall was called. The sharp-faced nurse took her place in the witness box and swore to speak the truth. She opened the Bible and daintily kissed an inner page, for fear of germs.

'Are you a district nurse?'

'Yes, sir, that's my profession.'

'All right, say what you want to say.'

The nurse proceeded composedly: 'I was called in to Mrs Probert's confinement two years ago last June. It was a premature child and Mrs Probert was very ill – in acute danger. Three nights after the child was born Mr Probert came to the door cursing and using the most filthy language I have ever heard. I think he was drunk. He was kicking the panels and carrying on like a madman. Mrs Probert was terribly upset. I went out and forced him away with Mr Kilminster's help. I believe Mr Kilminster locked him in the harness room and threatened to send for the police.'

'Do you imagine that this occurrence endangered Mrs Probert's life?'

'I certainly do. The next day she was so ill that we sent for another nurse.'

'Who is "we"?'

'Mr Kilminster and I.'

'I see. Is that all?'

'No, sir. The day after her husband cut off her hair Mrs Probert came down to show me.'

'Were there any marks on her?'

'Yes. Her shoulders were bruised, as if she had been held down by force.'

'No marks of blows?'

'Not actually. Her hair was ruined. She had very lovely hair.'

Easter did not question this witness, who cast him one venomous glance before she stepped from the box and made her way to the back of the court.

The next was Matt. While he was taking the oath the woman magistrate blushed for the third time. His wan face made her feel sentimental, and what a generous, noble man the nurse made him out to be!

Matt looked utterly lifeless. Phoebe was beyond attending to his testimony. Her strained eyes were immovably fixed on Easter.

'Do you employ Easter Probert as groom?'

'I did, but he left last week after receiving the summons.'

'Do you consider he has a good character?'

'I did,' he again replied.

'Would you give him one?'

'No.'

'What has made you change your opinion?'

'If I have changed it, it has no bearing on the case, I assure you.'

'Well, go on.' The magistrates regarded him dubiously.

Matt substantiated Mary's story of the night of November the fifth. The olive-skinned magistrate stared down his nose. The atmosphere was charged with unbearable suspense. The Bench, Matt, Mary, Phoebe, were all expecting an explosion from the dock. Mary, feeling sick and languid, leant against the back of her chair. Matt's inert gaze was fixed on the pewter inkpot. Again Easter declined to question the witness. He looked at Matt, he looked at Phoebe. He looked again at Matt and saw him with unabated hatred... stepping down from the witness box. He'd have him, in spite of all... this was the minute! Now then, Easter, tear out that eye and wrench away that tooth! He leant forward snarling like a dangerous animal, all his veins swollen, his ears singing with passion.

'Good Lord, I could never send a woman back to that!' thought the skinny reporter.

'I want to say something!'

'You can say it from where you are.'

Silence.

A hoarse indistinct word Easter let fall, and paused again. To Phoebe came the thought of a minister racked by experience, preaching on the casting out of devils. Easter's face worked. His eyelids descended and he clenched his teeth until black hollows showed under his cheekbones. Phoebe gazed and gazed at the harsh out-thrust profile painted white against the rose-coloured centre of the pointed window.

'If you have anything to say, say it. Don't keep the magistrates waiting.'

He looked at the magistrates, one after another, and with a gesture utterly strange to him raised one hand to his forehead.

'No, I haven't nothing to say. I pleaded guilty, didn't I? Oh, get it over, I want to get out!'

* * *

The six magistrates were interested enough in the case to dispute over their decision. The lady in grey, who continued to blush at intervals, as if some uncomfortable thought lurked within her secret mind, shared the reporter's conviction that everything had not been heard. It was a pity, she explained, that a name had been withheld. The black-browed magistrate for some reason felt a boldly expressed sympathy towards the brutal husband, but on talking it over with the others, he came to the conclusion that Probert would be none the happier for remaining yoked to his mate. He therefore threw in his word with the rest.

'And, of course, there's the child,' the chairman added.

A separation order was granted with fifteen shillings a week maintenance.

Driving his car towards the station, the black-browed magistrate overtook Miss Kilminster walking beside Probert. He was not inquisitive, but he wished he knew what they were saying. He saw the groom turn away, leaving Phoebe standing still under the dull slag wall. This parting was not casual; the magistrate believed he observed a poignant and final glance pass between them.

The first fifteen shillings were paid over, the second never. The following week Tom Queary was brought before a special meeting of the magistrates, charged with the murder of Easter, and committed for trial at the next Chepsford Assizes. He reserved his defence. It was related in court that Queary had attacked Easter with a pike, which he had driven into his eye. Easter died instantly.

When Phoebe heard of it she began to cry dreadfully and heavily, in a deathly senseless manner, as if every sob would kill her.

LIBRARY OF WALES

The Library of Wales is a Welsh Assembly Government project designed to ensure that all of the rich and extensive literature of Wales which has been written in English will now be made available to readers in and beyond Wales. Sustaining this wider literary heritage is understood by the Welsh Assembly Government to be a key component in creating and disseminating an ongoing sense of modern Welsh culture and history for the future Wales which is now emerging from contemporary society. Through these texts, until now unavailable, out-of-print or merely forgotten, the Library of Wales brings back into play the voices and actions of the human experience that has made us, in all our complexity, a Welsh people.

The Library of Wales includes prose as well as poetry, essays as well as fiction, anthologies as well as memoirs, drama as well as journalism. It complements the names and texts that are already in the public domain and seeks to include the best of Welsh writing in English, as well as to showcase what has been unjustly neglected. No boundaries limit the ambition of the Library of Wales to open up the borders that have denied some of our best writers a presence in a future Wales. The Library of Wales has been created with that Wales in mind: a young country not afraid to remember what it might yet become.

Dai Smith
Raymond Williams Chair in the Cultural History of Wales,
Swansea University

PARTHIAN

A Carnival of Voices

www.parthianbooks.com

LIBRARY OF WALES
FUNDED BY

Llywodraeth Cynulliad Cymru
Welsh Assembly Government

**CYNGOR LLYFRAU CYMRU
WELSH BOOKS COUNCIL**

LIBRARY OF WALES   SERIES EDITOR: DAI SMITH

WWW.LIBRARYOFWALES.ORG

LIBRARY OF WALES
titles are available to buy online at:

gwales.com
Llyfrau ar-lein
Books on-line